Digging

THE

Director

JENNIFER NICE

Books By
Jennifer Nice

Christmas At The Manor:
Merry Christmas Eve Eve
That's It In A Nutcracker
All's Fair In Love And Christmas

The Nice Romance Collection
(a series of standalone romances):
Digging the Director
A Scottish Christmas Dream
Let's Skip This Christmas
Yellow Petals At Christmas

The Of You Duology
The Magic Of You
The Heart Of You

JOIN US IN THE WOODS

For free stories and news, please join us in the woods at www.writeintothewoods.com/join-us

To all the people whose eyes are caught by silver foxes.

Ren tried to memorise the way they were walking, her distracted gaze fixating on comparing her choice of outfit with the woman who was showing her around. At the end of the day, it wouldn't matter if she wasn't dressed appropriately for working at a gaming company if she couldn't find her way out of the building.

'There's a kitchen here on every floor and each one has a fridge, coffee maker, all the usual. Just make sure you clean up after yourself.'

'Of course.'

The woman leading her around had introduced herself as Bonnie and had a short blonde bob and dazzling blue eyes. Ren, however, was more interested in her denim dungarees and white t-shirt. After a week – an actual week – of repeatedly changing her mind over which outfit to wear for her first day, Ren had gone with logic and comfort. They'd hired her as an academic and a scientist, so that was what they were going to get. She'd forgone the dresses she loved so much and chosen loose trousers with a shirt and a smart woollen cardigan, but because this was Ren, the shirt was blue and the cardigan was green. She'd also tied her long red hair back. She didn't know why, it had just seemed like the right thing to do.

But in every space, nook and cranny of the office building she'd seen so far was a mixture of men and women in smart-ish suits, jeans, t-shirts with slogans, dresses, heels, flats, sandals – sandals! In a Scottish October! – and Ren was beginning to realise that perhaps anything went here.

'This is our marketing team, you'll get to know some of them. And upstairs, top floor, is where we are, along with our development team.' Bonnie led Ren to the lift and up they went. Floor five. Ren unstuck her tongue from the roof of her mouth and wondered where the nearest toilets were.

'Have you ever worked in gaming before?' Bonnie asked.

Ren shook her head.

'No. This is all very new.'

'I bet. A nice, shiny, purpose-designed office building instead of a dusty museum. There's something very romantic about a dusty museum, though.'

Ren agreed.

'There is. But actually my last job was in a university.'

'Oh?'

'Yeah, they made a bunch of us redundant. I'd only been there a few months.'

'That must have been a shock. I thought you worked in a museum?'

'I did. The Natural History Museum in London. The dream,' said Ren, a little too wistfully. 'But my contract ended and they couldn't renew it.'

'You hoping they'll be able to hire you back after this contract is through?'

Ren smiled and shrugged.

'Maybe.' Not a chance in hell, she told herself. That wasn't going to happen, no matter how much she wanted it to. No, once this contract was done, she'd be back searching for something else again. She had twelve months but could probably only relax with a steady paycheque for nine of those. Just the thought of it was exhausting.

The lift doors opened with a ping and Bonnie led the way out. The top floor, much like the others, was decorated in the company's brand colours of green, yellow and brown. It was open-plan but with good distinction between the teams.

'As with the other floors, we're separated by the projects,' Bonnie explained, leading Ren into the open-plan office, between desks. The company was working on about six projects at any given time, Bonnie had explained on the first floor full of admin, HR and accounts. However, in this building, they were focusing on only two of those projects. 'This is the side you're interested in,' said

Bonnie, pointing to the right. 'This is our project and right here, this is your desk.'

Bonnie stopped at an empty desk, complete with laptop, docking station, a solitary drawer and a chair that had seen better days. Next to Ren's desk was an empty table and opposite was a man with his head down over his keyboard.

'Billy.' Bonnie rapped her knuckles on the table and the man looked up with bleary eyes. 'This is Billy, he's our project manager. Billy, this is Ren, our new consultant.'

Billy's brown eyes widened and he grinned, standing and offering Ren his hand.

'Our palaeontologist has arrived,' he said breathlessly.

Ren could only take it as a compliment as the heat rushed to her cheeks.

'Yes. Present and correct.' She shook his hand and resisted the immediate urge to curtsey. Who curtsied? What was wrong with her?

Billy blew the brown hair from his eyes and sat back down, the grin still on his face. It made him look boy-ish and harder to get a read on how old he was. Not that it mattered. Although he did have a lovely soft Scottish accent. One of the benefits of having to move to Edinburgh, Ren had decided while packing up her Essex flat, was the accent. It was hard not to think about whether she'd end up meeting a gorgeous man with a Scottish accent, no matter how much she tried to push the thought away.

Not Billy, though. Not the man sitting opposite her at work.

'Come on, I'll introduce you to the rest of the senior team and then I'll let you get settled,' said Bonnie.

'Later,' Billy said to Ren before lowering his head back to his work.

'This is my desk.' Bonnie gestured to a desk just behind Ren's, covered in papers and pens, and a notebook filled with doodles. Ren would have thought that the head art designer would have a clearer desk, maybe with a large screen and digital pen. But what did she know?

'Liam sits there. He's our head developer, in charge of creating the actual game.' She pointed to the desk opposite. 'Then, just down here is our executive producer, and the finance and marketing directors.' Bonnie showed her the way down a narrow corridor, pointing out two meeting rooms with glass panelled walls and – much to Ren's relief – the toilets.

At the end of the corridor were two square offices. Bonnie knocked gently on the first office door and then let herself in, Ren following. On the right, Bonnie pointed to a tidy desk and empty chair. 'That's Val's desk, she's the marketing director. She's often out doing events and things. And when she is here, she spends most of her time on the fourth floor with marketing. We don't really know why her desk is up here. And this is Harrison Calloway, our finance director.'

Ren tore her gaze from the window behind Val's desk looking out towards Edinburgh Castle and met the cool blue eyes of a man with silver hair, flecked with dark brown, and a short silver beard. Ren blinked and Harrison blinked back.

'Harrison, this is Ren Bradley. Our resident palaeontologist. Today's her first day.'

'Ah, the new kid.' Harrison held out a hand but Ren hesitated. Kid? Did he just call her kid? He couldn't be more than ten years older than her. Kid, indeed. His accent wasn't Scottish, or English. Remembering herself, she reached out and shook his hand. His skin was soft and warm, and he gave her hand a little squeeze before letting go. Ren hated when men did that. A shot of pleasure swept through her. How dare he do such a thing.

'Harrison is from New York,' Bonnie explained as if hearing Ren's thoughts. 'Be nice to her,' she added to Harrison.

'I'm always nice,' said Harrison, his eyes on Ren. 'What were you doing before this?' he asked.

'I was a university lecturer,' Ren told him.

Harrison raised one eyebrow slightly and gave her something of a half-smile that instantly hit her as charming but with a question mark.

'Gaming industry newbie,' said Bonnie. 'Harrison was too when he joined us. We'll teach you the ropes soon enough.' She flashed Ren a grin and then led her out. Ren glanced back over her shoulder as she followed, and hurriedly looked away when she discovered Harrison was watching her leave.

'He isn't nice to people?' Ren asked quietly before she could stop herself.

Bonnie laughed.

'He is. He's just very good at his job. A bit cut-throat, you know? Think Wolf of Wall Street.'

Ren stopped herself from looking back to Harrison's office.

'And this is our executive producer. He's our big boss, as high as it gets around here without going to head office,' said Bonnie, knocking on the remaining office door. Ren swallowed against her dry mouth and steeled herself. A muffled voice broke through and Bonnie opened the door revealing an office slightly bigger than Harrison and Val's with a glorious view across the old part of the city through large windows. If Ren had been able to move to the right a little, she fancied she would have a good view of Arthur's Seat. Which begged the question as to why Martin Clyde sat with his back to it.

Ren had met Martin at her interview and he was shockingly younger than she had expected of some-one so high up. There was something a little depressing about the fact that he was a whole year younger than her (according to his online profiles she'd found while snooping after her interview).

How did some people manage to get so far in life so quickly while others stumbled along, worrying how they would keep a roof over their heads?

'Good morning, Ren. Welcome!' Martin stood and shook Ren's hand. 'Bonnie's shown you around, Ren? Good, good. Well, we have our regular senior management meeting in a couple of hours. You're invited to them, they're every week. Someone will send the invitations through once you're set up. We're not expecting anything huge from you today, Ren, of course, but maybe the meeting will help you to orient yourself, yeah? Have you met Harrison and Val yet?'

'Harrison, yes. Val's not here,' said Bonnie before Ren could reply.

'Of course, of course. She said she'd be in late today, I forgot. She'll be here for the meeting though, you can meet her then, Ren.' Martin gave Ren a wide grin. 'So, go settle in. Any questions, just ask whoever's around. Really excited to have you with us, Ren.'

Ren nodded and thanked him, flinching at how often he spoke her name. Why did people do that? Did he have a bad memory? Was it a power play? Is that how people got to the top of the company hierarchy?

Martin went back to his work, dismissing them, and Bonnie ushered Ren back out into the corridor.

'Nice views these offices have, huh?' she asked, leading Ren back past the toilets and meeting rooms. 'This is where the meeting will be,' she added, pointing to the room on the left. 'Try not to get distracted but if you manage to get a seat on the far left and lean over a bit, you can just about see the castle.'

Ren gave a small laugh.

'Are you from Edinburgh?' she asked.

'No. I'm from Aberdeen, well, no, a town outside Aberdeen, but close enough. You're from the South East?'

'London,' said Ren. 'Or close enough.'

Bonnie flashed her a smile and then settled Ren at her desk.

'Billy. Could you give her a hand with her laptop? Get her email and everything up? I checked with IT yesterday, it should all be there, but you know what first days are like.'

Billy stood, gave Bonnie a mock salute and walked around the desks to Ren who was trying to get comfortable on her chair.

'I'll come get you for the meeting, okay? Until then, just familiarise yourself.' Bonnie gave Ren's chair a comforting tap and walked back to her own desk.

'Let's see here,' Billy murmured, opening Ren's laptop and typing in the generic password IT had left on a Post-it. 'You can change the password in a bit. Let's just set up the email and messages and stuff.'

Ren let Billy tap away at the laptop and waited

until he was ready to show her around her new digital office. It didn't take long. After Billy had returned to his desk, Ren spent another ten minutes going through the shared folders and attempting to figure out what she had let herself in for.

'Have you played any of our games?' Billy asked, standing and holding up a coffee cup.

'No,' Ren admitted.

'Wow, throwing yourself in the deep end.' He grinned and shook the cup at her. 'Coffee?'

'Please.' Ren dug around in her bag for the cup she'd brought and then followed him hastily over to the kitchen area and the coffee machine. 'You'll have to show me how it works.'

'Oh, it's simple. And maybe after the meeting, I'll get you in the gaming chair.'

'The what?' Ren's heart jolted.

'Don't panic. There's a room over there' – Billy pointed – 'with a few consoles and screens. It's a break area, technically, but I can show you the game we're working on so you know what we're talking about. In fact, if we have time, we can do it now. What do you think?'

Ren blinked. Her first day in a new job and she was going to be asked not only to bring her expertise to a senior management meeting but also attempt to play a game she knew nothing about on a console she had no understanding of. This wasn't just the deep end. This was more like shark-infested waters.

'Sure,' she said, her mind swimming, desperately trying to watch what buttons on the coffee machine Billy was pressing. 'Sure thing.'

Harrison was the second person to arrive at the senior management meeting. He'd been expecting to be the first.

'Morning, Val. I didn't see you come in.' He sat at the opposite end of the long table to the marketing director.

'I've been downstairs,' she said, not looking up from her laptop.

Harrison sighed softly through his nose and tapped his fingers against the table. Not a senior management meeting went by when he wasn't reminded of how glad he was that Val spent most of her time downstairs instead of in their supposed shared office. His gaze moved a fraction to his coffee cup and its cold remains.

'Gonna go get a coffee,' he said, standing and grabbing the cup. 'Want anything?'

'No, thanks.' She still didn't look up.

That was fine by him.

Harrison strode out of the meeting room, happy

to have claimed his seat and wondering where the others were. He entered the open-plan part of the office and found Bonnie on the phone. She gave him an apologetic shrug of her shoulders and then made a chatty motion with her hand. Harrison grinned. Liam's desk was empty, who knew where he was. Billy's desk was also vacant, along with the desk opposite his. The one Bonnie had been preparing the day before for the new starter. The new kid.

He hadn't meant to call her that.

He'd been startled by how attractive she was, by her red hair and then, when she spoke, by the fact that she wasn't Scottish as he'd been expecting. 'Kid' had just fallen out of his mouth.

Where were they all?

Harrison made his way to the coffee machine and started it up, scanning the office as he waited. There they were. Billy was in the break room, leaning over Ren, telling her what buttons to press as they attempted to play with the shambles that was the game they were currently working on. It seemed unfair to unleash it on the poor girl on her first day. The game was nowhere close to being playable yet. Harrison didn't know much about gaming, but he knew enough about making money to understand that the game was a long way from being finished, let alone profitable.

Taking his coffee, he paused to watch for a moment. Bonnie was still on the phone, Liam was still missing. Smiling, Harrison wandered over to the break room and leaned against the doorframe.

'You're gonna be late for the meeting.'

Ren jumped and turned to look at him. Billy glanced back to him and checked the time on his phone.

'Yeah. Okay. Well, that's where we're up to. What do you think?'

Ren stared at the screen as Billy shut it all down.

'Erm. Good,' she said.

Harrison held in a laugh. She didn't have a clue. Neither had he. He waited to see if anything more was coming.

'It'll be interesting to see where you're up to with it all coming together,' she said, climbing out of the chair and straightening her clothes. She avoided Harrison's gaze but he watched her intently anyway, as tendrils of hair fell out of her ponytail and she pushed them back behind her ears. She wasn't wearing any rings, he noted.

'Oh?' he asked when Billy remained frustratingly quiet. 'Got some suggestions?'

Ren gave a small flinch, then straightened and looked him in the eye. Her eyes were the dark green of the cardigan she wore; a cardigan which was adorable.

'I did spot a few inaccuracies,' she said.

Harrison laughed.

'That's one way of putting it.' He glanced at Billy who was gathering his things.

'Best get to the meeting,' said the project

manager. 'Don't want to keep Martin waiting.' He left the room, squeezing past Harrison. Harrison watched Ren turn her shoulders to go past him, following Billy, before taking up the rear, sipping his coffee and smiling to himself.

The meeting started with Martin introducing Ren to everyone she'd already met and then to Val and Liam, who finally turned up ten minutes late. Harrison leaned back in his chair, sipping his coffee as Martin worked his way through the agenda. First, an update from Billy.

'We're bang on schedule. And I've shown Ren some of the game we have so far. I reckon with her input and a little more of a push, we could even get ahead of ourselves.'

Harrison raised an eyebrow, filled his mouth with coffee and watched amused as Liam muttered something under his breath, which everyone pretended not to hear.

Next was an update from Val and her marketing department.

'We've been working on the pre-launch and launch campaigns and have a skeletal plan. We'll need more details before we can flesh it out, but here it is.' She brought up the campaign plans on her laptop connected to the large TV screen on the wall. They all stared up at it as she walked them through. It was standard stuff, nothing new, mostly because she didn't have quite enough detail yet. 'And I have events booked already so we'll be looking at getting some merchandise designed and we'll need a little play through.' She looked pointedly at Bonnie and Liam.

Bonnie didn't talk for long about the art design, essentially echoing what Val had said and claiming that she had stacks of files for Ren to work her way through. Ren smiled but a light in her eyes dimmed at the suggestion. Again, Harrison held back a laugh.

'Harrison? How are we doing?' Martin asked. He was leaving Liam till last. He always left Liam until last, because Liam had the most explaining to do.

Harrison cleared his throat.

'No show and tell today, I'm afraid. The numbers are looking good, the budget is holding strong and, as Val said, interest is growing. We already have a good number of pre-orders, and magazines and shops are interested in reviewing and stocking it. Just need to get the game finished, huh?' He gave Liam a playful look and got a scornful glare in response. 'I hope you won't be creating freebies for your events.' He turned on Val.

'We have a budget for freebies,' she told him.

'There's no money in free stuff,' he said. 'A play through, yes. Whet their appetite, push them to buy the full game. But don't go making crap no one wants that costs us money but doesn't make us money.'

Val rolled her eyes but Harrison was used to that.

'Hopefully our new scientist can help make it all more authentic,' he continued, looking to Ren who finally met his eyes. There was a hardness there and Harrison hesitated at the sight. 'The more authentic it is, the more chance we've got of selling the thing. Authenticity and gore,' he added to Liam. 'That's what'll make the sales.'

'Next you'll be wanting more sex in there,' Val muttered.

'Well, now that you mention it,' Harrison started as Martin shifted in his seat. 'We don't have to go getting desperate,' he told her. 'It's a dinosaur game. More teeth, less sex.'

'It's not *just* a dinosaur game,' Liam blurted. 'It's an MMORPG.'

There was a pause and then Ren slowly lifted a hand. Harrison's heart skipped at the sight. That was more adorable than her cardigan.

'Yes, Ren?' Martin ventured.

'Erm, sorry. What's an M...O...R...'

'An MMORPG,' said Liam. 'A massively multi-player online role-playing game. MMORPG. Basically you have servers and on each server you can have thousands of real people creating their own characters, or avatars, and playing the game alongside each other, with each other, and facing NPCs.'

'Non-playable characters,' Bonnie whispered to Ren who gave a resolute nod.

'And the dinosaurs are...NPCs?' Ren checked.

'Yes,' Liam almost snapped.

Harrison gave him a level gaze, not that the developer noticed.

'People can face dinosaur NPCs in the game, attack them or interact with them,' Bonnie explained. 'And some classes of characters can have them as steeds and pets.'

'Classes?' Ren murmured, sinking lower into her chair.

'We have a range of classes people can choose for their character or avatar. Each one with specific skills, abilities and items they can use—'

'And items they can buy,' Harrison cut in.

'Hmm. The classes are hunters, warriors, poachers, magicians... How much did you play?' Bonnie asked Billy.

'I just saw a man walking through a jungle spotting some...dinosaurs,' Ren explained.

'There's more to it than that.' Liam closed his eyes.

'Then maybe you should show her,' Martin offered. 'Remember, Ren is new to all this but she has valuable insight. Harrison is right, we need this to be authentic. I want feathers as well as teeth, people. Liam, you'll give Ren a proper walkthrough of what you have so far. Block out half a day for it, at least. Bonnie, block out a day to go through the dinosaur designs. Right, Liam, time for your update.'

And just like that, Harrison's part in the meeting was over.

As they spilled out of the meeting room, Martin went right to his office but everyone else went left. Val headed straight for the lift to return to the fourth floor while Billy collapsed in his chair with a grunt. Bonnie and Ren walked in front of Harrison.

'I'll send you the files so you can look through them and then maybe we can take a look together in a couple of days and you can give me notes? You can annotate them, or do whatever feels comfortable. How does that sound?' Bonnie asked.

'Perfect. Thank you.'

'And in the meantime, maybe Liam can give you a proper run down of the game?' Bonnie added pointedly.

Liam sighed.

'Like I have the time,' he moaned. 'I'll figure it out. Maybe one of my developers can walk you through it as they're working on it.'

'Whatever works for you,' Ren agreed.

They all took their seats except for Ren who ventured to the kitchen with her coffee cup. Silently, Harrison followed.

'Don't worry, you get the hang of it pretty quick,' he told her as she pressed the coffee machine into action. Ren hugged herself as she turned to him.

'Thanks.' It wasn't a smile she gave him although

maybe that's what she thought it was. Harrison studied her.

'Been in Edinburgh long?' he asked.

'No. No, I got here last week. Wednesday.'

Harrison whistled.

'Not even been here a week.'

'How long have you been here?' she asked.

'At this company? Three years. In Edinburgh? Yeah, three years.'

'Not three years working on this project, though?' Some of the hardness in Ren's eyes lifted, curiosity winning over.

'No,' he told her, unable to wrench his gaze from her. 'I started working in the centralised team – floor three – helping build the financial position of the whole company. Once I'd proven myself, they asked me to take over this project. They need it to be profitable and know that I can make that happen.'

'With no freebies,' Ren said in a low voice.

Harrison laughed.

'No freebies,' he repeated. 'And what a lesson for life that is.'

Ren frowned, wrinkles appearing between her eyes and her mouth twisting slightly. She took her coffee and moved out of Harrison's way.

'Guess I best go look at dinosaurs,' she said.

'But that's what you live for, right?' he asked, putting his cup in place and pressing the buttons for a coffee. When he turned back, Ren looked up into his eyes.

'Looking at pictures isn't quite the same as looking at rocks.'

Harrison blinked and then grinned.

'You'd rather be looking at rocks?'

There was a pause and then Ren smiled. Harrison tilted his head a little. That wasn't her true smile, he could tell. It was three quarters a polite, held-back smile. He wondered what she was holding back.

'I don't know,' said Ren. 'Let's wait and see.'

On her second day, Ren wore a dress. It was one of her favourites, hanging down past her knees, over leggings and ankle boots. She walked into the office feeling much more herself and smiled as Billy and Bonnie greeted her. Liam's desk was empty, as were quite a few of the other desks in the office. She'd managed to get in at quarter past eight, wanting to show willing on her second day without being too early. Having placed her coat over the back of her chair and turned on her computer, she ventured over to the kitchen to make herself a coffee. Billy followed her.

'Ready for round two?' he asked with a chuckle.

Ren's brow creased at the oddness of the remark but she gave him a smile nonetheless.

'Absolutely. Ready to spend a day looking through images of dinosaurs.'

Billy made a strange noise, as if a light-hearted laugh had been strangled on its way out. Grabbing a can of something fizzy from the fridge, he gave her a nod and meandered back to his desk. Her eyes followed him as he left and she tried to work out what had just happened. As Billy found his seat, her gaze found Harrison, walking through the hallway that connected their offices. Their eyes met for a moment across the large room and Ren wrenched herself away as her insides jolted. Blowing out her cheeks, she filled her cup with coffee, and as she turned to leave, Harrison blocked her way.

'Morning,' he said, a little too brightly.

'Good morning.'

Harrison glanced over his shoulder to where Billy sat hunched at his computer. With a smile, he traded places with Ren to make his own coffee at the machine.

'Met the real Billy this morning, huh?'

'The real Billy?' Ren had been about to amble back to her desk but at Harrison's words, she turned back to him, keeping her voice low.

'Yeah. Nice guy, don't get me wrong, but didn't anything about him feel a little forced to you yesterday?'

Ren gave this some thought while having a covert peek at Billy behind her.

'He was really helpful.' She looked back to Harrison. 'Is he...not normally?'

Harrison laughed.

Something inside Ren twitched.

Laughing was something the American did a lot, which seemed at odds with how Bonnie had described him. It wasn't just that, though. It was that his laugh was deep and full-hearted, if not full-bellied. Something about Harrison's laugh warmed Ren's insides and made her eager to stay by his side, ready for whatever he might find funny next.

As it was, there was only enough time to be reminded that his laugh had played in her head that entire evening before he was talking again.

'Oh, very helpful that one. As long as it doesn't take much time and it distracts him from what's important.'

Ren frowned.

'He avoids his work?' she interpreted.

Harrison looked down and met her eyes in a moment of silence.

'You'll see soon enough,' he told her, his voice a little gentle, his blue eyes dancing. And they were blue. Set against the silver of his hair, they were ice blue, but the dark flecks shining through the silver – the clue as to how Harrison might have looked ten years ago – made the blue of his eyes bright. Especially when he laughed, especially now as he softened a little.

Ren chastised herself for even noticing.

'The joys of a new job,' she murmured to fill the growing silence.

'Hmm. Must be a real shock to the system, huh? Going from a – university, wasn't it? – to some-where like this.'

Ren nodded.

'A little.'

'Have you ever worked in an office?'

'Of course. Palaeontologists work in offices. I had an office in the Natural History Museum, and at the university. It just...wasn't quite like...this,' she added, looking around as more people arrived and found their desks. When she turned back, Harrison's eyes were still on her, unmoving. 'There wasn't a break room with game consoles,' she explained. 'Or even a decent coffee maker. Hell, at the university we were expected to fill a kettle from the toilet taps.'

Harrison pulled a face.

'I can't imagine a better place to be made redundant from.'

Ren grinned before she could think.

'It was dire,' she agreed. 'And fairly toxic.' She glanced back to Billy. 'Would you describe this place as toxic?'

When Harrison didn't reply immediately, she turned back to him and there were those blue eyes, still watching her. He seemed to tear his gaze away, glancing over her to Billy.

'Not toxic, no,' he said, which Ren realised was exactly what someone would say if they were the toxicity in a workplace. 'Sometimes it's explosive,' he finished with a playful tone.

'At least you have an office of your own to escape to,' Ren said, realising she wasn't quite ready for the conversation to end. Harrison had shifted to make his escape back down the hallway, but at this, he stopped and turned back to her. A smile brightened his features, a grin that usually accompanied the deep laugh.

'True. If you ever want a moment to stare at the castle, my office is the best place.' Ren decided she had imagined him looking her up and down as he spoke, he was probably wondering where her stiff, academic style had vanished to. 'Or the roof,' he added, bringing his cup to his lips and sipping what must have been scalding coffee as he turned his back on her and wandered out of the open-plan area.

Ren watched him go and then shook the fizz out of her free hand. The day had already had a strange start and she wasn't even at her computer yet.

When she returned to her desk, Billy still had his head down and Bonnie had arrived.

'Good morning.' She gave Ren a grin. 'All recovered from yesterday?'

Ren nodded, smiling.

'Got my bearings, ready to get to work properly checking out your dinosaurs.'

'Great! I mean, there's a deadline and all, but other than that, no rush. Liam! Good morning.'

Even Billy looked up as Liam plonked a bag on his desk.

'You're early.'

Liam gave Billy a look.

'I was working until three this morning,' he said

bluntly.

'Well, that was silly of you,' said Bonnie, grabbing his mug from his desk on her way past. 'Coffee?'

'Gallons of the stuff, please.' Liam nodded. Then his gaze landed on Ren. 'If you're not too busy with Bonnie's designs today, I can introduce you to one of my main developers who's putting all the dinosaur artwork into the game. So we can make sure everything is...authentic.'

Ren didn't like the way he said 'authentic', given that it sounded like he was mocking her entire purpose for being there, but as it was only her second day and was in her job description, she nodded.

'Great. Whenever you're ready.'

Liam gave a huff and plonked into his chair, opening his laptop and immediately getting to work. Ren turned back to her own screen and, above their partition, Billy raised his eyebrows at her. She smiled back and they both got to work.

'No, Mum, everyone seems nice. The office is lovely. Everything's fine,' Ren spoke into the phone as she wandered back to the office.

Drizzle was falling on the city, turning every-thing a slightly darker shade. Clouds hung heavy, covering the top of Arthur's Seat in a light mist. That, along with the close alleyways and cobbled streets, gave Ren the impulsive desire to don a cape and stalk through the old town in an historic re-enactment. A cape with a hood, perhaps. And an umbrella.

This was the type of drizzle that got you soaked through.

She slowed as she approached the modern office building, standing out against the backdrop of the old architecture surrounding it. It wasn't the only new building in the vicinity but it still stuck out. Ren hadn't yet decided if she liked it or not.

'Are you making friends?' her mother asked.

'Hmm. Not yet. I was thinking about trying a dating app.'

'You know how I feel about online dating, Ren.'

'I know, but at least it'll get me meeting people?'

She could practically hear her mother pursing her lips down the phone.

'Yes, great, alone in the city and meeting men who are only after one thing? Oh, no. No dating apps. No online dating. No dating. You didn't go up there to meet a man, you went up to work. Find some nice girl friends. What about a yoga class?'

'Yoga classes smell of feet,' said Ren as a group of men walked past her and into the office. She looked up just as Harrison followed the group in. He gave her a strange look followed by a broad grin and doffed his coffee cup at her. She gave him a small, panicked wave.

'A book club, then?'

'Mum, yoga classes are full of women who don't eat sugar and book club women spend all their time drinking.'

'That's still better than axe murderers and rapists.'

Ren sighed. There was just no arguing with her mother.

'Fair point,' she said. 'Fine. No dating apps. I'll look for a wholesome female club to join, or something. Maybe I'll discover I've been secretly a lesbian all these years, two birds with one stone, then. Huh?'

'It would explain your awful taste in men.'

Ren looked up at the steel grey sky and took a moment to relish the rain on her face.

'Thanks, Mum.'

'After what Oliver did to you, I wouldn't think you'd want to try online dating. You need to figure out who you are again before you go finding a man.'

'I know who I am, Mum. And we agreed not to talk about Olly.' *The arsehole*, Ren added silently.

'True. We're not talking about that arsehole.'

Ren grinned to herself.

'What if I just need to get back on the horse?' she pondered.

'Oh, horse riding! You haven't done that since you were a child. What about horse riding?'

The very notion made Ren's legs ache.

'I'll think about it,' she lied. 'Gotta go, Mum. Lunch is over and it's raining.'

'Okay. Take care, love.'

Once off the phone and inside the building, Ren shook the water droplets from her hair and arms, and made a dash for the lift before the doors closed.

Back at her desk, she peeled off her coat and dug around in her bag for a hair brush.

'Ren?'

She turned to find Liam and a man behind her. Liam glanced at how wet she was and then his gaze travelled past her to the windows on the other side of the office. 'Raining?' he asked.

'More than it looks,' Ren told them, meeting the other man's gaze. He gave her a warm smile and Ren caught herself melting a little. As far as attractive men went, this one was gorgeous. Dark, soft brown hair with large eyes to match, full lips and a smile that deserved a Hollywood star.

'Hmm. This is Dougal. He's our main dinosaur developer, coding all of Bonnie's designs into the game. Doug, this is Ren, our...palaeontologist.'

Ren wondered if she'd have to give Liam lessons on how to say her profession without making it sound like she'd just crawled out of a slime-filled bog. Or the bog of eternal stench. She tried not to smile at her own silent pop culture reference.

Dougal held out a large hand with long fingers and Ren was acutely aware that her own hand was slick with rain as she took his and they shook.

'Nice to meet you,' he said, and the damn man had the softest of Scottish accents. He was tall too, the perfect height for her to melt into, and a little broad in the shoulders. Enough to suggest he knew what a gym was. 'Liam suggested I show you the game.' He glanced behind her to her computer. 'Come to my desk, it's all set up and we can get started.'

'Oh, erm, okay.' Ren glanced down at the brush in her hand and the empty coffee cup on her desk. Dougal followed her gaze and smiled.

'Go do what you gotta do, me and Liam need a chat first anyway.'

Ren grinned and made a stupid noise as she exhaled at the same time. She made her escape as quickly as possible, cursing the day she bought a coat without a hood to protect her hair from the Edinburgh rain.

As she jogged towards the toilets, Bonnie stepped out and they almost crashed into each other.

'Woah!' Bonnie held up her hands.

'Sorry!' Ren screeched to a halt.

'It's okay.' Bonnie studied Ren's hair. 'Got caught in the drizzle, huh?'

'Yeah, should have bought the coat with the hood.'

'You're not in Kansas anymore, Dorothy. Hey, I was thinking, you've only just moved here, right? Don't know anyone yet?'

Ren hesitated before answering.

'Yeah,' she said slowly.

'Want to go for a drink? I can show you the best spots.'

Ren stared into Bonnie's warm eyes for a moment too long. Could making friends be this easy? She could have hugged Bonnie in that moment.

'Yeah. That would be great. Thanks.' Ren tried not to gush.

'Okay, I'll grab your number when we're back at our desks.' Bonnie stepped aside and Ren was able to walk into the toilets as a calm, sane person who then, for a split second, forgot why she was in there.

Harrison had tried a number of ways to meet people when he'd first arrived in Edinburgh. He'd spent his weekends doing the tourist things, among throngs of other Americans who would be catching their next flight any day now, and his evenings joining (and leaving) clubs and meeting groups. By his fifth weekend, he'd completed the tourist traps and turned his attention to the game of golf. It seemed the thing to do, being a businessman in Scotland, and where better to meet his peers?

Harrison wasn't looking for a date; he was looking for a friend.

And he'd found one. During his second visit to the club, there had been a few other men at the driving range practising their swings. They had gotten talking to one another and suddenly someone suggested a game together. Among those men was Mac, a short, brown-haired man from Inverness whose family had been farmers until Mac broke the mould. Deciding he preferred the city to the fields of home, he'd qualified as an accountant and had worked his way up the ranks in financial firms in Inverness before moving to Edinburgh for a bigger slice of the monetary pie.

He and Harrison had clicked almost immediately.

They'd also discovered, by around hole five, that golf was mind-numbingly boring, and by the end of the game, they realised they both preferred to sit in the bar drinking than trying to skilfully hit a ball into a hole.

Given that the golf club membership was eye-wateringly expensive, they opted to continue their friendship by exploring the various pubs and bars the city had to offer, where there was no entrance fee and where single women who didn't look down their noses were allowed to tread.

Harrison downed the first half of his pint in one go as Mac watched, amused.

'Everything all right there, buddy?' Mac brought his own pint to his lips.

'I need your help,' Harrison told him.

'Oh? With what?'

An agreement had been made, some weeks after their first meeting and after a lot of beer had been consumed. Harrison had confessed all and Mac had made a proposal: Harrison would assist Mac in his career if Mac assisted Harrison in his personal life. His romantic life, to be more exact.

Mac leaned across the table to Harrison and

whispered, 'Is there a girl?'

Harrison nodded, staring into his beer.

'There's the potential of a girl,' he muttered.

'Well, we've been through this,' said Mac, sitting back and fiddling with the beer mat that should have been under his glass. 'If you truly like her, then you need patience.' He looked up at Harrison. 'Do you like her?'

'We wouldn't be talking about her if I didn't,' Harrison pointed out.

'Right,' said Mac, returning his attention to the beer mat, fraying its edges with his fingers. 'Is she cute?'

Harrison looked up at his closest friend and scowled.

'Right, right,' Mac acknowledged. 'Is she single?'

'I don't know.'

Mac leaned forward again.

'Does she have a friend?'

The men stared at one another for a moment and then Harrison laughed as Mac grinned.

'Remember the last time you felt like this?' Mac asked, sitting back again and twirling the beer mat between his fingers. 'You thought you liked her, she was single, you asked her out, and three dates in you realised she was only going out with you for your accent.'

'She wanted me to dye my hair,' said Harrison, squinting at the memory.

Mac gave a hushed laugh.

'Yeah. And she hated me.' He looked up and gave Harrison an expression of complete seriousness. 'That alone was a red flag.'

Harrison laughed again. He could always count on Mac to cheer him up.

'So,' his friend continued. 'What could be wrong with this one?'

Harrison blew out an exhale in a puff of cheeks.

'Oh, anything. I barely know the woman. She could be married. She could be gay. She could hate dogs.'

Mac pulled a face.

'She could be after your money,' he suggested quietly.

Harrison's brow furrowed and he filled his mouth with beer, shaking his head.

'No,' he said after swallowing. 'I don't think that's her.'

Mac narrowed his eyes.

'How long have you known her?'

'She started on Monday and today is Friday, so.. .yeah.' Harrison downed another mouthful.

This time Mac laughed, smacking his hand down on the table.

'Five days? Five days, Harry? Wow. You really do have a problem.'

Harrison gestured to himself. *I know! You know! That's why we're here.*

'Wow.' Mac whistled to himself. 'Five days. Okay, so she's pretty. She has to be. What else is there? Jeez, Harry, anything could be wrong with her. I'm here for you, mate.' He reached across the table to Harrison, nowhere near touching him but pointing a finger at him. 'No doing anything stupid. No asking her out, no nothing. Just be patient. You work with the woman? Just be professional.'

Harrison grimaced.

'Right.' He downed the rest of his pint, smacking his lips and wiping his mouth with his hand. 'I can do that.'

'You do it all the time,' Mac agreed.

'With women I'm not attracted to.'

'So, pretend you're not attracted to her. It's been five days, Harry. At least give yourself ten or something.'

Harrison smiled to himself.

'Another week? I can do that.'

'Make it a couple of months, just to be safe,' said Mac, his voice echoing a little as he spoke into his raised pint glass, letting another mouthful of beer disappear down his throat. He looked around the pub. 'Not sure about this place,' he said.

Harrison gazed around.

'It's quiet,' he said. 'Maybe that's a good thing.'

'Bar's full of miserable old men.'

'So's this table,' said Harrison.

'Speak for yourself.'

The men's eyes met for a beat and then they both laughed.

'It's Friday night, Harry,' said Mac, downing the

last of his pint. 'We need to go where the action is.'

Harrison's back disagreed as he went to move.

'Depends on the action,' he told Mac, watching his friend stand and pull on his coat.

'Somewhere with more chatter and more women.'

Harrison pulled a face.

'Well, the women aren't for you, are they,' said Mac, gesturing wildly for Harrison to get up and grab his coat. 'We won't talk to them. It'd just be nice to look at something other than your face or a possible future.' He glanced at the men huddled over their pints at the bar.

Harrison slid his coat on.

'Fair enough. But no dancing, no bachelor parties, no leaving me for a pretty face.' He smiled to himself and then had to straighten his lips as Mac caught him.

'Stag parties,' Mac corrected. 'And no leaving you for a pretty face. How about an ugly face?'

Harrison shrugged, following Mac out of the pub.

'No faces,' he told his friend. 'How do I get this girl out of my head?'

The Edinburgh street was cold and quiet. They were too far out of the city centre, even for a Friday night.

Mac dug his hands into his pockets and led the way. As they walked, the streets became more alive, the pubs they passed filtering music out into the night.

'How about that blues bar we found last week?' Mac ventured.

Harrison sniffed.

'Not sure I can cope with blues right now.'

'Nah, you're right. That won't take your mind off her. Another woman might.'

'No,' said Harrison, resolutely.

Mac looked over his shoulder to flash his friend a playful grin.

'How's work?' Harrison asked as Mac pointed to another pub. There were no drunken yells or loud music coming from the door so Harrison agreed.

Inside, the warmth smacked them in the face along with the smell of spilled beer and the clicking sound of pool balls tapping against one another. Two young couples were playing pool in the corner, a TV was playing in the opposite corner and between them were tables of people, young and old, having a drink and a laugh. This was more their place.

Harrison went straight to the bar and ordered two pints of the beer with the fanciest name while Mac found them a small table off to the side.

'They're doing another restructure,' Mac explained as Harrison seated himself opposite, the two pints and a packet of a crisps on the table. Mac opened the crisps, ripping the edge of the packet so they could both help themselves.

'Is your job in trouble?' Harrison asked.

Mac shrugged, crunching through a handful of crisps. Harrison watched and then glanced around for a menu. Did they do food here? A table nearby had bowls of fries. That would do.

'Don't know yet,' said Mac. 'But it's gotten people talking. Lots of people are starting to jump ship.'

'Hang on,' said Harrison, standing to return to the bar. 'Two bowls of fries incoming,' he said when he sat back at the table.

'Chips,' said Mac without thinking, staring off into space.

Harrison sighed and muttered under his breath, 'Fries.' Then he studied his friend. 'Are you thinking of jumping ship?'

Mac nodded, returning to the room as he lifted his pint.

'Don't suppose they're hiring at your place?'

Harrison gave this some thought.

'Not on my project,' he said. 'Not unless you want to change career, at least. We're after some junior animators and I think the cyber security team is hiring.'

Mac pulled a face.

'But the corporate team might be hiring too. Have a look on their website and if you spot anything I'll put in a good word for you. But' – Harrison leaned forward over the table – 'you should be aiming for a promotion out of this,' he told Mac. 'You need a pay rise, the next step up. Then, even if you don't get a new job, you throw it in your employer's face and *they'll* give you the pay rise.'

Mac gave Harrison a sceptical look.

'I don't think they'll do that during a restructure.'

Harrison shrugged, filling his mouth with beer. He'd had better but the taste could be improved with the chips that were now heading their way. Mac grinned at the woman who brought them over and thanked her in his most flirtatious voice, until Harrison caught his eye. Mac dived into the food as the woman walked away.

'Then see what's around. I'll have a look too. You want the next step, right?'

'Definitely,' said Mac with a mouth full of food. 'Need the beautiful house so I can provide for the wife and children I'll have one day, right?' He laughed bitterly and washed the chips down with a gulp of beer.

'One day,' Harrison told him.

'Yeah, one day we'll both find women who love us for us.'

Harrison sighed, picking at a knot in the wooden table.

'Just need to be patient,' he muttered.

'You think it's easier to find love when you're not earning as much?' Mac asked, watching his friend.

'I don't know yet,' said Harrison.

'It's been years since you took this job.'

'And I still haven't found someone,' Harrison pointed out, his mind immediately conjuring an image of Ren. 'Yet,' he added. The hardness in her eyes fascinated him. She seemed to put blocks up but soften as soon as he said anything that made her curious, and so far this week a lot of things had made her curious. Watching her eyes soften had become his new favourite pastime.

'Patience,' Mac's voice cut through his thoughts.

'Patience,' Harrison agreed, lifting his pint. Mac clinked their glasses together and both men drank deeply.

The thing that shocked Ren the most about how her new employer and team celebrated Halloween was that none of them had dressed as a dinosaur.

No, wait, it was that they celebrated it at all in the first place. What company celebrated Halloween?

'Was this Harrison's idea?' Ren whispered to Bonnie as they traipsed towards the meeting place.

'No. Why?'

Ren shrugged.

'Americans like Halloween, don't they.'

Bonnie gave her a sideways look.

'You don't like Halloween? How can you not celebrate Halloween when you live in one of the most haunted cities in Europe? I believe Harrison actually groaned when Martin suggested this. I'd be surprised if he showed up.'

Ren wished she'd had courage to not show up, but the pull of needing to impress her boss and the desire to make friends had won out. So there she was, bundled up in her coat on the last day of

October, walking through the centre of Edinburgh with Bonnie by her side as the evening darkness swept over the city. Ren shivered.

'Do they do this every year, then?'

'Pretty much.' Bonnie nodded before elbowing Ren and giving her a grin. 'C'mon. It'll be fun.'

Ghost tours, especially outside on a cold night, were not Ren's idea of fun.

They were meeting on the Royal Mile, which seemed harmless enough. The wide street was emptying of tourists and their teammates were easy to spot. There was Martin, a hand up to wave at them. There was Val with one of her managers, dragged along for the ride. Liam was nowhere to be seen but Dougal and a handful of developers seemed to have taken his spot. And there, near the back, was the broad-shouldered, silver-haired Harrison. His hands were dug into his pockets and his expression aptly depicted how Ren felt. Ren, however, plastered a smile on her face and greeted the people she'd gotten to know over the last two weeks.

Martin clapped his hands.

'Are we all here? We're all here,' he announced.

A woman in a dark cloak, hood pulled over her hair, stepped out of the shadows by the nearest shop front and greeted them all. She talked a little about what to expect and did a little health and safety chat, with just enough mention of the need to stick together to make Ren's stomach squeeze. She swallowed what was likely a lump of fear but tasted a little like bile, and gave Bonnie a weak smile as her new friend clapped excitedly.

They were led down the Royal Mile towards a crossroads and then away from the city centre. Ren matched her pace with Bonnie's.

'Oh, Ren, you should have been here last year. We did the Vaults. We should do the Vaults again,' said Bonnie with a small squeal.

'Never again,' came Dougal's voice from in front of them. 'Ever.' He glanced over his shoulder and flashed Ren a smile.

Stomach twisting with a jolt of pleasure, Ren took a shaky breath. She could just about cope with nerves and the last couple of weeks had taught her that she could just about cope with being close to Dougal's soft accent and warm scent, but she wasn't certain about mixing all three.

'What was wrong with the Vaults?' she asked.

'They're incredibly haunted and there are some mean ghosts in there,' said Bonnie, lowering her voice and thoroughly enjoying herself. 'Burke and Hare used to stuff their murder victims there before they sold the corpses.' She held up her hands in a lame impression of a spooky ghost.

'Right,' said Ren.

'It's pitch black and the place where a lot of people have died,' came Harrison's voice from behind. 'It's not a pleasant place to go.'

Another shiver ran over Ren.

'I'm glad we're staying out in the open air, then,' she murmured.

They reached the cemetery gates and the tour leader unlocked them, leading them inside. She started with a short history of the cemetery.

'Greyfriars is so named for the Franciscan monastery that was here until 1559,' she began, leading them to the front of the small church. 'The monks wore grey habits and so were nicknamed the Grey Friars.'

Ren had visited Greyfriars Kirkyard the previous weekend, wishing to get a lay of the land and see it in daylight before being subjected to the ghost tour. In the light of an October afternoon, it was incredibly pretty. There was a neat lawn with pathways leading visitors around the cemetery and to the two entrances. Dotted around were trees glorious in autumn yellows and golds. The sides were lined with huge mausoleums that backed onto wonky houses on the other side of the cemetery wall. At the top of the cemetery was a section that was blocked off, although Ren hadn't really understood why.

'You may have noticed,' said the tour guide in her low, gentle voice, 'that the cemetery is higher than the road we have just left. Over time, the cemetery became over-crowded until the festering smell of bodies piled upon bodies was deemed a health and safety issue, and the cemetery was closed.'

Ren pulled a face, looking down at her feet. The developers began making spooky noises under their breaths, elbowing each other. Ren followed the group as the tour guide led them down to the bottom of the cemetery and began telling a story about a lady in white. Ren stayed near the back of the group, focusing on the street lights that could be seen over the wall. Bonnie didn't appear to notice, she was near the front, hanging on the tour guide's story and giggling as one of the developers made their teammates jump.

Eager for anything that might help her not look into the shadows or think about ghosts, Ren pulled out her phone. Yes, it was rude, but her pounding heart needed the distraction.

Her attention was soon pulled from the tour when she noticed she had a handful of notifications.

The tour moved, slowly ambling up the path towards the church.

'You're not bored, are you?' Bonnie whispered, grabbing Ren's shoulders to make her jump. Ren shooed her away.

'No. No, I'm not bored, I'm just... I don't like this much,' she whispered back.

Bonnie accepted this, her gaze drawn down to the light of Ren's phone.

'Have you had responses?'

'Five of them,' said Ren, keeping her voice low.

'Ooh, don't look at them until we can look together.'

Ren gave Bonnie a look.

'Are we looking for a date for you or for me?'

Bonnie grinned.

'I thought you didn't want to go on a date?'

'I don't.'

'Then this is for me, isn't it. It's a bit of fun. You don't actually have to talk to any of them. If you don't want to. Unless they're hot. Are they hot?'

'I haven't looked.'

'No. Good. We'll look together over wine. It'll be a laugh. Relax.' Bonnie gave Ren's arm a squeeze and then skipped back into the group. Ren watched her go and did an accidental double take when she realised Harrison had looked back, catching her eye. He turned just as quickly and Ren became acutely aware that she was on her own. Thankfully, the group stopped and Ren caught up without having to break her stride.

'Let's go back to something nice, shall we?' asked the tour guide. 'Who here knows the story of Greyfriars Bobby?'

Martin put his hand up, looked around and slowly lowered his hand back to his side. The tour guide smiled.

'Bobby is the name of a little terrier dog who belonged to a policeman named John Gray.' The tour guide went on to describe how, after Gray's death, the dog guarded the man's grave for fourteen years until his own death when he was buried just outside the cemetery walls, near the statue of the dog they'd all passed on the way in. Ren listened with interest, despite already knowing the story. It was nice to listen to something that wasn't spooky, only a little sad. On her daytime visit, she'd noted the sticks people had left on a memorial to Bobby at the entrance, and had been forced to move on as a lump in her throat had forced tears into her eyes.

'And who here is a fan of Harry Potter?' the guide ventured.

Val and her manager put up their hands. The guide turned to them and began explaining all the spots of inspiration for the franchise that lay within the cemetery walls. It turned out there was a lot, so Ren peered back down at her phone.

'Not a Harry Potter fan?'

Ren jumped and turned to find Harrison next to her, glancing down at her phone and then meeting her eyes with a playful smile.

'Not really,' she admitted. 'Although I don't think you're allowed to say that. Especially here.'

Harrison shrugged.

'I'm not either.' He looked around at the darkness behind them. 'Are you enjoying the tour, though?'

Ren studied him for a moment, his face was covered in shadow but the nearby lights and the bright light from her phone lit up the silver in his hair and bounced from his blue eyes, turning them almost white. In that moment, there was a definite feeling of safety coming from the man.

'I am,' she said. 'I just...get freaked out easily.' She sighed, her shoulders lifting to her ears as a chill breeze swept over them. 'I didn't expect to see you here.'

Harrison returned his attention to her, his eyes searching hers.

'Oh? Why's that?'

'I don't know. Doesn't seem like your thing.'

Harrison laughed, a smaller, quieter version of his usual belly laugh.

'What does seem my thing?'

Ren looked the man up and down and gave another shrug.

'I have no idea,' she admitted. 'Golf?'

Harrison's eyes danced.

'Tried that, it's incredibly boring.'

Ren smiled before she could stop herself.

'Really? What do you like then?'

Another shiver ran through Ren and this time it was because Harrison raked his gaze over her.

'I like fine eating and drinking,' he told her. 'I'm here because we're going to the pub afterwards.'

'Oh. Of course.' Ren gave a nod and then ventured aiming a playful smile his way as the tour began to move on. 'You like wine?'

'Beer,' he corrected. 'You Brits do good beer.'

Ren raised an eyebrow.

'Never thought I'd hear an American say that.'

Harrison laughed again, only louder this time and something in Ren softened.

While Harrison wasn't sure what caused the hardness in Ren's eyes when they were in the office, this time he knew he could blame it on the ghost tour. Not that he was really listening to it. Being out in the cemetery at night was an experience. The air was cold and fresh, the stars above them twinkled whenever there was a break in the cloud, and it was quiet and peaceful. That alone was enough to warrant coming on this so-called ghost tour. The fact that he'd managed to make Ren's eyes soften again was the cherry on the cake.

He smiled to himself as the tour guide led them to the back of the cemetery and the Covenanters' Prison, pausing to explain the history. From the corner of his eye, he watched Ren listen attentively, her phone dark and back by her side.

He knew the history of the cemetery, he'd done this exact tour when he'd first moved to the city. Still, he didn't whisper in Ren's ear or attempt to engage her. Instead, he waited, watching her listen, and tried to ignore the developers winding each other up.

Eventually, their noise became so much that Martin turned, open-mouthed, ready to shut them up. Before he could, Bonnie wheeled round to face them.

'Oi!' she yelled.

The silence that followed swept across the cemetery. Harrison fancied that even the ghosts were waiting for her next words. Furious, Bonnie looked at each developer in turn.

'I know you're having a laugh but some people here are interested in learning the stories we're being told. And you're in a cemetery. Have some respect.' Bonnie turned back to the tour guide. 'Sorry about that. Please, continue.'

The tour guide was beaming at Bonnie. She cleared her throat and continued where she'd left off. Martin gave the developers a defiant nod. Harrison couldn't help but glance sideways at Ren and found that she was giving him a look, an expression that was to be exchanged. He did so, heart pounding as they both turned back to the tour guide, the smile he was holding back aching on his lips.

They moved on.

'On a dark night in the late nineties, a homeless man came into the cemetery seeking shelter,' said the tour guide as they moved slowly from grave-stone to gravestone. 'Breaking into a mausoleum that offered protection from the Edinburgh storm that was raging, he didn't take into account the rotten floorboards. Crashing through the floor, he found himself surrounded by the remains of several people. Victims, they say, of the Plague, illegally dumped and decomposing so slowly that they were not yet just bones. They were wet and sticky with flesh.'

Val and the manager she'd brought along gave a small squeal and then laughed.

'Yes, ladies. That's pretty much what he did,' said the tour guide. Lifting a hand, she slowly lowered the hood from her head revealing a shock of purple hair tied back. Harrison raised an eyebrow. Her hair had been green a few years ago. He took a moment to admire it and wished they were in the pub. 'He screamed and scrabbled and tore his way out of there, leaving behind his belongings and escaping the cemetery. But not before he had awoken something.'

In a hushed silence, the tour guide led them to a round mausoleum with dirty grey arches and a black domed roof, green with plants growing through the tiles. At the front, below a carved family crest, were slim black double doors. Harrison didn't blame the homeless man. It was the most sheltered place in the cemetery, save for the church.

'This,' continued the tour guide, gesturing to the mausoleum, 'is the Black Mausoleum and the last resting place of Sir George Mackenzie who persecuted the Covenanters – those who were imprisoned just over there – in such a vile, inhumane way that he was nicknamed Bloody Mackenzie. Now, I'm not keen on calling the man horrible, although he was. Why don't I want to voice my thoughts on him? Because...' The tour guide paused for a moment, looking from developer to developer to Val to Martin to Ren and, finally, to Harrison. 'Since the date that poor homeless man fell into a pit of remains and bones, people have had strange experiences. Right here, on this very spot. Even in the nineteenth century, his spirit was said to wait right here for passers-by and since that poor homeless man awoke something, people such as your good selves have been injured, scratched and cut by things that aren't there. They've gone faint. They've become sick. They've felt cold spots, smelt strange smells on the air and heard disembodied voices. We even recently had someone pass out.' She looked around them all again, holding each gaze for a second before moving on. 'The famous author Robert Louis Stevenson once wrote of Bloody Mackenzie that the man's soul is certainly in hell and sometime or other, the door must open.' She stopped, looking over her shoulder to the Black Mausoleum, and then she stepped away, as if into the shadows.

Harrison had to admire her acting. Val and her friend jumped forward and then screeched as one of the developers leaned over and tapped on the doors. Ren stepped back as Bonnie reminded the developers to stay respectful and to perhaps not incur the poltergeist's wrath.

Harrison scoffed, looking back for Ren. He found her on the path, near a lamp light, peering at her phone.

'You okay?' he asked, approaching slowly. 'You don't believe in ghosts, do you?'

Ren gave him a weak smile.

'Well, no, but...' She looked back to the developers, laughing with one another. 'This thing has to be nearly done, right?' she whispered.

'Nearly.' Harrison nodded. 'That should be the last story. I've been on one of these tours before. Same guide, in fact,' he clarified when Ren gave him a curious look.

One of the developers screamed and Ren jumped violently, her arm brushing against Harrison as she darted closer to him. Harrison smiled, holding out his hands as if to catch her but not touching her. Maybe a ghost tour wasn't such a bad thing.

'All right?' he asked.

Breathing hard, she looked up at him, a hand on her chest. She nodded.

'Hmm.'

He glanced down at the phone in her hand.

'You talking to someone?'

Ren followed his gaze.

'Oh, no. It's just a distraction.' She peered back

over to the Black Mausoleum where Bonnie was chatting to the tour guide, and Dougal and his colleagues were daring each other to knock again on the mausoleum doors.

'And that!' cried the tour guide, spotting what the developers were up to. 'Is the end of the tour. Please follow me if you don't wish to be locked inside here with the white lady and Bloody Mackenzie.'

Grateful, Harrison and Ren followed the group out and waited patiently while the tour guide locked the gates. Finally, she turned back to them, giving Martin and Bonnie a smile.

'Thank you so much. I really enjoyed that,' Martin told her.

'And thank you very much for joining me. I hope you learned something as well as getting a feel for some of our city's more famous spirits. Happy Halloween and a safe night to you all on this precarious evening.' The tour guide handed out leaflets to each of them, giving a brief overview of the other tours they offered. All of which Harrison had already done.

They gave the tour guide a short, quiet round of applause before going their separate ways. The tour guide heading to wherever she went next, presumably to gather the next group, while the Martin led the way towards a nearby bar. About time. Harrison needed a drink.

He and Ren took up the rear of the group and

once again, Ren checked her phone.

'We're away from the ghosts,' Harrison told her. 'You must be chatting to someone interesting.' Was it a boyfriend? A husband, perhaps? Or a girl-friend? His stomach twisted with the unasked and unanswered question hanging over him.

'Not chatting, no.' Ren sighed and did a little skip to go up on tiptoes, checking who was in front of them. 'It's silly, really. Bonnie convinced me to sign up to a dating app. She made my profile when we went out for drinks one night. I didn't think anyone would actually be interested but...I've had five matches.' Ren grimaced. 'I promised my mum I wouldn't join a dating app. But I want to meet people, you know?'

'I can think of better ways of meeting people,' said Harrison, a little harsher than he meant to. But a dating app profile meant that she was single. A part of him relaxed at the news. Not only was she single but she was interested in meeting someone.

Mac's voice sounded in his head. *Patience. You've known her two weeks.* And Mac had told him to wait. Harrison had to do as Mac said, that was the agreement they'd come to. So he bit his lip and pushed those thoughts aside.

'I told Bonnie that but she met her boyfriend using this app, so...' Ren drifted off.

'Are you going to meet any of them?' Harrison asked, his mouth now painfully dry.

'I don't know,' said Ren. 'I promised Bonnie we'd

go through them together.' She shook her head. 'No, of course I'm not going to meet them. It was just a bit of fun for Bonnie.' She flashed Harrison a grin and he smiled in return.

'Fun for Bonnie? That doesn't sound like good news for her relationship.'

Ren's smile faded.

'No, I wondered about that,' she murmured. She seemed to shake the thoughts away and glanced up at him. 'Have you made friends here?'

'I have.'

'How did you meet them?'

Harrison glanced down, meeting her eyes. There wasn't a trace of hardness there and it took everything he had to remember his promise to Mac.

'A failed game of golf, actually,' he told her. When she frowned, he added, 'We were at a golf club, we played a game and realised it was boring as all hell so we went to the bar and drank instead.'

Ren grinned.

'I like that. Although it's not helpful to me at all. So, I should try things I probably won't like in the hope of meeting someone I connect with?'

'You should try everything,' Harrison corrected. 'You never know.' He studied her for a moment, choosing his words carefully. 'Are you after a friend or a boyfriend? Or girlfriend?'

'A friend,' she told him, looking where she was walking. 'But I seem to be getting on well with Bonnie. I guess a boyfriend would be nice.' She glanced at her darkened phone again as Harrison's insides jolted. 'Friends are more important right now,' she added.

He nodded, trying not to appear too eager.

'And hey, you met a friend at work, you might meet a man at work.'

Ren glanced at the developers who were heading into the bar. Harrison followed her gaze, his stomach turning.

'Maybe. I mean, that does happen, doesn't it,' she said quietly.

'Yeah,' he mumbled as Dougal followed his colleagues inside, laughing loudly.

'Lots of people meet their husband or wife at work,' Ren continued. 'I've never been sure how that works.'

'No,' said Harrison, holding out an arm so that Ren would go ahead of him through the bar doorway. 'Me neither,' he added gently, following her in.

They'd spent too long in the bar on Halloween, telling each other spooky stories, daring each other to drink shots, admiring anyone who came in wearing a costume. Ren had managed to avoid a hangover – she had never been much of a drinker – but there was a quiet about the office that morning that suggested any raised voices would be met with groans.

Bonnie came half-trotting down the hallway that connected the open-plan office to the directors' offices and landed on her desk with a thump.

'Liam. Brace yourself.'

Liam looked up at her, his eyes widening.

'Harrison talked to Martin,' Bonnie told him, as if that made any sense. Ren, twisted in her chair, turned to watch Liam.

Apparently it made complete sense to him.

'Oh no. No, no, no.' He buried his head in his hands for a moment and then straightened, lifting his chin and taking a deep breath. Bracing himself.

'Senior team,' came Martin's voice. The executive producer had followed Bonnie through to the main office. 'Quick meeting, now.' He turned, leading the way to the meeting room.

A loud groan filled the office.

Slowly picking themselves up, the senior team trudged into the meeting room. Ren followed Billy in who followed Liam. Martin and Harrison were already seated and Liam glared at Harrison.

'What have you done?' he hissed.

Harrison didn't give anything away other than slightly narrowing his eyes.

An uneasy feeling swirled in Ren's gut and she swallowed a mouthful of coffee in a poor attempt to soothe it.

Val stormed in last, taking her seat and only acknowledging Bonnie and Martin. Ren attempted a smile at the marketing director but was ignored. *Fine*, Ren thought, *screw you.*

Once they were all seated, sipping their coffees, wincing at their headaches, Martin looked at each of them in turn.

'I know we're all still feeling the effects of last night. First of all, I want to thank you all for coming in and working today. I appreciate it. Liam, it's a shame you couldn't join us last night. It really was a lot of fun.'

Ren had to agree, not that Liam appeared bothered. He was still glaring at Harrison. Ren looked between the men and then studied

Harrison. There wasn't a hint of a hangover about him, but he'd only drunk a few beers and, by the sounds of it, his body was used to that.

'But back to business,' said Martin with a sigh. 'It has come to my attention that we are lagging behind.' His eyes met Billy's. 'You've been saying all this time that not only are we on track, but we could be getting ahead of ourselves, Billy.' He raised a questioning eyebrow and everyone looked down at the table.

Billy cleared his throat.

'According to my calculations, we are on schedule.'

'I would like to see your calculations,' said Martin shortly. 'Regardless, we are currently losing money as momentum builds and patience thins. We absolutely cannot afford to deliver this game late and, after a meeting with head office this morning, we cannot afford to lose momentum and make a loss.' He sighed again. 'Our competitors are bringing out new deals.'

'They're not the same game as us. We'll be unique,' Liam countered.

Martin shook his head.

'It doesn't matter. If they choose the other games because they're available when we're not, we could be losing players.'

'They'll still try us when we release and if we make it good enough, they'll stay. Just as always,' said Bonnie in a soft voice, although whether that was due to her hangover or an attempt to placate the others, Ren wasn't sure.

Martin and Harrison exchanged a look.

'What's he said?' Liam blurted.

Martin gathered himself.

'Harrison has done his job, Liam. He's shown me the figures and to be perfectly honest, recently I've been seeing more of the figures than advancements in the game's development.'

A tense silence descended upon the meeting.

'We're working on getting it right. If the game isn't right, we won't keep those players who buy during the launch,' said Liam with gritted teeth.

'No, well, there won't be a launch if we don't get this sorted.'

Everyone looked up at Martin. He shrugged.

'Head office orders,' he said.

Liam snapped back to Harrison.

'You sent *them* the figures?' he spat.

'That's my job. Maybe if you were doing yours, it wouldn't be a problem,' said Harrison before leaning forward on the table. 'You seem to spend every day and evening working on this game, Liam. We should be ahead by now. Just what have you been doing?'

Everyone turned to Liam whose face was turning the colour of a ripe plum.

'I've been making this game the best it can be,' he managed to get out. 'I've been working my arse off. Unlike you, I do it for the game, not the bonus I get if I go crawling to head office, kissing their arse.'

Harrison gave a half-smile and Ren watched with a sinking heart. Why was he doing this to them? Everyone had been getting along, everything had been going well. She'd been enjoying studying Bonnie's dinosaur designs and helping her to correct them, she enjoyed sitting with Dougal and watching his clever fingers adapt the code to bring Bonnie's designs to life. She hadn't even been here a month but she loved this job. Why was Harrison ruining it?

'And where exactly are the fruits of your so-called labour?' Harrison asked in a gentle tone that brimmed with ferocity.

Liam slammed his hands down on the table, making everyone jump.

'Now, hang on—' started Martin.

'You manipulative, money-grabbing bastard,' Liam growled. 'Anything for a quick pay out. How much are they going to pay you for this one, huh?'

Harrison didn't rise to that. He merely cocked his head ever so slightly to the side and asked, 'Show us what work you did last night.'

'What?'

'The work you did last night. You said you couldn't join us because you wanted to work more on the game.'

Everyone turned back to Liam, expectantly.

'That was an excuse,' said Liam, although some of the wind had been knocked from his sail. The man was visibly shaking and Ren clenched her hands into fists in her lap. This wasn't fair. 'I just don't like ghost tours.'

'So there's nothing to show,' said Harrison, that assassin smile on his lips again.

Liam opened and closed his mouth, but no words came.

'None of this matters anymore,' said Martin with a raised voice.

Beside Ren, Bonnie flinched, her hand going up to brush over her temple.

'Head office have issued new deadlines.' He looked glumly at Liam. 'We've got six months.'

'Six months!' This time it was Val who erupted. 'We can't...' She paused, thinking it through. 'No, okay. Six months. We can do that. Sure. Just about, though.'

Liam shook his head while Billy hurriedly went through files on his laptop.

'We can't,' he was saying. 'Look. All of my projections—'

'Were off,' Harrison told him. 'Because Liam hasn't been doing as much work as you think.'

'How do you know that?' Billy asked.

Everyone turned to Harrison. His keen blue eyes were still on Liam, watching the head developer squirm. Ren pressed her lips together to stop herself saying anything.

She'd been wrong. This place was just like the others. It gave the illusion of safety and then it pulled the rug from under you. It tore people down. This place was no less toxic than the rest. She glanced at Harrison, the only one in the room sitting up tall, then at Martin whose shoulders were slumped. Their boss had given his power away, she decided. He'd given all of his authority to an American capitalist who was now ripping the team apart.

Ren looked back down to the table and tried to focus on her breathing.

'You don't know anything about gaming,' Billy continued to Harrison. 'You don't even know how to turn the consoles on.'

'I've seen it,' said Martin before Harrison could speak. 'He's right. Your projections are off, Billy, and what's your excuse? You do know how to turn the consoles on. You do understand gaming. Why weren't you keeping tabs?'

'I...I was!'

'Six months,' Martin declared before Billy could say anything more. 'I'll email you all to confirm the new deadline. We're going to have to work hard, people.'

'And will we get paid overtime?' Bonnie asked. 'You know, all that overtime we were due on the last project that came four months late? All the overtime that Liam is due for this project?'

Harrison scoffed and Liam's jaw tensed.

'You will get paid overtime,' said Martin. 'Keep records of when you're working and what you're working on during those overtime hours, though. And if we can meet the deadline and the launch is successful' – he gave Val a look – 'there'll be bonuses available, too.'

'For everyone?' Bonnie asked, glancing sideways at Ren.

'For everyone,' said Martin, giving Ren a weak, quick smile. She tried to return it but failed. 'Everyone can go back to work. I'll send more details through later. In the meantime, can Billy and Liam please stay.'

With that, the others scraped back their chairs and silently filed out of the room and back towards their desks.

Val groaned, pushing a hand through her hair.

'This is going to be fine,' she mumbled to herself. 'A few tweaks to the plans, a bit of overtime, some working lunches.' She sighed.

'Good thing we had fun last night, huh?' Bonnie said, and Val laughed over her shoulder.

'We'll do it again to celebrate in six months!' she called, heading to the lift and the fourth floor to give her team the news.

'Is that what you meant about Harrison being cut-throat?' Ren ventured.

Bonnie nodded.

'It happens every now and then.'

'That was horrible.'

Bonnie searched Ren's eyes before leading her slowly to the kitchen.

'As Harrison would say, it's business.'

'But poor Liam,' said Ren. 'Is Harrison really just interested in the money?'

'Well, that is his job.'

'But he should be able to do it without ripping people to shreds and tearing them down,' said Ren, raising her voice a little higher than she meant to. She regained control of herself. 'He seemed so nice. I didn't realise he was a capitalist scumbag.'

Bonnie gave a sweet smile, refilling her coffee cup.

'He was a stockbroker in New York and now he's a finance director. Plus, he apparently comes from money. He's got wealthy, cream of the crop parents. Of course he's like that.' Bonnie turned away from the coffee machine and, a little out of sorts, Ren turned with her and walked straight into Harrison.

As if in slow motion, she looked up into his blue eyes and found not the cut-throat assassin staring down at her but the friendly man who had kept her company on the ghost tour the night before. Heart pounding, Ren swallowed on a mouthful of bile that leapt up her throat. How much had he heard?

'Excuse me,' he said, moving around Ren.

Ren opened her mouth to apologise but couldn't even emit a squeak.

'So, what's Liam been up to?' Bonnie asked, sipping at her coffee.

'I couldn't possibly say,' said Harrison, his back to them.

'You don't know, do you?' said Bonnie with a grin.

Harrison flashed them a smile over his shoulder.

'Pretty sure you girls have work to do.'

'Yeah. Thanks for that,' said Bonnie, still smiling before gesturing with her head for Ren to follow. Ren did as she was told, the apology still lodged in her throat. 'The next six months are going to be tough,' Bonnie told her as they reached their desks. Billy and Liam were still absent, although muffled raised voices could soon be heard from the meeting room. 'We should go out tonight.'

Ren stared at Bonnie.

'Tonight? But...you're hungover and we have all this work to do.'

Bonnie shrugged.

'Work hard, play hard,' she said. 'I'm gonna need a distraction tonight, before I start all this overtime we have no choice but to do. How about a gaming cafe? That'll be sort of work related.'

Ren shook her head in disbelief.

'Sure. Okay. Sure.' She wondered if it was safe to venture to the toilets near the meeting room. It sounded like Martin and Billy had forgotten they were at work and that people could hear them. 'Think I might just...go to the toilets on the fourth floor,' she murmured.

Bonnie listened for a moment and then nodded.

'I would.'

Ren turned away from her desk and again,

walked straight into Harrison as he made his way back to his office. Again, their eyes met as she lifted her gaze to him.

'Sorry,' she murmured.

He let her pass and she pretty much jogged to the lift, not daring to look back. Her stomach churned as she pressed the button to call the lift and a wave of homesickness rocked through her.

'Capitalist scum, huh? That's harsh.' Mac watched as Harrison took his first mouthful of beer and closed his eyes to savour it. 'Maybe she's not the one for you. I bet you're glad you waited now.'

Harrison didn't respond. He only tried to fill the yawning gap in his gut with more beer.

'Don't drink your feelings, mate,' said Mac.

Harrison met his eyes, swallowing his mouthful.

'So now you can move on, right?' Mac asked when Harrison still didn't say anything.

After a long moment, Harrison shrugged, staring into his nearly empty pint glass.

'Fancy another?' he asked.

Mac sighed and brandished his barely touched pint. Harrison ran a hand down his face.

'Maybe she'll come around,' he murmured quietly.

Mac leaned closer as he waited for the muffled words to make sense.

'Maybe,' he agreed, leaning back and sipping his

drink. 'Maybe there'll be someone else.'

'Why does this always happen?' Harrison asked.

Mac hesitated, probably wondering if the question was rhetorical.

'I don't know,' he said eventually. 'You're a good bloke, Harry.'

Harrison smiled but it was bitter.

'Yeah.'

'You are.'

Harrison shook it off, straightening his back, stretching out his arms and turning a new focus onto Mac.

'How's work? Any news on the restructure?'

'Not yet,' said Mac. Now it was his turn to drink sullenly. He brightened a little. 'But I saw the jobs you sent me. The salaries on them! You really think I should go for them?'

Harrison nodded.

'Absolutely. I'll help with the applications, if you like.'

'That'd be great, thanks.'

'No worries. That's what we do, right? I'm gonna make you rich and you're gonna...' Harrison sighed, searching for the right words while his heart squeezed in pain.

'Get you laid?' Mac offered.

Harrison shot him a look.

'Have you ever considered a one nighter?' Mac continued. Harrison's looks rarely put him off, it was one of the things that made Harrison sure that

Mac would achieve great things if only he had the confidence to pursue them. And Harrison would give him that confidence.

'Of course I have,' he told Mac. 'I've had a few of them, too. They don't do anything for me.'

Mac tutted, draining the last of his pint.

'You're just too much of a romantic.'

Harrison barked a laugh and they both considered their empty pint glasses.

'What do you think?' Harrison asked.

'Could have been better.' Mac smacked his lips. 'Another?'

Harrison nodded.

'Go for the most expensive this time.' He reached into his pocket and pulled out some notes, forcing them into Mac's hand as his friend started to argue. He pointed to the bar and then turned his back on Mac.

Sighing, Harrison stared down at the table and wondered what to do about Ren. It wasn't that he'd messed up, as such, just that she didn't have all the facts. But he could hardly share those facts; they weren't his to share. Maybe Mac was right. Or maybe she would come around. This would all blow over, it always did, and he would keep trying to get to know her. She'd see a different side of him, eventually. Unless she didn't, unless she wouldn't be open to talking to him now. Unless she took Liam's side in all of this. Unless she took Billy's side. Billy was the one who had looked after her on her first day, after all. Billy was kind and caring and quiet, in her eyes at least. Harrison couldn't compete with that.

He snarled to himself. He couldn't compete with fiction.

'Don't say no yet, but a couple of women just walked in and I think they might be the answers to our lonely night.' Mac's voice in his ear made Harrison jump. He looked up wildly, heart pounding.

'I can't, Mac,' he said as Mac placed the two pints on the table. 'Not tonight.'

'Okay, fine. But can I?' Mac gave Harrison an imploring look and Harrison blew out his cheeks.

'Knock yourself out.' He'd rather go home and Mac hitting it off with a woman would give him the perfect excuse.

In silence, they both sipped their beers and Harrison's eyes lit up. He studied the liquid in his glass, holding it up to the light.

'Now this one, I like,' he declared.

Mac agreed, drinking more.

'You're definitely gonna have to help me get one of those jobs, so I can keep buying this stuff.'

They laughed and a weight lifted from Harrison.

'Where are these women, then?' he asked, glancing around the pub.

Mac pointed and all that weight and heaviness landed hard back on Harrison's shoulders.

'No,' he said.

'No?'

'I work with them.' The words came out thick. His tongue suddenly too big for his mouth.

'Oh? Oh! Is one of them... Is it the blonde?'

That was the moment that Bonnie turned and met Harrison's eyes, her expression changing in recognition. Harrison swore under his breath.

'No. No, that's Bonnie.'

Mac turned to Harrison.

'The redhead? This girl of yours is a redhead, Harry?'

'Don't call her that and yes, that's Ren. And now they're coming over here.' Harrison turned to Mac and caught him waving to Bonnie, gesturing for her to come over. Harrison smacked his arm down. 'What are you doing?' he hissed.

'What? I can't meet them? Maybe seeing you out of work will help Ren see the real you,' he added in a hoarse whisper before turning to the women as they approached. 'Hey! My mate Harry here says he works with you.'

Mac beamed at them as Bonnie gave Harrison a look. Harrison's heart sank. He didn't dare look at Ren.

'Harry?' said Bonnie.

'Only my closest friends call me Harry,' Harrison told her.

'Aw, not me then? I could almost be insulted.' Smiling, with no resentment whatsoever, Bonnie turned her attention to Mac. 'Hi, I'm Bonnie. I've been suffering Harrison for three years.'

'Mac.' Mac took her hand and they shook. 'Also three years.'

Bonnie laughed and introduced Ren. 'This is Ren, not quite a month.'

'Want to join us?' Mac offered.

Harrison shook his head, still avoiding looking at Ren, but Mac ignored him. Again, Harrison sighed, and then he relented.

'Drinks?' he offered.

'Are you buying?' asked Bonnie, taking a seat. Ren did the same and finally, Harrison glanced up at her. She immediately looked away, putting her focus on a knot in the table.

'Sure. Go get another couple of these, Mac.' Harrison dug his card out of his wallet and Mac gave a mock salute.

'Absolutely, Mr Harrison, sir.' He took the card and vanished to the bar.

Bonnie watched him go, that playful smile still on her lips.

'Fancy meeting you here,' she said after a moment's pause.

'Fancy? I've been here a few times. Never seen you here before.'

Bonnie shrugged.

'Well, someone got our deadline shortened so I wanted a bit of fun before all the work starts. We went to investigate that new gaming café near the office but it was boring.'

'Boring? You're a gamer!'

Bonnie shrugged.

'It was quiet and expensive, not my ideal night out. So we thought we'd investigate somewhere a little more lively.' Bonnie looked around. 'It's nice in here.'

'Yeah, it is. Good beer, too.' Harrison glanced at Ren again and this time, caught her eye. She didn't respond although she held his gaze.

'Here we go,' said Mac, giving the women their drinks. 'What have I missed?'

'Nothing much,' said Bonnie. She glanced at Ren who gave the beer an experimental sip. Just like that, the hardness in her eyes lifted and she licked her lips, looking down into the pint with surprise. Harrison's stomach somersaulted at the sight.

'Hey, now that we've found you here outside the office, can you tell us the gossip?' Bonnie asked before tasting her own beer. 'Mmm, this is good. What is it?'

'The most expensive beer in the place,' Mac told her with a wink. The two of them clinked glasses and drank. Harrison watched on, amusement lifting the corners of his lips. His gaze found Ren again who flashed him a small smile before she returned to drinking.

'What gossip?' Harrison asked.

'Oh, come on. What's going on with Liam?'

Harrison shrugged.

'Damned if I know.'

'You must know. You worked out he hasn't been doing his job.'

'Yeah, because I asked his team to show me what he'd been doing and they couldn't. They were as surprised as me.'

'Why did you ask them?'

Harrison stared at Bonnie and she stared back. The insufferable woman had always been able to see through him. It was one of her many talents.

'Because, Bonnie, the figures don't lie.'

Bonnie studied Harrison for a second and then laughed, throwing her head back. She turned on Mac.

'Okay, fine. Tell me everything about Harrison that I couldn't possibly know from working with him.'

Mac grinned and did a subtle sideways glance at Ren before clearing his throat.

'Wow, where to start.'

'Nowhere,' said Harrison. 'There's no need for that.'

'Fine,' said Bonnie. 'So, Mac, what do you do?'

'I'm a finance manager,' he told her.

'Oh, you're kindred spirits,' Bonnie declared. 'That's sweet.'

'Harry's helping me,' Mac admitted, giving Bonnie an appraising look as he drank. 'We have a gentleman's agreement. He's helping me become rich beyond my wildest dreams.'

Bonnie laughed.

'And what are you doing for him?'

'Helping him find the woman of his dreams.'

There was a long pause as Harrison urged the ground to open up and swallow him. He jumped as sirens blared on the road outside, rushing past the pub. It wasn't quite the distraction he'd been hoping for. He buried his mouth in his pint and tried not to look at Ren, failing miserably. Unnervingly, she looked right back at him, the hardness had returned to her eyes but there was something else there too.

Bonnie laughed again.

'And are you qualified in helping him with all things romance?' she asked Mac, her tone lowering a little.

Harrison shot her a look. Wasn't she in a relationship?

'I would say so,' said Mac, matching her tone. 'I know a thing or two.'

'Your wife must be thrilled.'

'No wife.'

'Girlfriend?'

'Nope.'

Bonnie sat back and narrowed her eyes.

'Then how are you qualified?'

Mac laughed and gave her another wink, which, for some reason, satisfied Bonnie enough for her to ask no further questions.

'How about you?' he asked when all she did was sit back and study him.

'Also single,' she said.

Both Harrison and Ren snapped up to look at her.

'Are you?' Ren asked. 'Since when?'

'Since last night.' Bonnie swallowed a painfully large mouthful of beer. 'So be gentle,' she added to Mac who grinned so wide Harrison wondered if his face would split in half.

'What happened?' asked Ren.

Bonnie shrugged.

'It was a long time coming,' she said. 'As you know. But he didn't want to hear me talking about the ghost tour. He ended up snapping at me, told me to shut up about the stupid ghosts.'

Harrison frowned.

'Do you believe in ghosts, Mac?' she asked.

Mac gave this some thought, or at least he appeared to.

'I don't not believe in them,' he decided.

Bonnie seemed to accept this.

Ren, her brow creased with concern, went to ask another question, but Mac got there first.

'So, what do you do at Harry's gaming company?'

'Harry's gaming company?' Bonnie raised an eyebrow at Harrison.

'He just can't be bothered to learn the name,' he explained.

'I'm the head art designer,' Bonnie told Mac. 'An artist, actually. Qualified digital artist and graphic designer with a lifelong passion for gaming and a hobby in fine art.'

Mac raised his eyebrows.

'Wow,' he murmured, before remembering Ren was there. 'How about you, Ren? What's Ren short for? Or are you named after the bird?'

Ren smiled.

'Lauren,' she said quietly. 'But please, for the love of god, don't call me Lauren. And I'm a palaeontologist.'

Mac stared at her wide-eyed and then glared at Harrison.

'You never said she was a palaeontologist. That's amazing.' He turned back to Ren. 'What the hell are you doing at a gaming company?'

'Harry's gaming company,' Bonnie corrected, smiling into her beer.

'I honestly have no idea,' said Ren. 'My contract with the Natural History Museum in London ended and for some reason I went into academia and sort of lost my way. I should have moved to New York or something, gone to work at another big museum, but instead I took a job lecturing at a university, got made redundant and had a panic about money. So here I am.'

Harrison watched her.

'You're enjoying it, though, right?' he asked.

Ren met his eyes.

'I was,' she told him. 'I guess we'll see how it goes now that there's all this new pressure and a new deadline.'

Bonnie tutted.

'It happens all the time. It'll be fine. Six months of hard work and then things will go back to normal. Until it happens again. Don't fret about it,' she said.

Harrison agreed.

'And your work won't change much. It'll just mean things will speed up,' he explained.

'You'll have to do some quick thinking and fact checking,' Bonnie added. 'You're more than capable.'

Ren smiled and nodded.

'Fair enough. As long as it doesn't shorten my contract.'

'It won't,' Harrison told her.

'How is Harrison going to make you rich?' Bonnie asked Mac.

Mac grinned.

'A new job and stock market investments,' he said.

'The usual,' Harrison added, sharing a smile with his friend.

Bonnie leaned across the table.

'Can you teach me those things?' she asked.

'Sure, anytime,' said Harrison.

'How about now? We could both stand to earn more, right Ren?'

Harrison looked to Ren who met his gaze and smiled.

'Sure,' she said. 'I've never understood the stock market.'

A grin bloomed on Harrison's face.

'That's because I haven't explained it yet,' he told her.

'I've got a date.'

'I know,' said Harrison as Bonnie approached him with a big smile on her face. 'Mac told me.'

Ren followed Bonnie to join Harrison beneath the overhang of the Scottish Parliament building. It had been two weeks since Bonnie and Mac had met in the pub. Two weeks of working long, hard hours as the weather turned decidedly colder and greyer. Today was a prime example of that, as the clouds turned the sky a solid dark grey and a chilled wind swept through the city. Apparently, Martin was keen on work socials. Bonnie had suggested to Ren that this one might be cancelled, but Martin had been happy with the game's progress and wanted to 'reward' everyone. Ren wasn't sure that a team walk up Arthur's Seat counted as a reward. Especially in this weather.

At least it wasn't raining.

Near the entrance to the Scottish Parliament, opposite Holyrood Palace, were the entire marketing team led by Val, what appeared to be some people from accounts and HR, a team of administrators wrapped up in scarfs and cackling at something, a clump of developers and a gaggle of others who Ren didn't recognise. Billy skulked around the corner and did his best to avoid Martin, although he did catch Ren's eye for a moment. At first she thought he might join them, but he stayed put.

Liam was nowhere to be seen.

Bonnie waved to Billy.

'Are we ever going to find out what's going on with Liam?' she asked Harrison. He turned to look at Billy over his shoulder.

'No idea,' was all he said. He'd found a spot out of the wind and stood under the overhang with his hands deep in his pockets and a fetching woollen hat pulled over his head.

Bonnie gave him a look of frustration and then shook it away.

'Anything I should know about Mac? Is he trouble?' She grinned.

Harrison laughed.

'Do you want him to be?'

'Depends on the trouble, I guess,' said Bonnie. She narrowed her eyes at Ren. 'Just gotta find a date for you now.' She elbowed Ren in the side and Ren used the push as an excuse to move closer to the building and Harrison, and away from the cold edge of the wind. She sniffed.

'Nah, I'm good. Unless you think it'd get me out of this walk?'

Harrison looked down at her with soft, dancing eyes and smiled.

'Why'd you come, then? You're allowed to say no.'

'Am I?' Ren asked. 'Martin said this is a treat.'

Both Bonnie and Harrison pulled a face.

'You mean there won't be hot chocolate and cake at the top?' Ren asked, a smile tugging her lips. Bonnie laughed while Harrison gave her an amused look. Ren studied the people still gathering. 'I've never been up there. The view must be amazing, right?'

'Definitely. As long as the cloud doesn't dip any lower,' said Bonnie.

Harrison gave a shiver. Ren studied him as he looked up at the hill they were going to climb. They hadn't spoken much since she'd accidentally called him capitalist scum within his earshot, and Ren put that down to the fact that they'd both been working hard. They hadn't really seen each other in the kitchen, at least, not alone. They hadn't once shared the lift or met in the corridors. For two whole weeks, it was as if they would never speak again. Maybe that would have been the case if Bonnie hadn't led her over to Harrison as soon as they'd arrived that morning.

The silence was becoming awkward and Ren opened her mouth to ask an inane question when

Martin mercifully clapped his hands and gathered everyone around him.

'Welcome, everyone!' he declared, moving to stand on one of the higher walkways that doubled as a sitting place, curving around the fountains and grass outside the building, leading away to Holyrood Park. 'I'm so glad you could make it. I'm sure we'll all be warm soon, walking up there.' He glanced to the hill behind him. There was already a line of tourists, wrapped up in raincoats, trudging up the well-worn path. 'Take your time and keep an eye out for each other. And if you're struggling, keep in mind that we're going to the pub afterwards.'

That elicited a small cheer and Martin grinned, jumping off the walkway and leading them towards the path to Arthur's Seat. They fell in behind a group of tourists and soon the fitter people were near the front with Martin, while others lagged behind in clumps. Billy walked slowly until Bonnie caught him up and began chatting to him, forcing him to keep pace. Ren watched. She'd hoped that her and Bonnie would stick together on the walk, especially now that Bonnie was easily distracted from Ren's love life by her own upcoming date with Mac.

The wind picked up, cutting through Ren. She pulled her coat tighter, ramming her hat down over her ears and using the back of her gloved hands to wipe at her eyes.

'I'm not sure how I feel about Bonnie and Mac.'

Ren flinched, managing to control herself before it turned into a full startle and squeal. Still, she gave Harrison a dirty look as he appeared beside her.

'How come?' she asked, the wind whipping her words away. 'She's lovely and he seems nice. Is he not nice?'

Harrison smiled as he stared down at the ground, watching where he put his feet.

'Of course he is. Mac's a great guy. I love him like a brother. A little brother. Who needs a bit of looking after.'

Ren considered not saying the words that immediately jumped to mind, but they fell out of her mouth before she could stop them.

'I thought the two of you had a gentleman's agreement? That doesn't sound like a little brother to me.'

She looked up when Harrison didn't reply – maybe she hadn't heard him – and found him looking down at her with an amused half-smile.

'Damn,' he said, his blue eyes soft. 'You remember that, huh?'

Something inside Ren gave way and if it wasn't for the wind snatching at her nose, she would have forgotten to breathe. It was only for a moment and she recovered quickly, as if dazed, wondering what that reaction had been.

'Kinda,' she said quietly, watching where she was treading. 'Something about you helping him with his career. Which is nice. I wish I had someone like that.'

Harrison's smile vanished, replaced by an expression of serious concentration.

'I'd be happy to help,' he told her. 'What do you want? More money? To climb the ladder?'

Ren looked back to him.

'Is that all you want?'

Harrison met her eyes and they both stopped to stare at each other.

'No,' he said. The word was a whisper, instantly gone on the wind but Ren had heard it. Her stomach flipped, her chilled fingers fizzing. She blinked the feelings away and continued walking, aware that they were falling behind and the clerical team at the back were catching them up.

'What do you want?' she asked, unable to help herself. If this man, so desperate to do a good job and earn his precious money and bonuses, didn't want a bigger bank account or to climb higher, then what else could there be?

Harrison gave this some thought as they walked in silence, both becoming increasingly out of breath as they picked their way up the stony path.

'You know what I haven't really had much of? Not until I moved here, anyway,' he said.

'What?'

'Freedom.'

Ren raised an eyebrow and shot him a look.

'Money must buy freedom,' she said.

Harrison laughed and still, over a month later, the sound sent a jolt of something akin to pleasure through her. She chastised her body for its reaction and stared hard ahead as the path became a little rocky.

'Yeah. I guess so. Money meant I could move across the Atlantic and settle here.' Harrison paused and took a deep breath. 'Gotta give it to Scotland, it knows how to do mountains and weather.'

Ren laughed.

'New York has weather,' she said, shutting the smile down quickly as the wind blew cold air onto her teeth. 'You get snow and everything.'

'Not like here,' said Harrison. 'I spent last Christmas in the Highlands. Waking up every morning to snow on the mountains, and then one morning to snow on the ground. It was...' he paused, searching for the right word.

'Magic,' Ren finished for him.

He grinned at her.

'Yeah. Magic.'

'Are you going to do that again this Christmas?' she asked. Christmas in the Highlands sounded like a dream. A small part of her brain – the bit not engaged in conversation or trying to work out how she was going to get to the top of Arthur's Seat without vomiting – began wondering how to get her family to agree to travel to the Highlands one Christmas.

'Nah. I thought about it, though. My son's visiting this year, it's his first time in Scotland. So I figured we'd stay in the city. We might do a day's drive out that way though, just to show him what's there. It might tempt him to come back again next year.'

Ren faltered.

'You have a son?' she asked.

'From my first marriage,' said Harrison.

Ren gave a weak laugh.

'First? How many marriages have you had?'

'Two.'

Ren looked up to find not a hint of a smile on Harrison's lips. He was focusing on where his feet were going, his brow creased. He didn't look up at her at first, only when she refused to look away, and for a second their eyes met again until he turned to check out the view.

'This is a pretty good view,' he said. 'Shame we can't stop here. I reckon someone could make a lot of money putting a pub at the top of this hill.'

Ren smiled, looking over the top of the Scottish Parliament and Holyrood Palace to the ruined abbey behind.

'Are you going home for Christmas?' Harrison asked, turning to continue and forcing Ren to join him on the narrow path.

'Yeah, that was the plan. Only for a couple of days, though.'

'How come?'

Ren sighed.

'I don't know. Seemed like a good idea when I planned it. Maybe I'll go for longer.'

Harrison glanced at her.

'You don't want to go back?'

'It's not that.' It was that.

'You don't get on with your family?'

Ren squirmed and looked back to Harrison. Those blue cut-throat eyes were soft and curious, his arms shooting out as he slipped and regained his balance. Ren raised her eyebrows.

'You okay?'

He nodded, gesturing for her to continue.

'I get on with my family,' she told him. How much was she going to say? The only person she'd opened up to since coming to Edinburgh was Bonnie, but Bonnie was kind and safe. What was Harrison? 'It's more the friends side of things,' she said. 'And the questions that my parents might ask.'

'Right. Questions like...?'

Ren smiled to herself. She wouldn't have been able to let that lie either.

'Have you got a boyfriend yet? Oh no, you don't want a boyfriend right now. Focus on your career. When are you going to get a job in a museum? Have you applied? Are you doing any networking?' Ren sighed, her heart pounding, even though she was asking herself the questions and Harrison wasn't expecting any answers.

'Museum, huh?'

'Yeah.'

'Not the university?'

Ren stopped up short and Harrison skidded a little to stop beside her. He watched her eyes.

'Well, no...' she started. 'I guess...I don't know why. They know I hated the university job.'

'And working in a museum was the dream,' said Harrison.

'Yeah.'

'So what the hell are you doing at a gaming company?'

Ren looked up to find Harrison still watching her. She smiled and they continued walking.

'I was at a bit of a loss,' she told him as they climbed. 'My boyfriend dumped me the same week I was made redundant. In one week, I had no job, no prospects, no relationship and no idea what I was doing. It was a shock to the system.'

Harrison made a noise of disgust.

'He chose to break up with you when you got made redundant?'

'Yeah.' Ren sighed.

'Maybe he did you a favour.'

Ren gave Harrison a sideways look.

'So, I didn't know what to do and I got talking to a friend of a friend in the pub on a night out. He runs a game development company in London. I told him I'm a palaeontologist and he got excited, told me about the job going here, told me to apply and sent me the link. And, well, here I am.'

'You're here because of an act of desperation,' Harrison summed up before Ren had time to think.

'And an act of kindness,' she added. 'Who knows what I'd be doing if he hadn't told me about this job.'

'Don't you see it as a fresh start, though?' Harrison asked.

Ren smiled to herself.

'Yeah. I do. New job, new city, new friends.' She looked up to Bonnie in front, except that Bonnie and Billy weren't in front of them anymore. They must have gotten further ahead, somehow.

'New boyfriend,' came Harrison's voice. 'I mean, if Bonnie has anything to do with it, right?'

Ren sighed again.

'Oh god, yeah, that stupid dating app.'

'No good?'

'No, Bonnie didn't like any of them. Thankfully. But I'm still getting matches on there.'

'You could just, you know, not tell Bonnie,' said Harrison, giving her a playful smile.

'I tried that,' said Ren, lowering her voice to a whisper. 'Somehow, she knows.'

Harrison laughed his wonderful belly laugh and Ren's smile became a grin.

'Well, personally, I think you should drop the dating app,' he told her. 'Try things the old-fashioned way if you really want to meet someone.'

'What, like at a bar?'

Harrison shrugged.

'Worked for Mac and Bonnie. Maybe.'

'True.'

'Or at work,' said Harrison. 'Plenty of couples meet at work.'

'Also true. There were a few married couples at the university, although I'm not sure that's a great example.'

Harrison opened his mouth to say more when raised voices were carried down to them on the wind.

'That's enough! We're not discussing it!'

It was Martin's voice and the muffled words of anger that followed it sounded a lot like Billy.

Beside Ren, Harrison gave a deep sigh.

'Of course,' he muttered, striding a step ahead of Ren and searching the groups in front of them as they rounded the hill.

10

The path curved around the corner of the hill and flattened out onto grass. The main path continued to the right and another went past where the group were now standing, sloping gently back down to the road beneath. On Harrison's left was the glorious view across to Edinburgh Castle and the hills beyond. To his right was the glint of the sea in the distance. In front of him, and demanding his attention, stood Billy and Martin, facing one another and shouting into the wind. Bonnie was behind Billy, holding onto his arm, shouting at him to calm down. Val was standing behind Martin, her arms crossed, glancing back to her team who were pretending to admire the view. The developers were nowhere in sight which was typical. This was their boss's fault, but why should they hang around to help?

Harrison sighed through his nose and headed for Martin, calling for calm, and Martin finally turned his attention from Billy. Bonnie used this to her advantage, pulling Billy away.

'Come on, Martin, we're on a work social. Remember? Climbing Arthur's Seat, rewarding your teams,' Harrison told his boss gently. Out of the corner of his eye, he saw Ren wander over to Billy and Bonnie. Assured that Billy was in safe hands, Harrison continued to calm Martin down. Val remained by their side, saying nothing, as helpful as ever.

Behind them, her team were taking photos and videos of the views, presumably to upload to social media later that day with a caption about how wonderful the company was to work for.

Harrison gritted his teeth.

'He won't shut up about it,' Martin was saying. 'Keeps going on about how he's trying to do his best, but he's not, is he? Remember when he started, Harrison? He was brilliant, and then suddenly he wasn't. What the hell happened?' Martin groaned, rubbing his hands over his face. 'He says Liam won't talk to him and he can't do his job without Liam talking to him.' He stared up at Harrison. 'But you managed to figure it all out without talking to Liam. Why can't Billy do the same?' He growled. 'I need to talk to HR.' He looked around as if that was something he should be doing right that very moment.

'Well, hang on. You can talk to HR when we're back in the office,' Harrison told him. 'And I'm sure Billy is doing his best. Who best to go to about the game progress than the head developer, right? He's trying, Martin.'

'Keeps saying how he needs this job,' Martin grumbled.

'Well, there you go. He's worried about losing his job. He's stressed. You're stressed. We're on a hill overlooking the city, Martin. Look at that view! Take a deep breath. Forget about it all for now. That's for another day.'

Martin looked at the view and nodded. Little by little, his fists uncurled, his jaw untensed, a smile picked at the corners of his mouth.

'I'm sorry,' he said eventually. 'I guess it's all just bringing back...a bad taste,' he finished, glancing at Val.

'A bad taste?' Harrison asked before he could stop himself.

Martin nodded, his smile fading. Taking Harrison's arm, he pulled his finance director away from the others.

'It all just reminds me of a couple of years ago,' he whispered. Harrison's mind raced to catch up. Then Martin plastered a smile on his face and announced that they were continuing. The marketing team abandoned their photoshoot and followed him.

Val wandered over to Harrison.

'Thanks,' she said bluntly.

He studied her for a moment.

'He's still on about what happened a couple of

years ago,' he muttered.

The only thing Martin could have been talking about was when he'd told everyone he needed a break and they'd all had to report directly to head office for three months.

Val perked up and leaned closer to Harrison.

'Of course he is. You know Martin, he holds onto grudges.'

'Yeah, but—'

'Oh come on, didn't you hear? His husband had an affair with the HR intern at his work, of all things. A nice little fact he managed to hide all this time. Apparently he's forgiven but not forgotten, but since when does Martin forgive?' Val gave a small laugh and then followed her team and Martin to finish climbing the hill. Harrison watched her go, his mouth dry. Who had told Val about the HR intern? Harrison certainly hadn't. He'd made a promise to Martin he wouldn't tell anyone over a drunken evening shortly after Martin had returned to the office.

He needed a beer and something to eat, his stomach twisted and grumbled at the thought.

Over to the side, Billy shook his head at Bonnie and headed back down the hill, following the gradual slope instead of tackling the steep path they'd come up. Harrison didn't blame him.

Bonnie and Ren watched him go.

'Why didn't we come up that way?' Ren asked as Harrison wandered over.

Bonnie gave a sad laugh.

'Where's the team-building fun in that?' she said bitterly. 'The hell is going on?' She turned on Harrison as he joined them.

'Can't really say much here,' said Harrison. 'Maybe in the pub, later.'

'At least we made it to the top,' said Ren, looking out over the city. She turned to Bonnie and Harrison when they didn't reply and found them both smiling at her. 'What?'

'This isn't the top,' said Harrison, taking a moment to commit how Ren looked to memory. Her red hair wind-swept despite being held down by her hat. Her coat tight around her, her eyes widening at the prospect of more climbing. It was all he could do to stamp down the urge to reach out and hold her. Somehow, she'd managed to pull off looking beautiful even bundled up on a hill in the wind.

'That's the top.' Bonnie pointed up to the peak of the hill. Ren turned to the side, craning her neck up to look at it and the small figures of people who had managed to get there. Climbing the last steps was the development team.

Ren swore loudly but a gust of wind tore it from her and sent it down the hill towards the sea.

Harrison laughed.

'Yeah, I agree.' He looked up at the peak and then to the rest of their colleagues wandering up the path with Martin.

Bonnie growled, stamping her feet against the cold.

'I say we go grab a table at the pub,' she shouted into the wind. 'Who's with me?'

'Definitely,' said Harrison, glancing down to Ren. 'But you've never been up there.'

Ren shrugged.

'I'll come back in the summer,' she told him. She took out her phone to snap a quick photo of the view over the city, then she pushed past them both to amble along the gentle walk downhill.

Bonnie's phone rang a quarter of the way down the hill and she hung back to answer it. Harrison caught Ren up and they picked their way down together.

'Is it bad?' Ren asked. 'Is the company in trouble? Are our jobs in trouble?'

Harrison grinned.

'What? No! No, nothing like that.'

'Then why haven't you told us what's going on yet? I mean, what the hell was that about? Who has a big argument on the top of a hill during a work social?'

'Martin and Billy do,' Harrison told her. 'In the office, on the work social, down the pub, on the street outside the office. They always have. This is nothing new, it's just they have something fairly new to argue about now. Instead of why Billy isn't doing his job right, it's that Billy still isn't doing his job right. But now Billy can blame it on Liam.'

Ren gave Harrison a sideways glance.

'Because Liam hasn't been doing the work. Because...?'

Harrison grinned again, his gaze catching hers for a moment in a sidelong look before he went back to watching where his feet were going. She was clever. Of course she was, she had a mind that was trained to put pieces together. She was often so quiet that he could forget how clever she was, but then she went and opened her mouth and something inside him would melt.

'Because he's been doing something else,' he said cryptically.

Ren stared at him.

'Which is...?'

Harrison shook his head, still smiling.

'Wait until we're in the pub.'

The pub was warm and cosy, filled with the scent of beer and the soft laughter of friends chatting. Being out of the wind was extreme and Harrison had to take a moment to adjust to the stillness around him. He headed straight to the bar while Bonnie led Ren to a small table.

Martin would have reserved a big table for everyone at the pub they were supposed to be meeting at. Harrison wondered if they'd join them. He ordered a pitcher of his favourite beer and checked the pub's food menu.

'He suggested a nice little restaurant on the edge of the city,' Bonnie was saying as Harrison made his way over. 'I've looked up their menu. It looks perfect.' She made a small squealing noise. 'I can't wait. I'm so excited. I really like him. We've been messaging each other for two weeks straight.'

'Is two weeks enough time? You only just broke up with your boyfriend.'

'Two weeks is plenty,' said Bonnie. 'My ex was on the way out for a while. If I'd known Harrison was hiding Mac away, I would have ended it a long time ago.'

'Gonna pretend I didn't hear that,' said Harrison, placing the three glasses on the table along with a wooden spoon with a number on it. He vanished and returned a moment later with the pitcher. 'This'll warm us up,' he said, pouring some into each glass. 'And I ordered fries. Hope that's okay.'

'Lifesaver,' said Bonnie. Ren agreed.

When the three bowls of thick, triple-cooked chips arrived, Ren looked up at Harrison and said, 'Chips.'

He aimed a chip at her.

'Don't start with me,' he told her. 'I get enough of that from Mac.'

Ren grinned and Harrison mirrored it, shoving the chip into his mouth, his heart pounding.

'How much do I owe you?' she asked, dipping a chip into a big dollop of tomato sauce.

Harrison nearly choked on his chip. He recovered quickly, his still empty stomach flipping.

'On me,' said Harrison around his mouthful.

Ren went to argue and Harrison smiled at her as Bonnie got there first.

'Right, please tell us what the hell is going on. Please? Otherwise I'll start calling you Harry in public.'

'You don't call me Harry in private,' said Harrison, reluctantly turning from Ren, her cheeks flushed from the sudden warmth of the pub.

'I will do, if you don't spill the beans.'

Harrison chuckled and brushed the salt and grease off his hands.

'Fine. Here goes. Billy's bad at his job. Is this news to you?' he asked Bonnie. She shrugged. 'He wasn't asking Liam for updates, and when he did, Liam was vague about it all. Why was Liam vague about it all? Because he hasn't been doing the work.'

'We kinda know all this,' Bonnie complained. 'Why hasn't he been doing the work? Cathy in marketing says he's been shagging someone in the office instead of working.'

A silence fell over the table and Harrison did a small gesture of *well, there you go*. Bonnie's eyes widened.

'No! Who?'

'He's been sleeping with someone in the office instead of working?' Ren clarified.

'I don't think there was much sleeping going on,' Harrison said.

'Who?' Bonnie repeated in a tone that suggested she was doing her best not to scream. Harrison watched her, amused.

'Ally.'

Bonnie gasped, hands covering her mouth, sitting back in her chair.

'Who's Ally?' Ren asked.

'Little Alison?' said Bonnie, recovering quickly. 'Who just got married, like, five months ago or something?'

'Who invited us all to her wedding, for some reason.' Harrison nodded.

'Whose husband is gorgeous,' Bonnie told Ren. 'And she's been having an affair with Liam?' she asked Harrison. 'How on earth do you know that?'

'I told you,' he said. 'The figures didn't match up. Billy's progress reports didn't match up. So I went and asked one the developers and what he showed me didn't match up.'

'Yeah, yeah, but how do you know about Liam and Ally?' Bonnie pressed.

'I can't say.'

Bonnie looked like she might explode.

'Did you catch them at it?' Ren asked. Harrison smiled and did a subtle nod, his insides fizzing with a thrill of pleasure as he watched her quick mind working.

Bonnie whistled through her teeth.

'In the office?' Ren asked.

Harrison gave another slight nod, lifting his pint to his lips.

'While you were working late one night?'

Harrison drank and nodded again.

Bonnie laughed.

'Where were they?' she asked.

Harrison shot her a look as Ren gave it some thought.

'Not out in the open,' she mused. Harrison turned to watch her. 'In the meeting room?' she ventured.

Harrison pulled a face and ate a chip.

'No. Okay. Erm, on the roof?'

Harrison smiled but didn't nod. He glanced quickly at Ren, thankful she couldn't read his mind and see the fantasies he'd been having about taking her up to the roof to show her the view over the city. She frowned thoughtfully and popped a chip into her mouth.

'Not in the toilets?' said Bonnie.

Harrison nodded.

'In the men's toilets?' Bonnie asked, incredulous.

Again, Harrison nodded and then shrugged.

'It's clean in there,' he said. 'Or at least, it had just been cleaned.'

'Ew,' said Bonnie, and Ren laughed a little too loudly.

'So what's going to happen?' Ren asked. 'Liam's still the head developer and in charge of building the game, Ally's still in marketing.'

'Can't fire them for having an affair,' said Harrison.

'You can for not doing their jobs. Liam's still got his job. That's only because getting another head developer right now would take too much time,' Bonnie thought out loud. 'He's going to leave after this project, isn't he.'

'Wouldn't surprise me,' said Harrison. 'But honestly, I don't know much else. And I didn't tell Martin about what I heard in the toilets or who I saw coming out. I just gave him the figures and facts.'

'But he knows?' Ren asked. 'How does he know? Did Liam tell him?'

'Someone told him.' Harrison studied a chip before eating it. 'But it wasn't me. I don't care about that stuff. Just the numbers.'

He regretted those words instantly, filling his mouth with more beer and watching Ren grit her teeth.

'I wonder if they're still doing the sex,' Bonnie wondered, smiling to herself.

'Doing the sex?' Harrison repeated.

Bonnie laughed.

'Speaking of which.' She leaned across the table. 'Tell me more about Mac. What do I need to know?'

Harrison groaned and looked to Ren for help.

'Well, now, hang on,' she said, coming to his aid. His heart thumped for her. 'Do the figures show

how long this affair might have been going on for?'

Harrison smiled and fiddled with his bowl of chips.

'Might do.'

That caught Bonnie's attention.

'Oh god. Was it going on before she got married?' she whispered.

Harrison lifted his pint to his lips and gave one subtle nod as Bonnie's eyes widened and she became lost down the rabbit hole of office gossip.

Ren blew into her free gloved hand, looking up at the warm office building with yearning.

'Yes, Mum. I'm fine. I'm keeping warm,' she said into the phone once her mother let her get a word in.

'Are you coming home for Christmas?' her mother asked.

'Of course I am!'

'For how long?'

Ren sighed.

'I don't know. A couple of days? A few days?'

'What a waste of a journey.'

Ren looked down at her shoes.

'A week?' she offered, grimacing. 'I'm not sure I can get a week off. What with this new deadline and stuff.'

'They can give you a week off over Christmas, Ren!'

'I'll see, Mum. But a couple of days wouldn't be so bad, would it?'

'Better than nothing.' Her mother sniffed and Ren sighed again.

'I'll ask for the week,' she told her.

'Thank you.'

There was a pause.

'Mum?'

'Yes, sweetheart?'

'If I told you someone had been married twice, what would you think of them?'

There was another pause as her mother considered the strange change of topic.

'Lots of people have two marriages in their lives,' came the response.

'And two divorces,' Ren clarified. At least, she assumed there were two divorces.

'Oh. Well. I guess that happens too. Why? Have you met someone? Don't go out with someone who's already been divorced twice. You don't want to be number three, do you? Think about why those women might have divorced him.'

'Oh, so it happens but I'm not allowed to go out with them?' Ren double-checked.

'You can be friends with them,' her mother offered. It was her turn to sigh down the phone. 'Have you met someone? Why are you asking?'

'No reason,' said Ren, a little too quickly.

'Are you seeing someone?'

'Nope. Bonnie's still got me on this dating app, though.'

'And she's found you a double divorcee?'

'Well, no. She's found me a thirty-five-year-old council worker who seems very nice if not a little dull. But attractive.'

'But dull,' repeated her mother.

'Yeah.'

'So what's the point?'

'Well, you said I can't date the double divorcee.'

Her mother laughed down the phone, but it was tinged with hysteria.

'Do what makes you happy, Ren. Just do it safely. Be careful.'

'I will be, don't you worry. Public places and back up plans and Bonnie always knows where I am. I'll be fine, Mum. Whatever I do.'

'Good. Okay, then. Who's this double divorcee?'

'No one. Better go. Back to the grindstone. Speak to you later.'

They said their goodbyes and hung up. Ren trudged into the office, relishing the warmth as her nose defrosted. December had well and truly hit Edinburgh and the air seemed to be edged with ice. Still, the spirit of Christmas was spreading through the streets, and if it was possible for the city to be more magical, it could only be at Christmas.

Ren made her way up to the fifth floor where she found Dougal waiting at her desk, sitting in her chair.

'Hello. Have I been moved?' she asked, glancing at Bonnie who was on the phone and waved, and then at Billy who had his head down, ignoring them all.

'Yes, please,' said Dougal. 'To my desk.' He gave her a grin that was far too charming. 'I've got those two latest dinos to check. Are you free now?'

'Sure, hang on.' Ren ditched her coat and bag at her desk and then followed Dougal through the office to the developers' corner. He pulled up a free chair for her and she sat carefully, manoeuvring it closer to his computer. This was something they'd done countless times over the last two months, and Ren was now used to Dougal's cluttered desk. The smell of him never seemed to change either, a mixture of cologne and coffee that seemed to have the ability to both attract Ren and make her a little hungry. As always, he picked up an elastic band that seemed to live by his mouse and began fiddling with it as he spoke.

'Right, here we go. The Apatosaurus. Nice long neck.' Dougal tapped away at his keyboard, the elastic band stretching as his fingers danced. 'Here he is.'

'He? I think you'll find all the dinosaurs are female,' said Ren with a smile.

Dougal laughed.

'How do you know they're all female?'

'Somebody goes out into the park and pulls up the dinosaurs' skirts,' Ren finished for him.

Grinning, Dougal pulled up the fully coded Apatosaurus and sat back to let Ren study it. She moved closer, taking the controls to turn the beautifully designed dinosaur just as Dougal had taught her.

'Gorgeous,' she said. 'Do you know what Apatosaurus means?' she asked as she checked the dinosaur's dimensions.

'Nope.'

'Deceptive lizard,' Ren murmured.

'Ah, a suspicious type.'

Ren laughed and Dougal grinned, looking at her sideways.

'What made you want to study giant lizards?' he asked.

Ren frowned.

'Dinosaurs aren't lizards.'

'Literally in the name.'

'Because once upon a time, someone thought they were reptiles.'

'What are they, then?'

'Dinosaurs. Like birds are avians. We're mammals. Frogs are amphibians. Lizards are reptiles. Dinosaurs are dinosaurs. Of course, there were mammals back then, really small ones. And there were giant reptiles. Like plesiosaur.' Ren caught sight of Dougal's confused expression. 'Nessie,' she explained.

'Oh, cool. Nessie's a reptile, not a dinosaur.'

'Exactly.'

'You ever been to Loch Ness?' Dougal asked.

'Nope.'

'I love it there,' he told her, leaning forward and

taking back control of his computer. 'We should go sometime.'

'Oh, okay.' Ren's mind whirred. What did he mean? Go there sometime together? Alone? With friends? As a group? As a couple? As a date? She said nothing, waiting to see what he would do next.

In her pocket, her phone beeped. She jumped and Dougal looked down as her hand automatically went to answer it.

'Everything okay?'

'Yup.' It was another damn notification from that dating app. Ren was going to delete the thing, especially if all it had to offer was attractive but potentially dull council workers.

Dougal said nothing more on the subject of a visit to Loch Ness and they went through the next dinosaur quoting only lines from the Jurassic Park franchise to each other.

'Brachiosaurus next,' said Dougal as they finished up. He clapped his hands. 'And then a carnivore, please. I like the carnivores.'

'The Gallimimus after that, I'm afraid.'

'Ah,' said Dougal, a grin blooming on his undeniably kissable lips. 'They're the ones that are flocking this way.'

Something in Ren shifted and she almost asked him about the Loch Ness visit when another developer called his name.

'Sorry, duty calls.' Dougal flashed Ren a grin and turned to his colleague.

Ren left the development team, fighting the smile from her face. Was she really attracted to Dougal? Was there something there?

Lost in thought, she rounded the corner and skidded to a stop.

'Sorry,' she said to Harrison who rocked back on his heels to stop himself colliding with her.

'I apologise now, right? That's how Brits do it? We both apologise? Even though neither of us did anything wrong?'

The smile won the fight and Ren grinned.

'Pretty much.'

Harrison studied her.

'What have you been up to?' He glanced behind her to the development team.

'Quoting Jurassic Park films,' Ren told him. 'While checking the coding of the latest dinosaur designs. Don't worry, it's all work.'

Harrison gave her a strange lopsided smile.

'Right. It's going okay, then?'

'All on schedule,' Ren said with a nod. 'The Brachiosaurus needs some work, but the Apatosaurus is done.'

Harrison blinked at her.

'Good, well, if I knew what that was, I'd give a cheer or something. Glad the apatchosaurus is done.'

'Apatosaurus,' Ren corrected.

'Yeah, that.'

Ren's phone beeped again from inside her

pocket. She sighed, pulling it out.

'More dating app notifications?' Harrison asked, watching.

'No. No, a message from this guy I'm going on a date with.'

Ren was busy reading the message – *'Can't wait for our date. What are you up to today dinosaur girl?'* – when she noticed the tension in the silence that had fallen between her and Harrison. She glanced up to find him staring through her, eyes glazed.

'You okay?' she asked.

He seemed to shake himself.

'Hmm? Yeah, no, I'm fine. Work stuff. So, you have a date. That's...exciting. When?'

'Thursday night,' she told him. 'Straight from work, too. I haven't quite got my head around that yet. Bonnie was peering over my shoulder and telling me what to say. Sort of wish she was coming on the actual date to do the same.'

Harrison gave her the fakest smile she'd seen since moving to Scotland.

'And you're sure it's safe to be meeting this guy?' he asked, his words stilted as if his teeth were gritted.

'Yeah. We're meeting in a restaurant. Bonnie's on standby as my emergency out, if I need it. But he seems nice enough. Divorced a couple of years ago, new to the dating scene, nervous as hell. He hasn't sent me a picture of his... Well, he hasn't said or done anything horrible.'

'Yet,' said Harrison.

'What?'

'Nothing, nothing. Great, well, I hope you have fun. And be careful. And... Best get back to work, huh?'

Without waiting for a response, Harrison strode past Ren and disappeared into the development team without once glancing back. Ren watched him go, wondering what that had been about, something heavy settling in her gut.

'She's going on a date, Mac,' Harrison hissed into his phone as he pushed open the door to the stairwell. It was as private a place as Harrison could find in the building, but even so, his words echoed a little.

'What? Who with?' Mac's alarm took Harrison by surprise and there was a moment of quiet as Harrison worked out the misunderstanding.

'Not Bonnie,' he growled. 'Ren. Ren is going on a date. You told me to hold off and I did, and now she's going on a date with some other guy.'

'Oh! Oh. So, Bonnie isn't going out with someone else?'

'No, Mac. She's been grinning like an idiot since your first date. It's annoying how happy she is. Okay?'

Mac chuckled down the phone.

'Well, if you were having sex with me, you'd be grinning too.' An awkward pause followed before Mac added, 'You know what I mean.'

'What do I do?' Harrison asked. There was no point trying to keep the desperation from his voice. His mind had already offered him options. He could stall her on Thursday, find some work that only she could do and tell her it had to be done there and then. Other than locking the doors and pretending the lift was out of order, that was his best idea so far.

'Okay, calm down. Who is she going out with?'

'Some guy Bonnie found her on a dating app.'

'Oh, well, that's easy. That won't go well. You'll be fine.'

Harrison stopped.

Was it that simple?

'How do you know?' he asked, his voice almost resembling something normal.

'Want me to talk to Bonnie about it?'

Again, Harrison paused.

'I don't know. Can I not just go and ask Ren out right now?' He glanced back to the door. 'She'll be back at her desk.'

'So you really, seriously like her, huh?'

'Really, seriously, Mac. She's clever and she's sweet and she's beautiful. And if this date of hers goes well, what then? I'll have missed my chance. It's been nearly two months, nothing's changed.'

'Has she given you any indication she'll say yes?' Mac asked.

Harrison thought on this, sighing, running his hand over his face.

'Yes? No? I don't know. What kinda sign?'

'Anything. Bonnie told me to be gentle with her, for crying out loud.'

'Yeah, Ren isn't quite as obvious as that.'

'Or she is but she isn't giving you those signs.'

Harrison's chest squeezed painfully.

'What if she says no,' he said in an almost whisper.

'You'll still have to see her every day,' Mac told him gently. 'You need to really think about this, Harry. You like this job, right? So you need to tread carefully.'

Harrison nodded, despite Mac not being able to see him.

'Tread carefully. I can do that,' he murmured. 'And I can ask her out now?'

'Well, I mean...maybe wait and see how this date of hers goes? If you ask her out now, she might still go out with this guy. And if it works out between them, then it won't really matter if you ask her out or not.'

'Thanks, Mac. That's very comforting.'

'Sorry, mate. Go ask her out. But tread careful. Good luck.'

Harrison thanked him before mentioning a job he'd found that had Mac's name written all over it. He promised to send it over and then hung up. Making his way to the kitchen, he made himself a coffee and took the opportunity to watch Ren working at her desk. He had two days before her impending date and not a moment to spare.

Thursday came around far too quickly and Harrison still hadn't quite worked out what he was going to do. Mac was no help, not now that Bonnie existed to distract him. Harrison had considered enlisting Bonnie's help, but something in his gut told him that was a bad idea. No, he was on his own and today was the day.

The day itself was annoyingly spent in meetings with Martin and head office. Harrison barely had time to pour himself a drink, let alone ask Ren if she wanted to join him in pouring said drink. If that was even how he was going to ask her.

Getting into a relationship had never seemed this difficult, and Harrison blamed it entirely on Mac's stupid advice that he should wait. If he'd just asked Ren in that first week, maybe they'd be happy right now, smiling idiotically, spending every evening in bed together.

Which was why he was imagining Ren in his bed as he walked through into the open-plan office and spotted her collecting her bag from her desk.

Harrison stopped.

She was changed for her date. The thick jumper and jeans combo had been replaced with a short green dress, black tights and a wrap-around cardigan that floated down over her curves. And she did have curves. The jumper and jeans had hidden them, but this dress clung to them. Her winter coat covered most of her, but Harrison had seen enough to make his mouth dry.

She made her way to the lift and he followed.

'Hold the elevator!' he called as she stepped inside and the doors began to close.

Heart pounding, swallowing on nothing to keep his stomach steady, Harrison stepped in beside Ren and she let the doors shut on them.

'Lift,' she said.

Harrison tried to laugh but it came out as a wheeze.

'Yeah, sorry. Lift,' he managed.

They stood quietly for a second that felt like a minute.

'You look good,' he said, his tongue sticking to the roof of his mouth. 'Got that hot date tonight, huh?'

'Yeah. Is it too much?' Ren asked, opening her coat a little to reveal the dress so he could pass judgement.

'Not at all,' said Harrison, his eyes grazing over her until they lifted and met hers. 'You look stunning.'

She smiled and thanked him.

'What does this guy do again?'

'He works for the council. Something about the city's environmental strategy. I can't remember his job title. Sounds interesting, though. Maybe.' Ren didn't sound convinced and Harrison's insides flipped.

'I can think of more exciting jobs,' he said, looking straight ahead. 'I bet you'd have more fun on a date with me than with him.' He snapped his mouth shut.

When she didn't respond immediately, he glanced down. She was looking back up at him with those soft, curious eyes and a smile tugging at her lips.

In a parallel universe somewhere there was a Harrison who didn't fight the urge to kiss her in that moment. And she would kiss him back. That Harrison would lift her up against the wall of the lift, press against her as she wrapped her legs around him, and there'd be a mad rush to straighten their clothes when the doors opened.

Harrison jumped as the lift doors opened with a ping.

'Yeah,' said Ren, stepping out into the foyer of the building. 'I probably would.' She turned to look back at him, eyes dancing.

Harrison forced himself to breathe.

'Although,' she continued. 'I wouldn't be able to tell unless I went out with this guy, I guess.'

Harrison frowned.

'I...I guess.'

'Unless...' said Ren, glancing around the reception area. 'That would probably be rude, to go out with this guy just as an experiment.'

'Yeah...'

'Even though I'm actually only going on this date to shut Bonnie up,' said Ren, watching him.

'Yeah?'

'Which seems a little silly now that she's so preoccupied with Mac.'

'Yeah.'

Harrison had never been so lost for words in his life. That wasn't true. His memories decided at that moment to show him a sixteen-year-old version of himself, asking out his first wife. In the end, she'd had to ask him out.

'So,' said Ren, pulling Harrison out of his thoughts. She glanced out at the dark evening of Edinburgh beyond the windows. 'I'd best get going.' Her eyes met his again.

Harrison needed a moment.

'Yeah. Okay. Well, stay safe, whatever you do.'

The corners of Ren's mouth dropped a little and Harrison panicked, realising his mistake.

'Have a good evening,' she told him, looking him up and down before turning away and leaving the office. Harrison watched her go, helplessly willing himself to find words that just wouldn't come.

Back in the lift, travelling up to the fifth floor, Harrison screamed the worst swear word he knew.

Had he just asked her out? Had she just said yes? The more he thought about it, replaying the conversation over and over, the more it had sounded like a yes. And still, he'd sent her away on that stupid date with another man.

Harrison rubbed his face and looked up as the doors opened on Martin following a shouting Billy and Liam into the office from the direction of the meeting rooms. It took everything in Harrison not to close the doors and run out after Ren. Instead, he stepped off the lift and gave Martin a nod as his boss gave him a panic-stricken look.

'What's going on?' he asked, and then wished he hadn't as Liam and Billy turned on him and a fountain of words fell out of Billy's mouth.

The office was quiet, even for a Friday, and Ren walked slowly to Martin's office. She'd been summoned and being called to the executive producer's office on a Friday morning didn't seem a cause for celebration. Her gaze was pulled into the meeting room as she wandered past, if only for the fleeting view of the castle. Then again, into Val and Harrison's office. Val's desk was empty, of course, but Harrison was there. His head was down, flicking through a document on his monitor, and he didn't notice her.

Ren had spent the previous evening thinking about their conversation in the lift. The more she thought about it, the more it felt as if he'd asked her out. The more she considered a date with Harrison, the more she wished she'd been firmer in her response.

She wasn't sure where it had gone wrong.

Ren took a deep breath before knocking on Martin's door and, at his call, she entered, closing the door behind her.

'You wanted to see me?' It seemed like the thing to say.

'Yes, please take a seat.'

Ren did so. Martin smiled at her from behind his desk. 'No need to worry, Ren. You're not in trouble. In fact, you've been doing a fantastic job.'

'Oh, thank you.'

'Yes, and I noticed you've been helping Billy out by filling in the parts of the project management that your work covers.'

'Oh, erm, I...'

'It's okay. It's good.'

'Oh, erm. Good.' Ren squirmed in her seat.

'Billy isn't in today,' said Martin. 'And I was wondering if you would mind taking a look at his schedules and forecasts, see what you make of it.'

Ren hesitated, trying to take this in.

'You want me to look at what Billy has been doing?'

'Yes.'

'Can I... Do you mind if I ask why?' Ren cleared her throat and shifted in her seat again.

This time Martin squirmed a little. He bit his lip and then straightened his back, lifting his chin.

'There's a possibility that Billy will need help, as of Monday. You've shown promising signs that you'd be good at the job and I'd like to offer you the opportunity.'

'Oh. Okay.' Ren's mind whirred.

'Take a look at what he's got today and have a think over the weekend. Sound good, Ren?'

'Okay.'

As Ren left Martin's office, she instinctively looked left, wondering what Harrison would say. If anyone could give her good advice on this, it was him.

He wasn't at his desk. She checked his office but it was empty. He wasn't in the kitchen either, and Ren sat at her desk, sure that he would pass her eventually.

He didn't. Ren didn't see him for the rest of the day.

Since moving to Edinburgh, Ren's weekends had been spent either quietly on her sofa or out with Bonnie. After Bonnie and Mac had fallen into bed with each other, Ren tended to spend her weekends alone. Weekends in December weren't that bad, though. She had Christmas presents to buy and festive streets to explore. She spent Saturday relaxing and avoiding the crowds, scouring the internet for advice on what to say to Martin on Monday, trying to work out if she should talk to Billy and resisting the temptation to disturb Bonnie. Instead, she'd spoken to her parents. Martin had agreed for her to go home for a week over Christmas, much to her relief, but she had a feeling it might mean being flexible when it came to helping Billy with his work.

On Sunday, after a light lunch, she ventured out into the chilled afternoon air. A month after moving to Edinburgh, she'd left her swish holiday flat to move into a long-term rental in Stockbridge, deeming it worth the extra money to have a one bed flat in such a beautiful central position. It was the basement garden flat, although the garden was more of a courtyard, but outside space was nothing to scoff at. She planned on filling it with potted plants and bright colours in the summer, but for now she was content to decorate her front door with a wreath and some fairy lights. It brightened up the little area where the concrete steps led up to the street above.

She walked through Stockbridge, heading straight towards the city centre until she reached Princes Street where she could cross the road, hesitantly avoiding the trams and buses, and head down into the tranquil Princes Street Gardens where she promptly stopped. She'd forgotten the Christmas fair had arrived. The park was crammed with stalls and people, tourists and locals alike, enjoying the beginning of the Christmas magic in the city. The colours were bright, fake snow had been placed over flower beds and music screamed out. Further down, a large ride was throwing people around far too close to the Scott Monument for Ren's liking. Ren shook her head and continued on, opting to walk around the park.

She wandered towards the Old Town to find some shops that her family wouldn't find in England. Climbing The Mound, she took a right to take a sneaky peak at the nice houses that lined the road to Edinburgh Castle. Once on the Royal Mile, she fell in behind a small group of tourists and began working her way down.

She went at her own pace, letting the tourists overtake her, dodging out of the way of photos being taken and then popping into a shop if she thought there would be something inside that her parents or brother would like.

She had a couple of presents in her bag when she reached St Giles' Cathedral, where they'd grouped on Halloween evening to meet the ghost tour leader. The road was eerily quiet compared to the usual weekend bustle. Most people were down in the gardens at the fair. It meant that Ren could take her time, looking up at the architecture, enjoying the atmosphere and a strange peace.

When she looked back to street level, concerned she would fall down a step or walk into someone taking a selfie, she caught sight of Harrison.

Her heart leapt into her mouth and before she had time to think, she'd raised her hand to catch his attention. It was in that moment that she realised he wasn't alone. She lowered her hand, ready to slink back into the crowd, but it was too late. He'd seen her.

Smiling, Harrison approached and Ren did the

same, until they met in the pedestrianised road.

'Hello,' said Harrison.

'Hi. Sorry, I didn't realise you were with some-one,' said Ren, glancing at the person who was following Harrison.

'No problem. This is my son, come to visit his old man for Christmas. Jackson, this is Ren. We work together. Ren, this is Jackson.'

Jackson had softer features than Harrison but he had his father's eyes; a cool but sharp blue, offset by dark hair. He was young, early twenties at a push, and Ren found herself wondering if Harrison had been this handsome at that age.

'Hi,' said Jackson, giving her a nod.

'Hi. Is this your first time in Edinburgh?'

Jackson nodded.

'What do you think?' Ren asked.

'It's cold.' He offered her a smile.

Harrison laughed, lifting Ren's spirits and pulling her attention back to him.

'I was looking for you on Friday,' she told him. 'I wanted to talk to you, and then Martin called a meeting with me and I...wanted to ask your advice.'

Harrison's eyes turned from warm and soft to curious.

'Oh?' He glanced at his son and pulled his coat tighter around him as the wind blew down the Royal Mile. 'Well, we can talk on Monday,' he said as Jackson looked at him. 'Or we could get out of this cold and go get a drink somewhere?'

Ren bit her lip.

'Oh, I don't want to intrude or take up any of your time together.'

'It's okay,' said Jackson. 'I'm here for a month.'

'And he's dying for an excuse to look at his phone and have a coffee. Huh?' Harrison elbowed Jackson playfully. His son gave him a smile, subtly agreeing.

'Coffee would be good. If you're buying.'

Harrison laughed again and turned to Ren.

'What do you say? Get out of the cold?'

'Sounds good,' said Ren before she could think on it more.

They found a bustling coffee shop nearby, the warm smell of Christmas spiced coffees hitting them, and Harrison pointed out a table for Jackson to grab while he and Ren stood in the queue.

'I really don't want to be in the way, are you sure about this?' Ren checked as they waited. She eyed up the glass covered display of cakes.

'Of course. Like Jackson said, he's here for a month. Gotta make the most of coming all the way across the Atlantic, right? He's trying to figure out what he does next. He's in college but he's not enjoying it. Turns out he's got a bit of an entrepreneurial spirit about him these days and he's taken a liking to Scottish whisky. He arrived Friday and we're already planning a trip around some distilleries he's found.' Harrison smiled to himself. 'Bit of a chip off the old block in some ways.'

Ren watched Harrison and realised she was

developing a silly grin. She wiped it away.

'Think he'll go start his own distillery?'

Harrison's eyes danced.

'Maybe. Maybe. Probably not in Scotland though, which is a shame. I'd like to see more of him. But that's my own fault. It was my decision to move here, away from him.'

They moved forward in the queue.

'Why did you do that?' Ren asked.

Harrison seemed to realise what he'd let slip and snapped his mouth shut, studying her for a moment. She waited, patiently, while he made a decision.

'I needed a fresh start,' he admitted. 'And Jack was eighteen, an adult, planning on college, starting the next phase of his life. I wasn't seeing him as much. Hell, his mum and stepdad weren't seeing him as much. He was always out with friends, as it should be. And I...I needed this. Maybe I could have waited another year, but, actually I don't think I could have.'

Ren glanced away as she found the words for her next question.

'What did you need a fresh start from?' she asked quietly.

'My second divorce,' said Harrison, just as gently. His tone made her look back up at him. 'Look, what happened in the elevator on Thursday, I—'

'Next!'

Both Harrison and Ren jumped. The space in front of them was empty and Harrison leapt forward, giving his order to the barista. He turned to Ren to ask what she wanted and then he paid, waving Ren's protests and her money away.

They returned to Jackson, removing their coats and taking their seats. Harrison gave Jackson his gingerbread latte and a large chocolate chip cookie. Jackson glanced up from his phone and smiled.

'Thanks.'

'No problem.'

'Yes, thank you. You really didn't have to pay,' said Ren. 'It could have been my treat.'

Harrison softened as he looked up at her. She watched as a thought flashed across his eyes and then he asked, 'How did your Thursday night go?' He glanced at Jackson, consumed by his phone. 'The date,' Harrison clarified.

'I didn't go,' said Ren, sipping her coffee.

Harrison snapped back to look at her.

'You didn't? How come?'

'I got to thinking,' Ren told him. 'I was only going on that date because of Bonnie, and Bonnie's attention is elsewhere now. So what's the point? I guess I could have gone and found out he was a nice guy. I could have had a nice time with a nice guy that maybe could have led to a nice second date. But, I feel like I've been there, done that. Nice is nice, but it doesn't really cut it, you know? I want a bit of fire.' She slowly met Harrison's eyes. 'I think you're right. I would have had more fun with you,' she added, hoping that Jackson wouldn't read too much into that, or perhaps that he wouldn't hear her.

It wasn't just Harrison's eyes that softened this time; his features shifted, a smile pulling on his lips, and he leaned towards her a little. Her heart quickened but she remained still, and then Harrison seemed to remember his son and leaned back.

'Well,' he said, glancing down at his coffee. 'I'm glad you didn't go.'

Ren smiled.

'Me too,' she murmured.

For a moment, they stared at one another until Jackson cleared his throat and picked up his drink. Pulling themselves away, Ren turned to her own drink and Harrison glanced around the coffee shop.

'So, what did Martin want?' he asked.

Ren's body calmed.

'It was weird. He wanted me to go through Billy's work yesterday and he asked me if I wanted to start helping Billy out as of Monday.'

Harrison smiled and Ren's eyes widened. 'You knew about this?'

His smile became a grin.

'Yeah. Sorry, maybe I should have mentioned it but it happened Thursday evening, after you left, and I didn't see you Friday. Otherwise I would have warned you. Maybe,' he added, filling his mouth with coffee.

Ren scoffed at that.

'Billy's not getting fired, is he?'

Harrison shifted in his seat.

'Not to my knowledge, but he's not doing his job. I may have noticed that you were already helping him a little and pointed it out to Martin. Which I won't apologise for,' he added quickly as Ren opened her mouth. 'Billy is more than capable of doing a good job, he's done it before. But the last year or so, he's been sloppy. If we're going to meet this deadline and make this project a success, everyone needs to be on their A game and Billy's holding us back.'

Ren's chest squeezed, a shot of pleasure shooting through her that caught her off guard.

'You really are cut-throat, aren't you,' she murmured.

That took Harrison by surprise and he stared at her with widening eyes.

'What does that mean?'

Ren smiled to put him at ease.

'It was how Bonnie described you on my first day. When she told you to be nice to me, I asked her if you weren't nice. She said you were but you were cut-throat. A Wolf of Wall Street.'

Harrison chuckled.

'Geez, you work as a stockbroker, do a good job and suddenly you're a Wolf of Wall Street?'

'Aren't you?' Ren asked gently.

When Harrison met her gaze, something happened in her gut that she couldn't deny. She wished Jackson wasn't there, or that he would go away for just five minutes. Just long enough for Ren to... To what? To ask Harrison out?

And what then?

She couldn't blindly act on some physical reactions with a man who not only worked with her but was higher up in the company than her. Especially not if what he'd said about Liam and Ally were true. Could she?

Liam and Ally hadn't lost their jobs, but the office was certainly not as bright and bubbly as it had been. What if something similar happened? What if it became so miserable, having to see the face of a failed romance or one night stand or whatever this could be, every day, that she had to quit her job? Where would she go? What would she do?

The questions must have shown on her face because Harrison's smile faltered, a frown growing between his eyes.

'I guess I am,' he said eventually. 'Do you want to help Billy?' he asked, getting back on track.

Ren blinked, trying to disperse the questions her mind was throwing at her.

'Erm, I don't know. I guess, if it helps. Yeah.' She recovered and leaned on the table towards Harrison. 'But will that change my contract? Should I ask for more pay? I don't want to work extra hours for free.'

Harrison smiled but he also now seemed distracted. The almost hurt look in his eyes would haunt Ren over the Christmas period, and she would regret not having said anything in this moment.

'No, Martin'll split your work, but if it becomes official, then you should ask for a new contract, job description and pay review. Definitely get a pay rise out of it, if you can. We can cross that bridge when we get to it.' He flashed her a weak smile. 'Don't worry, I'll help where I can.'

Ren leaned back. This hadn't gone how she'd wanted.

'Thanks. I appreciate that.'

A tense silence fell over them and Jackson glanced up at his father over his phone.

'So, Jackson, what are you studying at college?' asked Ren, desperately trying to find her way through the tension.

Harrison leaned back, happy to let his son take over as Jackson put his phone down and joined the conversation.

'Accountancy and economics,' he said, glancing at his father. 'Thought I might follow in Dad's footsteps but it's boring as hell.'

Ren gave a small laugh.

'Yeah, I'd find that boring too.'

'What do you do?' Jackson asked.

'I'm a palaeontologist.'

His eyes widened.

'Nice. How did you end up working in gaming?'

'I have no idea,' said Ren, glancing out of the window at the city. It was starting to rain, drops of water clinging to the window. 'The dream was to work at the Natural History Museum in London, and I got there but on a short contract. It got extended a few times and when a permanent job came up, well, I didn't get it. My boyfriend at the time got it, actually.'

Out of the corner of her eye, she noticed Harrison look up at her.

'That must have been hard,' said Jackson.

'It was.' Ren nodded. 'He knew how much that job meant to me. He'd started out as a geologist but moved over to palaeontology. He'd already been talking about trying another department. He always struggled with the fact that palaeontology doesn't just cover dinosaurs. He was a little...flaky.'

'Then how did he get the job and you didn't?' asked Harrison.

Ren looked at him but didn't answer, lifting her coffee cup to her lips instead and widening her eyes. *Why do you think?* they asked.

Harrison pulled a face.

'Any number of reasons,' was the official answer she gave. 'He was connected, people knew him. I'm the quiet little studious one who sits in the corner working her arse off. No one notices those people.'

Harrison sighed through his nose.

'Anyway, my contract ended and the funding

changed, so I was out of the dream job. I managed to get a lecturing job at a university which I'm pretty sure was actually in one of the circles of hell. Which I guess wasn't so much of a problem as I got made redundant a few months later. And that boyfriend broke up with me the same week, because that's how my life goes. I guess I forgot to break up with him before, so that was my fault. Then a friend of a friend knew about this job – I was applying for everything and anything – and I finally got lucky again.' She caught Harrison's eye and attempted a warm smile.

She got a flicker of something in response.

'See, I think that's why I'd like to be my own boss,' said Jackson. 'None of that being messed around by assholes.'

Harrison grinned.

'Sounds good to me,' he told his son. They clinked coffee cups and drank. Ren watched, smiling, her mind whirring.

14

'Have you asked her out yet?'

Harrison finished pouring the ale into the pint glass and popped the bottle into the recycling bin, closing the cupboard and carrying the full glasses into the living room of his penthouse West End apartment.

'What?' He handed Jackson one of the glasses and settled himself in his favourite armchair. His son, sprawled on the sofa, sipped the ale and gave the glass an appreciative look.

'Nice,' he said. 'I like this one.'

'Thought you might,' said Harrison, raising his glass to his lips.

'I said, have you asked her out yet?'

'Who?'

Jackson raised an eyebrow at his father.

'That woman we met. Who you work with. You bought her a coffee and dragged me with you, remember? It was only, like, a week ago or something. Have you asked her out yet?'

'What makes you think I want to ask her out?' said Harrison, avoiding eye contact with his son.

Jackson puffed out air in a half-laugh.

'Erm, because it's obvious you're into her? You were happy she didn't go on a date with some other guy and she literally told you she'd rather go out with you. So, what's the problem? Don't you like her? She seemed nice, she was pretty.'

Harrison smiled to himself.

'She did say that, didn't she.'

Jackson laughed.

'She did! So, what's up?'

'It's complicated.' Harrison sighed. 'We work together and we see each other most days, for the most part. Not that we've seen much of each other recently. Which is my fault, I guess. Bringing all the problems to Martin and head office's attention so they brought the deadline forward. Everyone's working themselves to the bone. Every time I've tried to catch Ren on her own this week, she's been neck deep working with Billy or Bonnie or with the developers.' Harrison pulled a face. 'I guess I didn't really think all that through.'

Jackson drank as his father spoke.

'I have no idea who any of those people are,' he told him. 'Is the only complication that you work together? What, you're worried it'll all fall apart and you'll still have to see her?'

Harrison levelled his gaze at his son.

'That's a part of it.'

Jackson pulled a face.

'I don't know why you work there, anyway. Didn't you have to take a big pay cut for this job? What's the point? Ask this chick out and if it all goes wrong, leave. Let's start a business together. Whisky and ale by the Calloways. A father and son family business, brewery and distillery. We could take over the world.' Jackson grinned.

For a heartbeat, Harrison's world stopped. He stared at his son in thought.

'"Whisky and ale by the Calloways" isn't a name,' he said eventually.

Jackson gave this consideration as he drank some more.

'Calloway Whisky and Beer,' he offered.

'Calloway Beer and Whisky,' Harrison countered.

His son grinned at him.

'Seriously, what do you think?'

Harrison drank and smacked his lips.

'Show me a business plan, and I'll think about it.'

'Deal,' said Jackson. 'Hey, I'll show you a business plan if you ask that chick out.'

'Don't call her a chick,' Harrison warned. 'Her name's Ren.'

'Like the bird?'

'Short for Lauren.' Harrison smiled.

'Lauren Calloway has a nice ring to it,' said Jackson. His smile fell as his father's expression dropped. 'Sorry, Dad.'

'It's okay. Nothing to apologise for.' Which was true but still, Harrison's stomach was in his throat.

'They won't all be like her, you know. This Ren seemed nice. Kind. Hey, she offered to pay, didn't she? That's a good sign, right?'

Harrison nodded.

'She always offers to pay. She also thinks I'm capitalist scum.'

Jackson's eyes widened.

'She said that?'

'Yeah, a while ago now, but yeah.'

Jackson shrugged.

'People change their minds, Dad.'

'I guess,' Harrison murmured, replaying that coffee shop chat in his mind, as he'd done repeatedly every day for the last week. That moment when she'd leaned towards him, when her eyes had softened, when he'd wondered if she was feeling the same as him, that same urge. That moment when something dark had crossed her eyes, when her smile had fallen at some unspoken thought. 'Women are complicated.'

'I hear that,' said Jackson, draining the last of his ale. He drank too fast in Harrison's opinion, who was only half way through his own pint.

'Oh yeah? What do you know of women? You got girl trouble?' Harrison smiled to himself.

'I might be seeing someone.'

Harrison snapped up to look at his son.

'You didn't tell me that! Who is she? What's she

like?'

Jackson shrugged.

'She's hot, a year younger than me, not happy that I want to drop out of college.'

Harrison grinned.

'Well, well. Hang on, let me get you another drink. I want to hear how you met.'

Jackson rolled his eyes as his father walked past, grabbing his empty glass.

'Of course you do,' he muttered.

A hopeless romantic. That was what his first wife had called him, rolling her eyes exactly the same way Jackson often did. Harrison had considered the label a good thing back then. Being a hopeless romantic had led him to his first love, had driven him to propose to her when they were too young and reckless, to believe he could marry his first love and that would be it.

Hopeless had been right, perhaps.

It wasn't until four months into his second marriage that he realised exactly what his problem was. His first wife had laughed in his face when he'd brought it up with her, declaring him a wonderful idiot for taking so long to figure it out.

Harrison Calloway fell in love too quickly.

He'd been lucky with his first wife and desperately unlucky with his second. Did it alternate? It was difficult now, three months after meeting Ren, to not wonder if this could be a case of third time lucky.

He was getting ahead of himself. Harrison didn't need Mac to tell him that. What he needed was to ask Ren out, or to at least talk to her, to find out if she felt the same way. Just the idea made his heart thump.

He spotted her around during the last week before Christmas, at her desk or in the kitchen chatting to Bonnie. He watched her during meetings, his mouth dry whenever she glanced over at him, a smile playing on her lips. Yet, there was never a moment to talk.

He caught her in the lift once, only for the doors to open and three members of the marketing team to spill in, chatting away and laughing at some joke Ren and Harrison had missed.

'Can we talk?' he managed to ask in a hushed tone on their last day in the office. He'd approached her from behind, catching her off guard in the kitchen. She turned, a flash of panic in her eyes before she agreed. As he moved to lead her to a meeting room, Billy appeared, searching for her. Ren crashed into the back of Harrison and stayed close to him as Billy asked for her help. She gave Harrison an apologetic look as Billy pulled her away, and that was it. They didn't see each other again.

At five o'clock on that last day before Christmas Eve, Harrison rushed into the office to find it practically empty.

'Damn it,' he shouted.

'What? What happened?'

Harrison spun to find Bonnie still at her desk, packing things into her bag.

'Oh, thank god. Is Ren gone?'

'Yeah, she had a plane to catch. She's gone home for Christmas. Why? You need her for something?'

Yeah, thought Harrison, *something*.

'I need to talk to her. I've been in a damn online meeting with head office for the last goddamn three hours. Those assholes don't seem to know it's Christmas.'

Bonnie groaned in sympathy and pulled out her phone.

'I'll ask if I can give you her number. Hang on. She's probably still at the airport.' She tapped out a message and hit send.

Harrison held his breath.

'Looking forward to Christmas with your son?' Bonnie asked as she finished packing, closing her bag and pulling on her coat.

'Yeah. It's gonna be a quiet one,' said Harrison, staring at her phone on the desk. 'How about you? Are you seeing Mac?'

Bonnie smiled, her eyes going distant.

'Of course. I'm heading up home to Aberdeen tomorrow, so tonight's my last chance to see Mac until New Year's Eve. We're going to see in the New Year together, though.'

'Spending Hogmanay in the city?' Harrison asked, smiling. He'd done the same the year before, drunk too much and had limited memories of the beginning of the year. But the memories he did have were good ones.

'Oh no. We'll be spending it in his bed,' said Bonnie, grinning widely and giving him a wink.

Harrison pulled a face.

'My best friend and some woman I work with,' he muttered.

Bonnie feigned an insulted expression and made to throw her phone at him. Magically, it beeped and drew the attention of both of them.

'She says yes. Give me your phone.'

Swallowing on nothing, Harrison handed over his phone and watched as Bonnie typed in Ren's number.

'Use it wisely,' said Bonnie. 'Don't bombard her with work.'

'Yes, boss.' Harrison flashed her a grin as he took his phone back, glancing down at Ren's name and number. 'Thanks for this. Appreciate it.' More than Bonnie could know. 'Have a good one.'

'Merry Christmas!' Bonnie sang, walking past Harrison and heading for the lift.

Harrison would have watched her go but he was still looking at Ren's name in his phone, already trying to compose a message to her in his head.

He still hadn't messaged her two days later, on Christmas Day. Standing in the kitchen, Christmas music playing faintly on the system he'd set up in the first weeks after getting the keys to his apartment, he downed the last of his beer and stared at his phone.

'Merry Christmas! Hope you're having a good one.'

It was a simple message with no expectations. He'd spent a good forty-eight hours considering it and now he was stuck.

'What can I do?' Jackson wandered in, bringing in the last of the Christmas dinner plates and putting his hands on his hips to survey the damage. 'You'll shout at me if I stack the dishwasher, right?'

'Yup,' Harrison mumbled, not looking up.

'What're you doing?' Jackson moved to read the message on Harrison's screen and Harrison didn't stop him. 'Is that to Ren?'

'I don't know whether to put a kiss. Should I put a kiss? Is that too much?' asked Harrison. Where was Mac when he needed him?

'You like her, right?' asked his son.

'Yeah.'

'You want her to know you like her, right?'

'Yeah.' Harrison sounded less convinced.

'Give her a kiss, then.'

Harrison's thumb hovered over the 'X' key.

'What if she doesn't feel the same way and I just make things awkward?' he asked in a rush.

Jackson shrugged.

'Your finger slipped. Make a joke of it.'

Harrison's heart squeezed in a painful jolt as he gave a singular nod, pressed the 'X' key and hit send. Exhaling in a puff, he threw his phone onto the worktop and opened the dishwasher.

'So, what can I do?' Jackson repeated.

'There's traditional British Christmas pudding in the fridge, get that out and put it in the microwave.'

Jackson pulled a face.

'There's whisky in it,' said Harrison.

Jackson went to the fridge and found the Christmas pudding, reading the label curiously. Harrison finished loading the dishwasher, leaving space for the pudding bowls, and then fetched the cream from the fridge.

He nibbled his bottom lip as he went and realised his son was watching him.

'What?'

'Promise me you'll ask her out when you're back at work.'

Harrison hesitated, staring at his son. Jackson sighed, taking the pudding over to the microwave.

'Dad, you've got to be brave in love. Remember? You told me that.'

'Yeah, well, I was an idiot back then.'

'You were brave when it came to Mom.'

'Yeah. I was,' said Harrison slowly.

'And you're not rushing this. And so she might say no, but she might say yes. And how will you know if you don't ask? Don't let one bad experience keep you from being happy.'

One bad experience. That was one way of describing it. Not that Harrison would ever describe years of embarrassment, pain and watching his money being leached from his bank account as 'one bad experience'.

'Ask her out in the New Year,' Jackson continued. 'Promise me.'

'Fine. Yes, I promise,' said Harrison, but Jackson didn't look convinced.

'Ask her out and I'll send you a business plan,' his son reminded him.

Harrison met his eyes and felt a bubble of the most painful kind of love rise inside him; the kind of love no woman could ever provoke.

'You're a good kid,' he managed to say in a low voice.

Jackson grinned.

'Thanks. Can you remind Mom of that when she tries to convince me to stay in college?'

Harrison chuckled.

'Will do.'

The microwave pinged and both men froze as, on the worktop, Harrison's phone lit up at the same time. Cautiously, Harrison moved to his phone, picked it up and opened the message with Ren's name on it.

Then he laughed, making Jackson jump as he lifted the Christmas pudding from the microwave. Jackson dropped the pudding on the worktop and rushed over to read the message over his father's shoulder.

'Merry Christmas! Hope you and Jackson are having a good one too! It's strange being back in England. For some reason I have the urge to listen to bagpipe music. Did Father Christmas bring you anything nice? xx'

'Two kisses,' Jackson murmured. 'You're in.'

Harrison grinned to himself, rereading the message over and over as his heart pounded and his legs threatened to bounce. Fingers trembling, he typed out a response.

'I think Santa's forgotten about me. How about you? xx'

Harrison typed the two kisses purposefully and hit send as Jackson turned his attention to sorting out the cream for the pudding.

'What do I do with this?'

'Err.' Harrison glanced up. 'Whip it, I think.'

Jackson stared at him until Harrison sighed, placed his phone down and took the cream off his son.

He'd barely started whipping it when his phone

lit up again. He thrust the bowl into Jackson's arms and reached for Ren's reply.

'The usual, which is always nice. My feet won't get cold in the Scottish winter, let's put it that way. I'm glad Bonnie gave you my number. I wish we'd gotten to talk before I had to leave. I checked in on you but you were in a meeting xx'

Harrison's heart leapt into his throat and he leaned back against the worktop, blowing out his cheeks. How far should he take this conversation? Should he offer to call her? Should he wait to tell her how he felt?

He wanted to do it in person, he realised. He wanted to see her face. Carefully, he typed a message.

'I ran out of that meeting but you'd already gone. We can talk properly when you're back? I've been thinking about you. Kicking myself for making us all work so hard that I can't seem to catch you for a chat anymore.'

He realised after he'd hit send that he'd forgotten the kisses. Then he reread his message and fretted as the long seconds passed. Finally, the app told him Ren was typing a reply and Harrison held his breath.

'Don't kick yourself for doing a good job. I've been thinking about you too. We'll have to try extra hard to catch each other for chats when I'm back. Hey, is it snowing there?'

And just like that, Ren and Harrison were deep in a conversation that would last the rest of the evening and into the night.

'Why are you always on your phone?' Ren's brother, Phil, whined as she read another message from Harrison.

'Sorry.' She only had a couple of days left with her family before she would be back in the office with Harrison, and yet her fingers ached to talk to him.

'All the Scottish men she's been meeting.' Phil rolled his eyes at their mother who raised an eyebrow at Ren.

'Not someone from the dating app?' she checked.

'No. I deleted that,' Ren told her, glancing down at her phone and Harrison's unanswered message.

'The double divorcee?'

Ren pressed her lips together and her mother sighed.

'Two divorces? How old is he?' her brother quipped.

'I don't know. In his forties,' murmured Ren. 'Late- or mid-forties, I guess.'

'And already divorced twice?' Phil pulled a face in what could almost constitute caring for what happened to his big sister. 'Sounds like a keeper,' he murmured sarcastically.

Her mother agreed and Ren sighed.

'There's more to him than that,' she told them.

'I would hope so!' Her mother was making them bacon sandwiches for breakfast and Ren had poured orange juice into four glasses, handing one to her brother sitting at the kitchen table.

She joined him at the table, an image of Harrison filling her mind, his voice in her ears. She smiled until her brother caught her.

'Okay. But nothing may come of it,' she warned them. 'His name's Harrison and I work with him. He's the project's finance director.'

Her mother's eyes lit up.

'Oh? Harrison's a nice name.'

'Hmm. He's from New York and used to work as a stockbroker, I think.'

Her mother's expression fell.

'Oh. Like an investment banker? With two divorces?' She pulled a face.

'He has this incredible laugh,' Ren continued. 'And...I don't know. There's something about him. I met his son a couple of weeks ago. He's nineteen or twenty or something. They seem to get on well.'

'Hang on, how did you meet his son? Bring your child to work day?' asked Phil, smirking. Ren shot him a look.

'I bumped into them on the Royal Mile, while out shopping,' she explained. 'Harrison offered to buy me a drink, out of the cold, so I joined them in a coffee shop. It was nice.' She smiled to herself again and this time, her mother caught her. 'It's been difficult at work, recently. There's been some fighting. What I told you about the head developer having an affair and me helping out the project manager? The project manager and executive producer, the big boss, keep getting into fights for some reason, but Harrison always manages to calm it down. He's the one who figured something was off, about the head developer.'

'Is he the reason you've been working all the hours, too?' asked her mother.

Ren kept her mouth shut, which told them all they needed to know.

'Good morning!' Her father swept into the kitchen, his hand trailing around his wife's waist as he reached for the coffee pot. 'What have I missed?'

'Ren's in love with some old bloke she works with who's been divorced twice and used to be an investment banker.'

Ren glared at her brother as her father slowly turned to look at her, an eyebrow raised.

'Oh? You haven't mentioned a boyfriend.'

'He isn't my boyfriend. There's nothing going on,' said Ren, wishing she hadn't mentioned Harrison at all. She glanced down at his still unanswered message.

'But you want there to be?' her mother checked.

Ren sighed.

'I don't know,' she said. 'He seems to like me – he asked for my number from Bonnie, we've been messaging each other since Christmas Day. And when I'm around him, I just...' She glanced up at her mother. 'Feel safe,' she finished.

Her mother smiled.

'Just be careful,' she warned Ren. 'Is he your boss?'

'Not directly. But I am worried about the fact we work together, kind of closely. Do you think that would be a problem?'

'Yes,' said Phil.

'No,' said her mother.

'Maybe,' said her father.

Ren looked from one to the other, waiting for someone, anyone, to expand on their response.

'What if you break up?' asked her mother. 'I think you should go with your gut, but be careful.'

'Especially with your track record.' Phil smirked again and Ren looked for something to throw at him.

'Phil has a point,' said her father, taking a bacon sandwich from his wife. 'Make sure he's not using you and that he's going to take care of you. How much older is he? Is he the gross boss looking to seduce his secretary?'

'No!' Ren took her breakfast as her mother passed it over. 'He's not that much older than me.

And I'm not a secretary! I'm not sure what he would use me for.'

'Sex,' said Phil around a mouthful of sandwich.

Ren picked off some of her crust and threw it at him. It bounced off his head and Phil turned angrily to their mother who raised a finger.

'You're grown-ups. I'm not getting involved, but stop fighting in my kitchen.'

Phil glared at Ren who stuck her tongue out at him.

'He's a gorgeous man with money and a New York accent living in the city. I'm pretty sure he could have any woman he wanted if he was just after sex,' Ren said, staring down at her breakfast. 'Plus if that's what it was, he would have made a move by now. Right?'

'Probably,' said her father, grimacing each time the word 'sex' was uttered.

'A New York accent?' asked her mother, and she and Ren shared a look which left them both grinning.

'Yuck,' said Phil, watching them. 'I'm getting out of here. I'm going to meet my mates. Thanks for breakfast, Mum.' He stood, leaving his crumb-filled plate on the worktop, and strode from the room.

'What are you up to today?' Ren's father asked her. 'Meeting up with your friends?'

Ren's stomach turned and she placed her half-eaten sandwich on the table.

'No,' she said. 'No, I'll just stay home, I think.'

Her parents exchanged a look that she probably wasn't supposed to see.

'Have you spoken to any of them since you moved to Edinburgh?' her mother asked gently, sitting in Phil's recently vacated chair and taking a bite of her own sandwich.

Ren shrugged.

'Sort of. We talk but they often don't respond. Or they cut it short. They're busy. Especially right now. They've got their own families. Can I not just stay here?'

'Of course you can.' Ren's father patted her on the shoulder. 'I'm going to pop to the shop.' He left without asking if Ren wanted to join him.

Ren's mother took her plate to the sink and left it there, wiping down her hands.

'In that case, I think I'll give Justine a call. I promised her we'd chat after Christmas. Will you be okay?'

Ren blinked and nodded.

'Yeah. Sure.'

She watched as her mother left her alone in the kitchen with a half-eaten bacon sandwich, and then sighed deeply. Picking up her phone, she reread Harrison's last message.

'What are you up to today? I'm being dragged to a distillery by Jackson. Didn't think any would be open this week! xx'

A soft smile picked at Ren's lips and she typed a reply.

'Today I'm wishing I hadn't come home for a whole week. Where's the distillery? I'm sure he doesn't need to drag you to somewhere with alcohol xx'

She placed her phone on the table and watched it as she finished her breakfast. Harrison replied before she took her last bite.

'Up near Aberdeen. I'll hide if I see Bonnie. And I don't like what you're implying there! I don't like all alcohol. I like beer. I'm beginning to get whiskeyed out. Do you want to come back early? Has something happened? xx'

Ren sighed, her finger stroking the screen as if that would magic her back to Edinburgh.

'Whisky.'

She hit send and grinned to herself, laughing as the reply came through.

'One day we'll be in New York together and I'll be able to correct you all the time!'

She reread that message a few times, wondering

how to respond.

'Nothing's happened. My family have lives, my friends have their own families, my only available friends are also friends with my ex. I'm sitting alone in the kitchen right now with no idea what to do. And I've never been to New York so you'd have to teach me how to speak the lingo.'

Ren placed the phone down and stared at it. The app told her Harrison was typing and she waited eagerly for his response to come through.

'I'd offer to call you right now and teach you the lingo if I wasn't about to get in the car. I'm sorry you're on your own.'

Ren smiled softly, her stomach flipping.

'Enjoy the distillery. And don't worry, I'll go annoy my mum in a bit. Make her regret asking me to take a week off! You can teach me the lingo when we're back in the office?'

She fretted over the question mark at the end. He'd be getting in the car, he wouldn't be able to respond. And then her phone lit up.

'It's a date xx'

Ren grinned, staring at the message. She replied with two kisses to end the conversation and free Harrison to spend the day with his son. Then she sat back and considered her own reaction. How would she face him back in the office after all this? With a smile? With an urge to kiss him? With a reminder that he promised they'd talk?

Ren's hand hovered over her chest as her heart pounded and a small voice in the back of her head sent out a warning message; *this might not end well*, it said, *be prepared for it to not end well*.

It was just past seven thirty when Harrison strode off the lift and onto the empty fifth floor. He paused to breathe in the air of a new year in the building and headed straight for his office. Leaving his coat and bag by his desk, Harrison turned his laptop on and slowly made his way to the kitchen. His plan was to make a coffee as slowly as possible and drink it while watching his colleagues return to the office, until Ren appeared.

She walked off the lift at eight o'clock and headed straight to her desk. Harrison carried his nearly empty cup over to her and said in a low voice, 'Happy New Year.'

Ren jumped and turned, a grin blooming on her face when she saw it was him.

'Oh, don't creep up on me like that!' She held a hand to her chest and Harrison chuckled.

'Sorry.'

For a blissful moment, they smiled at each other.

'You're in early,' said Ren, her eyes glancing

down to his coffee cup and absent coat.

'Yeah. Glad to be back in the city?' he asked. Behind him, a gaggle of developers stepped off the lift and wandered noisily to their corner of the building.

'Morning!' shouted Dougal, waving.

Ren waved back and Harrison watched him, dropping his smile.

'It's good to be back in Edinburgh. It's weird, isn't it. It almost felt like coming home when I got off the plane,' said Ren, taking her own coffee cup from her bag along with her lunch. She slipped off her coat and headed for the kitchen. Harrison followed.

'Why is it weird?'

'Well, it's a bit soon, isn't it? I thought it might take longer.' Ren put her lunch in the fridge and started up the coffee machine. 'How long did it take for Edinburgh to feel like home to you?'

Harrison leaned against the worktop and watched some more people arrive.

'Probably about a year,' he admitted. 'But I came from a land much further away than you did.'

Ren laughed and they switched places at the coffee machine.

'Happy New Year!' yelled Bonnie as she stepped off the lift. Half the office's occupants cheered at her and she walked to her desk laughing.

'I'm glad I'm back,' murmured Ren, grinning and taking a deep breath. She glanced at Harrison, meeting his eyes. 'Is Jackson still here?'

'Yup. For another week. I left him in bed this morning. He knows his way around the kitchen now.'

'What are you up to today?' she asked quietly.

'Oh, the usual first day back stuff. Remembering my password, checking emails, figuring out what my job is again, trying to catch a quiet moment with you so we can talk.' Harrison's gaze lingered on her as his words trailed off. His mouth was dry again but his coffee was too hot to sip yet. Should he ask her now? No time like the present, right?

'I'm free now,' she murmured before he could ask. His heart thudded.

'Okay,' he said, looking around. 'Meeting room?'

Ren frowned.

'My kingdom for a meeting room without glass walls,' she muttered before looking up at him brightly and saying, 'Sure.'

Harrison paused for a moment to appreciate her and she smiled back up at him, her eyes soft, a twitch of her eyebrow wakening him. Taking a steadying breath, Harrison began to lead the way to the meeting room at the back of the office just as Martin stepped off the lift.

'Good morning, everyone. Bonnie! Have you seen Ren? Ren! There you are. Billy's not coming in today. Apparently he's sick. Who gets sick on the first day back at work after Christmas? Anyway, that's what he's going with. And I really want to hit this year running. Ah, Harrison. Good, you're here too. Senior meeting in half an hour!' he shouted through the office, making Bonnie jump. 'And Ren, a word now, please. I need you to take over from Billy today, and we need to talk about your contract.'

Martin marched off toward his office before Ren had a chance to open her mouth to reply. Mouth finally open, but no words coming, she turned to Harrison who swallowed on a lump in his throat.

'My kingdom for a time machine,' he murmured under his breath, but she heard. She flashed him a weak smile and closed the gap between them.

'Later,' she told him. 'We'll talk later. Yeah? After the big meeting, maybe? And, oh god, my contract. What do I say?'

Harrison closed his eyes for a moment, trying to gather his wits about him.

'See what he's proposing. Originally you were only going to take over a day from Billy, to help him out, but... Well, I don't know what's happened this morning. If you're not comfortable about the contract or the pay, ask to think about it and then come to me.'

Ren stared up him with large eyes, and for a moment he thought she might hug him. Instead, she nodded, biting on her lower lip in such a way that in an ideal universe it would have resulted in them both somewhere private, pulling on each other's clothes, his lips on her hot skin.

'Thanks,' she said, breaking his thoughts. 'You have no idea how much I appreciate it.'

'Anytime,' he whispered.

She gave him a longing look that he couldn't help but return, and then she took her coffee down the corridor to Martin's office.

Harrison had the sudden need to sit down.

'Hey!' Bonnie skipped over to him, past him and over to the coffee machine. 'Good Christmas?'

'Yeah, yeah. You?'

'Very,' said Bonnie.

'And how is Mac?'

'You haven't talked to him?' Bonnie glanced at him over her shoulder.

'No. I didn't want to interrupt you both and my son's still here. Why? Everything okay?'

'Yeah, it's great.' Bonnie turned to lean back against the worktop while the coffee machine did its thing. She crossed her arms and her eyes glazed as she grinned at her memories.

'Don't wanna know,' said Harrison, holding up a hand.

Slowly, Bonnie came back to the office, her grin fading.

'Sounds like we're back in the deep end straight away,' she murmured before groaning. She perked up a little and Harrison followed her gaze to watch Liam saunter in.

'Morning, stranger,' said Bonnie, her tone a little too harsh. Liam shot her a look and then scowled at

Harrison. 'Senior manager meeting in, ooh, probably twenty minutes now.'

'Have you heard from Billy this morning?' Harrison asked him.

Liam sighed loudly, dropping his bag by his desk and wandering over.

'Happy New Year, Liam. How was your Christmas, Liam? Oh, I'm great, thanks. Nice to be back and all that.'

Bonnie and Harrison stared at him, Harrison's eyes narrowing as he gritted his teeth.

'No, I haven't heard from Billy. Actually, I haven't spoken to him in a while.'

'He hasn't been checking on the game development?' Harrison asked.

Liam shook his head.

'Not to my knowledge.'

'Son of a—' Harrison turned, balling his hand into a fist and wishing there was a punch bag nearby.

'What is up with him?' Bonnie asked. 'Seriously?' She turned on Liam. 'Do you know?'

Liam shrugged.

'A while back, we used to go out drinking together and I told him...' Liam glanced up at Bonnie and Harrison. 'About Ally.' He sighed. 'And he told me that he was fed up. He was looking for another job. And that was it. I don't know if he actually applied for anything. But he's still here.'

'He's called in sick today,' Bonnie told him.

'Martin's asking Ren to take over.'

'Take over?' Liam frowned.

'Not for good. But we need a project manager,' Harrison clarified. 'So if Billy wants to keep his job, he should come in and actually do it. You might want to tell him.'

Liam glared at Harrison and then slowly turned to Bonnie who was watching them both as if she was desperate to ask a question. She took Liam looking at her as permission.

'So, you and Ally. What's going on? Are you still. ..?' She waved her arms around to finish her sentence.

Liam tutted, rolling his eyes, but he didn't walk away. Harrison waited to see if he would answer Bonnie with him standing there and when he didn't, Harrison made an excuse and headed to his office. Bonnie would tell him later, anyway.

He lingered outside his office door, peering in through the glass of Martin's office to where Ren was sitting opposite the executive producer. Martin was talking, because of course he was. Sighing, Harrison went into his own office and prepared for the meeting. Logging into his laptop, catching up on emails, sipping his coffee. His son messaged him to ask if there was more orange juice so Harrison suggested he venture to the local shop.

Fifteen minutes passed before Martin and Ren appeared outside, and Ren glanced in to Harrison as Martin led her to the meeting room. Harrison jumped up to follow them.

Martin headed to the toilets so Harrison dipped into the meeting room with Ren and purposefully closed the door behind him.

'How did it go?' he asked, keeping his voice low, just in case.

Ren rubbed her hands over her face.

'I think I need to talk to Billy,' she told him. 'Martin's really angry with him. He wants me to go fifty-fifty with the job but I don't see how that'll work with Billy.'

'Is he getting a new contract drawn up?'

Ren nodded.

'He's going to head down to HR after this meeting.'

'What have you agreed to?'

'I told him I need to think about it,' said Ren proudly.

Harrison grinned.

'Atta girl.'

Ren glanced around, peering through the glass walls to see if anyone else was coming.

'We probably don't have time to talk now, right?' she murmured, stepping over to him. 'About... everything.'

Everything. Yes, Harrison wanted to talk to Ren about everything. His chest fluttered and he opened his mouth to ask her to dinner that evening when Bonnie burst into the room and shut the door behind her.

'So, Liam talked to me,' she said quickly. 'Oh, Ren, how did it go with Martin?'

Ren and Harrison stared at her for a moment and Harrison considered just how bad it would be to push Bonnie back outside so he and Ren could be alone again.

'I'll tell you later. What about Liam?' Ren asked.

Bonnie checked the coast was clear behind her.

'He's still sleeping with Ally,' she whispered hoarsely. 'She's left her husband!'

Ren covered her mouth with a hand while Harrison pulled a face.

'And a very merry Christmas to him,' he muttered.

'That's that, then,' murmured Ren. 'Nothing else'll happen now. Liam and Ally will probably get married and have a horrible story of how they got together.'

Harrison watched her, leaning towards her without thinking. A horrible story of how they got together. Just how would his and Ren's story go, he wondered. Would they ever get that moment alone? Harrison sighed so hard that both Ren and Bonnie turned to him, but only Ren seemed to understand what the sigh had been about. She gave him a sweet, soft smile and appeared to almost reach out a hand to him.

'I doubt that'll be it,' Bonnie added quietly, checking behind her again. 'I reckon Martin won't let it lie.' She gave Harrison a meaningful look and then wandered further into the room, pulling out a chair to take a seat.

Martin entered a second later, greeted Bonnie and took up his usual seat. With a longing look to one another, Harrison and Ren sat next to each other and Harrison resisted the urge to take her hand under the table.

Ren did a strange hop in an attempt to see if Harrison was in his office without Martin seeing her from his. Both men were at their desks. Ren spun and slid into Harrison's office in a move that she was pretty certain deserved an award. Breathing hard, she pressed herself against the wall and checked to see if Martin had noticed her.

He hadn't.

When she turned back to the room, Harrison was watching her with laughing eyes and an amused smile.

'What was that?' he asked.

'We need to talk,' she told him. 'And we keep getting interrupted.'

'So you thought you'd come in here Mission Impossible style?' Harrison laughed. Ren relaxed, although it did nothing to calm her nerves.

'It's working, isn't it?' She walked into the office, peaking at the view of the castle.

'It is.' Harrison's tone had softened, drawing her

attention back to him. He looked her up and down, and Ren's mouth went dry. Looking around, there was nowhere to sit other than a small sofa up against the wall. Ren went to it and sat facing Harrison at his desk. He swivelled his chair to her. 'So, finally, we can talk,' he said, breaking the silence.

Ren nodded.

'About...that,' she said. 'But also – and I feel horrible for this – but Martin wants me to sign my updated job description today and I can't get hold of Billy.' She gave Harrison a pleading look.

'Why do you feel horrible about it?'

'Because I don't want to take advantage of you.'

Harrison grinned and then tried to wipe the smirk from his lips.

'So it's not because you feel bad about Billy?'

'Oh, yeah, I guess there's a bit of that,' Ren admitted. 'But he's not here, is he? And he hasn't been doing his job, has he?'

They both jumped at a knock on the office door and Martin appeared. Ren's stomach turned.

'Ren, good, I was about to come looking for you,' said Martin, sparing Harrison a glance. 'Billy's gone and gotten himself signed off sick for a month. How are you feeling about that contract?'

Ren gawped, opening and closing her mouth, searching for the words. Harrison looked from her to Martin.

'Is she getting a raise out of this, Martin?' he

asked.

Martin twitched, as if Harrison was an annoying fly buzzing near his ear.

'No.'

'Then what's in it for her? She's a palaeontologist, not a project manager. Sure she'd do a good job, but she came here to make the dinosaurs authentic and she's doing it brilliantly. Why should she add to that?' Harrison leaned back in his chair as Martin fidgeted.

'There's the budget to consider,' he tried.

'You're telling me,' said Harrison, waving a hand over his laptop screen full of figures and charts. 'There's leeway.'

Martin sighed.

'Fine. I'll talk to HR about compensation.'

'And her hours stay the same,' said Harrison. 'Part-time palaeontologist, part-time project manager, same hours as before.'

Martin nodded.

'Yes. Yup.'

Harrison looked to Ren.

'Sound good?'

Ren stared at Harrison, her mouth still open. Harrison turned back to Martin.

'Go talk to HR, Martin, and let Ren know when it's ready for her to sign. But we need to hear about that pay rise first.'

Martin gave Harrison a look that had a hefty hint of betrayal about it before nodding, closing the door and disappearing down the corridor towards the lift.

Harrison and Ren turned to one another.

'That was amazing!' Ren breathed. 'Where have you been all my career?'

Harrison laughed his wonderful belly laugh.

'Just gotta have confidence. What's the worst that can happen? You do a great job, you're on a contract and they need you.' He studied her for a moment. 'You haven't managed to talk to Billy?'

'No.' Ren sighed. 'Bonnie gave me his number but it just rings and rings. I've messaged him and they're being marked as read, but he's not replying. I don't know what else to do.'

'Nothing,' Harrison told her. 'You've done more than you should. Let it go.'

Ren shifted in her seat.

'I guess.' She looked out the window. The view was even better from the small sofa. 'If I were you,' she murmured, 'I'd move my desk over here for that view.'

Harrison grinned.

'And get no work done,' he ventured.

Ren considered the view again.

'Good point.' She turned to him and their eyes locked. 'So, good Christmas?'

Harrison smiled.

'Better than I thought.'

'Oh?'

'Yeah, ended up chatting to this woman I work

with.'

'Oh.' Ren fought the grin battling to get onto her face. 'What about your son?'

Harrison nodded.

'He was also there.'

Ren laughed.

'Is he setting up a whisky distillery yet?'

'Oh, don't get him started on that,' said Harrison, stretching his arms above his head. 'He hasn't shut up about the idea. So, err, did you have any interesting conversations with a guy you work with over Christmas?'

Something inside Ren melted.

'I did,' she breathed.

'And... Did you... I mean...' Harrison frowned to himself as Ren smiled.

'You're as bad at this as I am,' she declared.

Harrison looked up at her.

'I'll have you know that I am excellent at asking women out,' he told her.

'Oh? Is that what you're trying to do?'

A smile spread across Harrison's lips.

'I'm a little out of practice.'

Ren said nothing, smiling at the man sitting across the room, waiting for him to ask her.

'If it helps,' she said when he appeared a little stumped, 'I'll say yes.'

Harrison grinned and Ren's body tingled with anticipation.

'Dinner,' he told her.

She nodded.

'Okay. Tonight?'

Harrison's expression fell.

'Damn. I'm taking Jackson to the airport to-night.'

'Oh, that's okay. How about—'

A loud rapping on the door interrupted Ren and they both turned, expecting to see Martin. Bonnie let herself in, out of breath.

'There you are,' she told Ren. 'Billy's on the phone for you. And Dougal's looking for you.' She turned to Harrison. 'Thought you said you had a meeting with head office this afternoon?'

Harrison leapt forward in his chair to check the time.

'God dammit,' he muttered, waking up his laptop.

Ren went to follow Bonnie out, her gaze lingering on Harrison.

'Later?' she murmured.

Crest-fallen, Harrison nodded. 'Later.'

Ren hung up the phone with a deep sigh and Bonnie immediately wheeled her chair to sit next to her.

'What happened? Why do you keep sighing? What's going on?'

Ren almost laughed, but the frustrated knot in her stomach meant that it would probably come out as a scream.

'I need to talk to Harrison, but we can't seem to get a moment, Billy's being an arse and says I can have his job but he's not quitting yet – what's his problem? – and now I have to go find Dougal to see what he wants.' She rubbed a hand down her face. 'I'm not sure I can do two jobs at once,' she added quietly.

'Sure you can. You'll be great,' Bonnie told her. 'And it'll probably only be until Martin can get shot of Billy, then they'll be able to replace him properly. And the thing with Dougal will be fun, right? Dinosaurs! What do you need to talk to Harrison about?'

Ren realised her mistake and thought fast.

'He's helping me with the new contract.' It wasn't a lie so Ren left it at that.

'Ah, okay. I thought maybe something was going on.' Bonnie gave her a sideways look. 'But then, for a while I thought there was something going on with you and Doug. Probably for the best there isn't anything.'

'Why do you say that?' Ren asked, her stomach heaving up towards her throat. She swallowed hard to settle it.

'After everything that's been going on. With Liam and Ally.'

'But that's nothing. That's fine now. Isn't it?' Ren lowered her voice, checking behind her, but Liam's desk was empty.

'I don't know,' said Bonnie. 'Maybe at any other office.' She glanced around them and Ren did the same, not knowing quite who they were looking for. Bonnie leaned in close to whisper. 'The problem is Martin.'

Ren frowned.

'Why?'

'A couple years back, he went off the deep end and disappeared off sick for a few months. It got bad. Harrison pretty much held the place together and helped him get back on his feet.'

Ren's heart jolted at the mention of Harrison and she twisted her lips to stop the smile that automatically began to appear.

'Problem is, it's just recently come out that the reason he went off the deep end is because his husband had an affair with an intern in his office.'

Ren looked up into Bonnie's eyes.

'So? Did they work it out?'

'Oh, yeah. Martin forgave him after he begged and pleaded. They're in counselling, last I heard, but all is well. Except it turns out that Martin made him change job. Val told me just before Christmas. Apparently, he broke down on her one evening when they were working late.'

Ren sighed.

'Poor Martin.'

'And now he doesn't look too keenly on work-place romance. You heard Martin and Billy arguing? My best guess is that Martin's anger has been misplaced. It's aimed at Liam but what could he do? Billy was the one talking back. Now look where we are.'

Nausea swirled in Ren's gut.

'So Martin doesn't like workplace romances but he's letting Liam and Ally get on with it?'

Bonnie smiled.

'For now,' she told Ren before pulling away.

Ren's hand went to her stomach as the room did a little spin around her.

'You all right?' Bonnie asked as Ren paled.

Ren nodded.

'Just, erm, a bit overwhelmed, I think.'

'Come on.' Bonnie grabbed her coat. 'Let's go get some fresh air and get out of this place for a while. We'll go to the coffee shop on the corner. Anyone want anything?' she asked quietly so no one would hear. 'Good-o. Let's go.'

Ren grabbed her coat and, casting a fleeting look behind her towards Harrison's office, she followed Bonnie out.

'Harry! It's been too long. We need to drink beer together. How about tonight?'

The doors to the lift closed, leaving Harrison alone, travelling up to the fifth floor. In one hand was a coffee, in the other was his phone, pressed against his ear.

'Sorry, I can't,' Harrison told Mac. 'I dropped Jackson at the airport last night, managed to have a last drink with him before his flight, came home late, now I'm at work late and I'm going to ask Ren out to dinner tonight.'

There was a long pause. Harrison raised his eyebrows, wondering if Mac would respond before the lift doors opened.

He didn't.

The doors opened with a ping and Harrison strode onto the fifth floor.

'Then we'll have two reasons to celebrate!' claimed Mac.

Ren wasn't at her desk. Harrison glanced around

and caught sight of her in the kitchen with Bonnie. Both of them waved to him and he managed an awkward-hands-full wave back before heading to his office.

'Well, hold your horses,' he told Mac. 'I've been trying for months to ask this woman out and the Powers That Be keep interrupting. Wait, two things? What else are we celebrating? You and Bonnie?'

Mac laughed.

'Nah. You remember that job you helped me apply for before Christmas?'

Harrison stopped.

'Yeah?'

'Had the interview yesterday and they called first thing this morning to offer it to me.'

Harrison whooped, nearly spilling his coffee. Through the glass doors, Martin gave him a look and he quickly disappeared into his own office, closing the door behind him.

'That's fantastic, buddy! Congrats. You're taking it, right?'

'Absolutely. Massive pay rise and all.'

'Ah, fantastic. I'm sorry we can't celebrate tonight.'

'That's all right. I'll celebrate with Bonnie tonight. Although let me know if Ren says no, we can still go out.'

Harrison laughed but his stomach twisted at the thought.

'Funny,' he told Mac. 'I'll let you know how things go. And, hey, don't mention Ren to Bonnie, yeah?'

'Sure thing. Although I'm going to have to tell her at some point, you know.'

'You can tell her on your wedding day.'

This time it was Mac's laugh that had an edge to it.

'Good luck, mate.'

'Thanks. See you soon.'

Harrison hung up and looked down at his desk. His insides were a jumble of butterflies but he still had a meeting to prepare for. A meeting that started in – Harrison checked the time – ten minutes. Groaning, he pulled up his chair, switched on his laptop and thanked those same Powers That Be that he'd been able to go through the figures for today's meeting while head office had droned on and on the day before, keeping him from Ren.

Harrison was first in the meeting room. He was just settling himself when Bonnie, Ren and Val entered. He exchanged a quick, secret glance with Ren before tuning into Bonnie and Val's conversation. Something about Ally taking some time off.

'Everything okay?' Bonnie asked Harrison.

He nodded, stopping himself from asking about Mac's new job.

'You?'

Bonnie grinned and nothing more was said.

Liam, Martin and another man entered the meeting room and the door was closed behind them.

'Welcome, everyone. Good morning.' Martin bustled to his seat. 'You all remember Ari from head office. Oh, apart from Ren, of course. Ren, this is Ari. Ari, Ren. Ari is our head writer, he's based in London. Did all the storyboards and then packed his bags, huh, Ari? But he's back now to check on everything. Liaising with the music team, as well, aren't you? Oh, but that can wait until the meeting's gotten started, of course. Ari, this is Ren, our palaeontology consultant and she'll be taking over from Billy as project manager. And of course, that'll be discussed later in the meeting, too.'

Ari turned to Harrison and widened his dark eyes ever so slightly, enough that Harrison had to cover a smirk with his coffee cup.

'Hello, Ren,' the writer said. 'And thank you, Martin. Nice to know nothing much has changed around here.'

Martin gave him a confused look which he immediately shook away, and started the meeting.

The news of Ren taking over part of Billy's work was left until last. Once Val and Liam had given their updates, Ari had discussed at length what he would be doing in the month he was staying in Edinburgh and the major changes to the story he was making. Bonnie had shown the latest designs for something new Ari was introducing, and Harrison had bored them with the latest budget news and pre-order sales figures. Finally, Martin turned on Ren.

'As some of you know, Billy has been signed off sick for the month.' Martin sighed. 'It's incredibly frustrating, but I'm hoping to find a silver lining by getting our project management well and truly updated and sorted out before he returns. I've asked Ren, who has been doing a fantastic job with our dinosaurs, to take over Billy's work for the month he'll be off and to then effectively job share with him when he returns.'

'So, erm, Billy will go part time?' Bonnie asked.

Martin pursed his lips.

'We'll see. Ren is still on a contract, the end date is still the same. But she's been doing such a fantastic job and is so organised, maybe she'll choose to stay with us. Hmm?'

They all turned to Ren who gave Martin a quick smile and murmured, 'Maybe.'

Harrison fought against his own smile, his gaze lingering on her as everyone else turned back to Martin.

'It's a little bit of a new world, so we'll see how it goes. No overloading poor Ren, help her out where you can.' Martin spared a look at Harrison who nodded. 'And, Ren, I'm really happy about this. I think good things will come of it. Is there anything you'd like to add?'

Everyone turned on Ren again and she sank into her chair, shaking her head.

'Nope. All good,' she murmured.

Harrison caught her eye and resisted the urge to wink at her. Her cheeks flushed, which only added to the temptation.

'Excellent. In that case, does anyone have any other business?' Martin looked around. Bonnie and Val shook their heads, Liam kept his down, Harrison and Ari shook their heads, and then Martin turned back to Ren.

'All right. I do have one last thing. It's Ren's birthday today!'

Harrison snapped round to look at Ren who was staring at Martin with wide eyes. Martin produced a small cupcake with a candle in it from somewhere, took a box of matches from his pocket and tried to light one. After a few tense moments, Liam pulled out a lighter and lit the candle.

'Thank you, Liam,' said Martin stiffly. He grinned up at Ren. 'Happy birthday, Ren! Everyone!'

What followed was an intensely uncomfortable rendition of 'Happy Birthday' as Ren sank lower and lower, her cheeks growing redder, her eyes hardening. Harrison didn't sing. He watched her, feeling the concern and a part of her anxiety bubbling away inside him.

The cake was passed down to Ren who managed a stiff, wonky smile.

'Thank you, Martin,' she managed through gritted teeth. 'How did you know?'

'Oh, I found out from HR while I was sorting out your new job description,' said Martin, grinning, evidently proud of himself. 'Go on. Make a wish. Blow out the candle.'

'I don't actually celebrate my birthday,' said Ren.

A thick silence fell over the table.

If it affected Martin, he didn't show it.

'You don't have to blow out the candle,' Harrison murmured to Ren.

'But then your wish won't come true,' said Martin.

Everyone turned from Martin to Ren. She glared at the executive producer and then, in a short puff, blew out the candle.

Martin clapped his hands as all the angry words filled Harrison's head.

'Wonderful! Wonderful. Well, that's it. Until next time.' Martin gathered his things and was first out of the meeting room.

Liam and Val left quietly, wishing Ren a happy birthday. Ari gestured to Harrison that he'd see him later and Harrison nodded. Ren was staring down at the cupcake, taking deep, steadying breaths.

'Are you okay?' Bonnie asked.

Ren nodded.

'He shouldn't have done that. It can't be legal, getting your birthday from HR. Can it?' Bonnie looked to Harrison. 'Can I do anything?'

Ren shook her head.

'No, no. I'm fine. Honest. Want a cake?' She offered the cupcake to Bonnie who hesitated.

'You don't want it?'

'No.'

'Where was he keeping it? I didn't see him come in with it,' said Harrison.

'He had a bag with him when he came in,' Bonnie explained. 'You really don't want it?'

'No. Here.' Ren handed Bonnie the cupcake, candle and all.

Bonnie left the office, glancing back to Harrison as she went. He gave her a comforting smile. *I got this.* Bonnie gave Ren one last concerned look before leaving, the door closing behind her.

Harrison moved to sit next to Ren and waited to see if she would talk. When she didn't, he put a hand close to her on the table.

'What can I do?' he asked.

Ren smiled and sniffed, wiping under one eye although Harrison couldn't see any tears.

'I'm okay,' she told him. 'Just took me by surprise, that's all. But hey, at least I got given a cake instead of having to bring them in, right? What the hell was that about?' she hissed at Harrison.

He watched the emotions flow through her.

'If I had to guess?' he ventured. 'I'd say that cake was a bit of bribery. Take no notice. Martin's self-centred. He's concerned about him and his job, and that's it.'

'In front of everyone,' Ren growled.

'Yeah.'

They were both quiet for a moment. Harrison's fingers tapped quietly on the table between them, and Ren seemed to watch unless she was actually staring through the table. Harrison couldn't tell.

'So, you don't celebrate your birthday?' he asked, wondering how she would react. He prepared himself for her anger but she only shook her head. With a sigh, she seemed to relax, trailing a hand onto the desk, leaving it close to his.

'No. I've had some bad experiences so I just... stopped.' Harrison stayed quiet as Ren thought. 'I used to try and really enjoy my birthdays,' she continued. 'I tried throwing myself parties, but something always ruined it. I tried having quiet nights in or out with close friends, but they'd cancel last minute. Once, at university, my so-called best friend went home for the weekend and completely missed my birthday. I'd organised a night in, bought a big cake, everything. I had to eat it on my own.' Her voice drifted off and Harrison's chest tightened.

'I'm sorry,' he murmured. 'But hey, Edinburgh isn't like that.'

Ren gave a sad smile, glancing up at him.

'I know,' she whispered. 'Bonnie wouldn't do that. Unless Mac offered her something better, huh?'

Harrison shook his head.

'No, I know Bonnie and I know Mac. Trust me, if Bonnie had known it's your birthday today, they'd have both organised a surprise party for you tonight.'

Ren pulled a face.

'She didn't know though, right?'

Harrison smiled.

'If she did then she didn't invite me.'

Ren looked back to the table and their hands, almost touching. Harrison followed her gaze.

'So, you're not doing anything tonight? You're not celebrating?' he asked tentatively.

Ren shook her head.

'Nope. Birthdays are for a night in alone, watching a film, eating cake.'

Harrison studied her as she continued to stare down at the table.

'Do you want to go out for dinner?' he asked, and the world around him stopped.

Slowly, Ren looked up at him.

'For my birthday or as a date?'

'A date,' said Harrison, not daring to breathe.

'Just the two of us?' Ren asked.

'I hope so.'

Softly, slowly, a smile bloomed on Ren's face. It turned into a grin and hit her eyes which had grown watery. The sight of that grin released Harrison to breathe again.

'Dinner sounds good. No birthday surprises,

though.'

Harrison shook his head.

'Just you and me,' he told her. 'Italian?'

Ren pulled a face.

'Steakhouse,' she said, and if Harrison hadn't fallen in love with her before, he certainly did in that moment. He grinned at her and, without thinking, reached forward, placing his hand over hers. She entwined her fingers with his and he squeezed gently.

'I know just the place,' he told her. 'Shall I pick you up?'

Ren searched his eyes.

'Isn't it in the city?'

'Yeah.'

'I live in Stockbridge. I can walk.'

Harrison gave a nod.

'Fair enough. I live in West End. I can pick you up on my way.'

Ren gave a soft laugh.

'Okay. That would be nice.'

Reluctantly, Harrison untangled their fingers.

'We should probably go do some work. I'll book us a table, let you know where we're going. Is seven okay?'

Ren nodded, brushing absent tears from her cheeks.

'Anytime,' she murmured, flashing another smile at him.

They left the office together, Ren disappearing

into the toilets to freshen herself while Harrison headed to his office. Martin's office was empty and Val was evidently back on the fourth floor. Harrison gave himself a moment to celebrate, dancing over to his desk and silently cheering himself on. Pulling his phone from his pocket to inform Mac of the good news, he discovered a message from Jackson.

'I'm home. I'm definitely coming to Scotland again. And I've emailed you the business plan. Now go ask that girl out.'

Grinning so wide it hurt, Harrison fell into his chair and replied to his son.

'Good. Can't wait for you to come back. Will take a look at the business plan now. And already done. We're going out tonight.'

Harrison sat back and stared at the castle through the window, his mind already planning that evening, the nerves bubbling away. He wouldn't be getting much work done today.

Ren stared at her reflection in the full-length mirror. The good thing about going on a date with someone you had known for around three months was that you didn't need to make a good first impression, you'd already done that bit. The bad thing was that Harrison had pretty much been exposed to every decent item of clothing Ren owned.

She'd opted for her favourite dress, which she'd last worn in the office a week before, but this evening she wore it as if it was summer. There was no jumper over the top, no leggings underneath. Yes, she was going to be cold but she'd decided it would be worth it. The dress was full of colour, to remind him of who she was, but cinched in at the waist because if they weren't in the office then she could show off her figure. During a panic about how the evening might end, she'd lost an argument with herself and pulled on a pair of tights. Even though the dress was long, the Edinburgh wind would seek out any bare flesh. She wore flats as they'd be walking through the city, and she would put a scarf and coat over the top of it all. Her long red hair flowed down her back, freshly washed and dried, and her make-up...well, it looked as it did every day and he seemed to like that.

He hadn't messaged her about the reservation he'd made, instead he'd caught the lift with her, sliding between the doors just before they closed as she headed down to the third floor to talk to someone about Billy's work. Alone in the lift, he'd given her the name of the restaurant and they'd discussed what time he'd pick her up. She'd given him her address, and there had been a wonderful moment when they'd smiled at one another and Ren had wished that he'd kiss her. Then the doors had opened and she'd been forced to go back to work.

Ren jumped at the knock on her front door. Smoothing down her dress and taking a slow, trembling breath, she left her bedroom and answered the knock. Harrison smiled at her, his gaze travelling over her dress until he met her eyes again.

'Good evening,' he said. 'You look amazing.'

Ren almost laughed but kept it in. She managed to not curtsey at the compliment, but the holding back meant that she missed a beat and Harrison tilted his head a little.

'You okay?' he asked.

'Yes. Yup.' She grinned at him. 'Good evening. You look amazing, too.'

Harrison was wearing his usual half-suit. That is, the trousers that belonged to an expensive suit – the rest of which was presumably hiding in his wardrobe – and a slightly less expensive shirt, buttoned up. It was a different shirt to the one he'd worn to work and his coat was different too, but left open.

'Won't you be cold?' Ren asked, grabbing her bag and keys, locking the door to the flat behind her.

'Nah. I'm from New York, where the rain and snow hit us with everything they have. I'm more worried about you being cold.'

'Nah. I'm from near London, mate. Bit of taters don't bother me.'

Harrison stared at Ren and she laughed. 'That's a no to the cockney accent?' she asked, returning to her normal voice.

'Actually, I'm a little turned on.'

Ren laughed harder and Harrison grinned, holding out a hand. She took it and they walked down the street towards the steakhouse Harrison had found.

'Taters?' Harrison asked eventually.

Ren had been enjoying the warmth from his large hand encompassing hers, the ease with which he had offered it, the jolt of pleasure that had coursed through her as their skin had touched.

'I don't know,' she admitted. 'It means cold, I

think. My dad's London born, he always says it's taters when it's cold. I might have used it wrong.'

Harrison laughed that belly laugh, squeezing Ren's fingers, and she grinned, helplessly, moving to walk closer by his side.

'Thank you for picking me up,' she said, glancing at the city around them. 'It must be a bit of a walk from West End? West End,' she added, shaking her head. 'Of course you live in West End.'

'It's no problem, and what does that mean?' asked Harrison, holding her back as a car whooshed past them before they crossed the road.

'I don't know. You always wear suits and you like expensive beer and you have a sexy accent and you live in West End.'

Harrison gave her a sideways glance and smirk.

'I have a sexy accent, huh?'

Ren snapped her mouth shut and looked up at him. He was smiling down at her, his blue eyes dark but soft as he studied her in the evening city light.

'Yeah,' she relented, exhaling. 'You do.'

Harrison chuckled, looking back up to where they were heading.

'And I like good beer, not necessarily expensive beer. Craft beer, preferably. I wear suits because I'm a finance director and that's what directors should wear, and I live in West End because...'

Ren looked up at him.

'Because?'

Harrison fought a smile and glanced down at her

again.

'Because I can afford to.' He shrugged and Ren laughed.

'See! You can take the stockbroker out of New York...'

Harrison watched her, that smile still pulling at his lips.

'Go on, finish that.'

'I'm not sure how,' Ren mused. 'But you can't take the New York out of... No, that's not right.'

Harrison didn't laugh, as such. He made a noise of amusement and slowed his pace, making Ren slow with him. He squeezed her fingers again so that her breath caught.

'Does it bother you?' he asked.

'What? No, why would it?'

Harrison shook his head.

'No reason. I just wondered. Would you still have agreed to this evening if I lived somewhere else?'

'Harrison, I agreed to this before you told me you lived in West End.'

'True. And would you have agreed if I didn't wear a suit every day?'

Ren looked Harrison up and down, smiling, biting her lower lip.

'Of course. Actually, I'm fascinated to see what other clothes you have. I mean, I know I've seen you out of work, but still. '

Harrison laughed, letting go of her hand and wrapping an arm around her waist in a strange, possessive sideways hug. He enveloped her and she took a moment to relish the warmth and safety the position offered. Then, he stepped away and took her hand again.

'Sorry,' he murmured.

'Don't be.'

Their eyes met and they both quickly looked away, grinning.

The warmth and noise of the steakhouse embraced Ren. She slipped her coat off, sitting opposite Harrison at their little table for two.

'This is nice.'

'Yeah, one of my first discoveries when I moved here. I try and keep it for special occasions.'

Ren picked up the menu and glanced down at the options. They ordered drinks and, when they arrived, Harrison let Ren take a sip of the beer he'd ordered.

'Nice,' she said.

'Can you taste the difference?' he asked.

Ren considered lying, if only for a moment.

'No. Sorry, beer tastes like beer.'

Harrison grinned.

'That's okay. A dinosaur is a dinosaur.'

Ren went to argue but laughed instead.

After some deliberation, they ordered their food; sirloin steak and chips for Harrison, burger and chips for Ren. Settling into a comfortable silence,

Harrison sipped his beer while Ren studied the rest of the restaurant.

'So, forgive me, but you haven't done anything for your birthday today? At all?' Harrison finally asked.

Ren quietly looked back to him. For a moment she was dazed by how handsome he was, the light shining from his silver hair, his cool blue eyes bright as he watched her, his beard neatly trimmed around lips that she had to tear her gaze from.

'Not really,' she told him. 'I spoke to my parents, of course. And I had to tell my mum not to call me later, as I'll be out. Which led to more questions.'

Harrison raised an eyebrow.

'You told them about me?'

Ren nodded, filling her mouth with drink.

'What have you told them?' he asked when she didn't say anything.

Ren struggled.

'Oh, you know. That you're clever and kind, from New York, have a son, and that you were a stockbroker with two divorces,' she added quickly, raising her glass to her lips again.

Harrison's eyes widened.

'Why did you tell them that?' he blurted.

Ren gave him a pained look.

'Because...' She sighed. 'Okay.' Leaning forward on the table, Ren looked straight into Harrison's eyes. 'I like you,' she told him. 'I think I've established that. But you've been divorced twice and, it just…' She drifted off, trying to find the right words. 'What happened?'

Harrison searched her eyes for a moment and then took a gulp of beer.

'All right,' he said. Ren sat back in her chair to await the story. 'I met my first wife when we were sixteen. I fell in love hard, but thankfully she's always been sensible. I thought she was it, for the rest of my life. We were engaged at eighteen, married at twenty purely because she decided she wouldn't marry me until she was twenty. By the time Jackson was born, I was at the beginning of my career in finance. I'd found something I loved and that I was good at and…' Harrison pulled a face at himself. 'And it's the type of career that demands all the hours. I'm ashamed to say I wasn't around much when Jackson was little. His mom practically raised him alone to begin with. We would argue, she was angry, understandably. And I tried to do better. I'd work eighty-hour weeks and get up early at weekends to spend the whole forty-eight hours with my son, before doing it all again. Nearly killed myself. And it wasn't enough. I guess we were too young. You do a lot of growing up in your twenties, especially when there's a baby involved.'

Ren nodded, although she couldn't relate at all. Harrison's eyes softened at the mention of Jackson and her heart somersaulted.

'We grew apart,' Harrison told her. 'We grew up and we grew apart. We tried to stick together. There was still love there, and Jackson is our world. We tried counselling, took advice from anyone and everyone, but in the end she wanted out. So we got divorced. We're still friends. She's actually one of my closest friends, but there's nothing between us anymore. I still always made time for Jackson. She remarried a few years later and they're still together.'

Ren offered Harrison a smile.

'Makes sense,' she said gently. 'You were kids when you got together.'

Harrison nodded and then sighed heavily.

'And the second marriage. Well, that was a mistake. I met this woman who was gorgeous and fun, and I fell in love. Or I thought I did. Everything felt right in the beginning. We got married after about six months. Yeah, I know, too fast. We hadn't even known each other a year when the credit card bills started going through the roof. She had a good job but one day she just quit. I thought she wanted to start a family, turned out she wanted to go to Monaco.'

'What?' Ren frowned. 'She quit her job for a holiday?'

'She quit her job to live it up,' Harrison said. 'I kept trying to talk to her about it, but she... Well, talking was difficult.'

'Why?'

Harrison shifted in his seat.

'She, erm, she used sex a lot,' he admitted,

avoiding Ren's eye. 'And she'd take advantage of my long hours. She'd disappear on shopping trips and when the credit card bill came in, she'd…'

'Take her clothes off?' Ren offered.

Harrison nodded.

'And I was an idiot, in my late thirties, and I'd been waiting to fall madly in love since my first marriage fell apart. I mean, I kept falling in love but it would usually fizzle out after a week, a month, a couple of months, but that time…' Finally, he lifted his gaze to her. 'I just wanted that rush again, you know? That feeling of knowing you're with someone who you love and who loves you. Who will be there for you, who you can keep safe. Who you can have fun with.'

Ren nodded.

'I get it,' she murmured, casting her mind back to previous relationships. 'And you're so desperate to hold on to that feeling, and so scared you won't get it ever again, that you hold on to that person. Even though they're completely wrong for you.'

Harrison's gaze was intense as a silent understanding passed between them.

'Did you finally confront her about it?' Ren asked quietly, painfully wanting the conversation to be over but needing the answers.

Harrison nodded.

'Yeah. I did. Massive argument. Screaming at each other. She told me what was the point if she couldn't have some fun? I asked her if she'd want me if I didn't have money. She said no. Basically, it came out she was with me for my bank account and my family connections. That was that. I packed my things and left. We got divorced. However many months later, I applied for a job here in Edinburgh and three years ago I moved here. Took a huge pay cut, pivoted my career and left my son behind, but I got away from it all. From her and our friends and. ..' Harrison shook his head and drank deep from his beer.

Ren stared down at the table, processing his words.

'I'm sorry,' she said, keeping her eyes down. 'That's awful.'

'Yeah, well, I promised myself I wouldn't repeat any of it,' Harrison continued. 'Told Mac the whole story soon after we met and he offered to help me out if I helped him with his career.'

Ren lifted her gaze to Harrison.

'How does he help you out?'

A soft smile touched Harrison's lips.

'Well, he stopped me from asking you out the moment I met you.'

Ren smiled.

'The moment you met me, huh?'

'God, yeah. You're beautiful and you're clever and you're sweet. And I've done well, right? Managed to wait, what? Three months? Just in case I was wrong again and the feelings went away.'

'But they didn't?' Ren asked softly, her heart

pounding.

'No, they didn't. If anything, they've gotten stronger.' Harrison evidently stopped himself, glancing around the restaurant.

'I'm not like her,' said Ren quietly, before she'd even considered the words.

Harrison snapped back to her.

'No, I know.'

'I would never hurt you like that. Or string you along. Or spend your money.'

'No, I know,' Harrison repeated, slower this time, reaching across the table to her. She took his hand and squeezed it.

'Was it a messy divorce?' she asked after a moment of watching their fingers entwining.

'One way of putting it.'

'Is she still in your life?' Ren looked up into his eyes and his softened.

'Hell no.'

Ren grinned.

'Good.'

A shadow fell over the table and they were forced to let go of one another as their food arrived.

Harrison didn't want dessert. He wanted Ren. To take her home, or be invited into her home. To sit on the sofa, to kiss her mouth, to slip the straps of that dress down over her shoulders and run his lips over her skin. But it wasn't his birthday.

'I'll have the chocolate fudge sundae, please,' Ren ordered before looking to Harrison.

'Just a coffee for me, thanks,' he told the waiter, who wrote it down, took their menus and disappeared.

'Should I have asked for a second spoon?' Ren gave Harrison a smile that made his heart skip. He chuckled.

'Nah, it's your birthday. It's all yours.' He leaned forward on the table. 'Did you make a wish? When Martin was being an ass? Did you wish for Martin to stop being an ass?'

Ren laughed, leaning forward on her arms to be closer to him.

'I didn't make a wish. I didn't want to give him

the satisfaction. But if it had been happier circumstances, I think I would have wished for this.'

They smiled at one another, reaching out again and entwining their fingers.

'I should have asked you earlier,' Harrison murmured.

Ren shrugged.

'When? We barely saw each other in the run up to Christmas.'

'Yeah, and that was my fault.'

Ren gave Harrison a sweet smile.

'You were doing your job. And you're damn good at your job. If you weren't, maybe we wouldn't be sitting here now.'

A rush of warmth flooded through Harrison. He glanced down at the table, eager to find something that would calm his insides.

'So, the big question,' he started.

Ren's eyes widened.

'Why dinosaurs?' Harrison asked with a grin.

Ren smiled, looking down at their fingers stroking against one another on the table. She removed her hand so she could pick up her drink. Harrison left his hand on the table, waiting for her to return.

'Because, dinosaurs,' she offered, grinning over her glass. When Harrison simply raised a questioning eyebrow, Ren put the glass down and looked around, giving it some thought. 'My mum used to take me to the Natural History Museum when I was little,' she started. 'We used to go visit Dippy in the main entrance and then I'd drag her through to the dinosaurs. Every time. And when I hit my teens and she would ask what I'd like to do during the school holidays, I'd drag her back there and stare at the dinosaurs. People used to buy me books about them and I would just soak it all up. My friends were all off talking about ponies and then chasing boys, and I had my nose in a book about dinosaurs. When our teachers started talking about university, I knew I wanted to study palaeontology but there weren't many universities locally offering it and those that were—' Ren whistled through her teeth. 'I'm not actually that clever. Not by their standards. There was no way I would get the grades to get in.'

Harrison sipped his beer, his brow creased.

'So what did you do?'

'Well, first I panicked. I went around asking all the teachers but they didn't know what to do. A few of them told me to choose something else. My biology teacher told me to study biology or life sciences. They were doing their best but it was all pretty useless. And the internet wasn't what it is now, so I panicked again. And then my mum called up one of the universities that offered palaeon-tology and asked for advice. Because *she's* the clever one.'

Harrison smiled.

'Where you get it from,' he suggested. Ren made a *pfft* noise. 'So what happened?'

They paused as Harrison's coffee was placed in front of him and a large sundae glass filled with vanilla and chocolate ice cream and large pieces of chocolate brownie, covered with chocolate sauce and whipped cream was placed in front of Ren. Her eyes widened as the waiter put it down.

'Wow,' she murmured. 'Thank you.'

'Might need two spoons after all,' said Harrison, watching her eyes.

She gave him a look before picking up her spoon and offering him some of the cream. He declined.

'The university suggested that I get some experience, learn as much as I could and apply as a mature student.' Ren spooned a heap of cream, chocolate sauce and ice cream into her mouth, and Harrison had to wait until she swallowed before she could continue. Her features broke out in pleasure and Harrison watched, a smile tugging at his lips. He stirred his coffee with his teaspoon and glanced at the sundae.

'Try it,' Ren offered again, pushing the sundae glass closer. This time Harrison took full advantage and heaped whipped cream and ice cream onto his tiny spoon. It wasn't quite enough, so he went in for more as Ren continued her story. She didn't argue or pull back, so he sneaked out a chunk of brownie while she was distracted.

'So, that's what I did,' she said, loading her spoon

up again. 'I took a year out and worked part time in an office as a temp and volunteered the rest of my time at the Natural History Museum. It was bliss, for about half the week. I tried my best to get to know people and did everything I could to be involved. Someone there suggested I do a degree in archaeology instead. It would teach me dig techniques and about the technology used, but I didn't want to waste my student loan. But that did give me the idea to go on some digs. No dinosaur digs, but I volunteered at some Roman and Anglo-Saxon dig sites. Even uncovered a piece of bone at one. It turned out to be dog bone.'

'So, after the year you applied to university?'

Ren shook her head.

'Nope. They said I should apply as a mature student. I ended up spending three years doing all the volunteering I could, taking short courses, talking to people, throwing everything I had at it. All while working horrible temp jobs to pay for it all.'

Harrison pulled a face.

'It was worth it, though?'

Ren shrugged.

'I was terrified I wouldn't get in. I honestly didn't know what I would do. I'd sort of resigned myself to working in the Natural History Museum gift shops or café or something. If I did that full time, it would pay the same as my part-time office job. And by that point, I'd been in my last so-called temp job for a year. They'd already sort of promoted me and wanted to make me permanent.'

Harrison stole another bite of ice cream.

'What was that job?'

Ren grimaced.

'Erm, assistant project manager.'

Harrison burst out laughing and the couple at the next table jumped, giving them looks. He ignored them.

'Suddenly it all makes sense,' he told her. 'Didn't the museum have any project management jobs going?'

Ren shook her head.

'I thought of that. But that wasn't the dream, was it? And no, no vacancies like that came up while I was job hunting. Anyway, I got into university by the skin of my teeth. I gave up the temp job so I could keep volunteering while I was studying. Suddenly everything was going to plan.' Ren sighed, staring at her melting sundae. 'I graduated and managed to get a proper job at the museum. I ended up going back and forth a bit. I got a secondment elsewhere, and then placed on a really exciting project that took me across the country at one point. I spent a year in Canada working at the Alberta University on a project. I loved that. Then, I met my ex. He was a geologist on a fixed-term contract which kept getting renewed, and then he got promoted. Blah, blah, blah. We didn't actually get together until a few years after we'd met. Which was stupid of me.'

'Oh? Why's that?'

'All the signs were there. I should have known not to take things further with him.' Ren dug her spoon into the ice cream. 'But he was clever and attractive and I mistook his talking over me all the time for confidence.' Ren rolled her eyes at herself. 'I used to be a bit of a pushover.'

An image of Ren putting her hand up to ask a question during their first senior meeting landed vividly in Harrison's memory.

'He took advantage of that,' he murmured.

'Yeah. He definitely did.'

Harrison shook his head, popping another spoonful of chocolate ice cream into his mouth. Ren offered him a chunk of brownie and, after checking she was sure, he took it and let it melt on his tongue.

'Anyway, idiot me got into a relationship with him and then after a year of everything going okay, he decided he quite liked dinosaurs too. He did a few courses, applied for a short-term job in the palaeontology department and got it. His dad used to work quite high up in the museum, that's all I can put it down to. Anyway, then a permanent job came up and we both went for it. It was my dream job, a permanent palaeontologist position at the museum. No more wondering what I'd do when my contract ended, I could have focused on working my way up. We had a big fight about it and why he was applying. And then he got the job, my contract ended, they didn't renew it and here I am.'

'I know it sucks,' Harrison murmured. 'But I'm kinda glad it worked out that way.'

Ren glanced up at him and he winked. She grinned and licked her lips, finishing off the sundae and sitting back, patting her full stomach.

She exhaled in a puff.

'Next time we come here, I'm wearing an elasticated waistband.'

Harrison's heart jumped.

'We,' he murmured, and Ren gave him a look.

'You'd want to come back with me, right?'

Harrison almost threw the paper napkin that had come with the sundae at her.

'Of course I do!'

He asked the waiter for the bill and then he reached across the table. She took his hand and he stroked her fingers with his thumb.

'You worked so hard to get to where you are,' he said. 'It's not fair.'

Ren sighed.

'Life isn't fair. Sometimes I feel like I'm just not meant to be a palaeontologist. I'm beginning to feel like I'm supposed to be a project manager,' she groaned.

'I dunno,' said Harrison. 'Your name is going to be on this game, right under the title Palaeontology Consultant. That has to be good for something.'

Ren grinned.

'Yeah. Maybe it'll boost my street cred.'

They met one another's eyes and laughed.

When the bill arrived, Harrison pulled out his wallet and made a noise as Ren found her bank card.

'Absolutely not, put that away. It's your birthday, apart from anything else. This is my treat. Plus, I've been waiting three months for this. If you don't let me pay, I'll be mortally offended'

'Mortally offended?' Ren smiled. 'Can't have that.' She put her money away. 'Thank you. I'll get the next one, though.'

Harrison grinned to himself as he paid the bill.

The temperature had dropped since they'd entered the restaurant and a fresh Edinburgh breeze lifted up the hem of Ren's dress as they stepped out onto the street. Ren pulled her coat and scarf tighter around her. Unable to offer anything else, Harrison wrapped an arm around her waist and pulled her in close. Something inside him shifted as Ren stepped further into him.

They walked like that for a while in silence, heading towards Stockbridge and Ren's flat. The city at night bustled around them as tourists moved from restaurants to bars or back to their hotels, and groups of friends laughed from one pub to the next. Harrison kept an eye on all of it, steering Ren around the people.

'Do you think you'll ever want to move back to

New York?' she asked when they found the street quiet, leaving the bars and restaurants behind them.

'No,' said Harrison, feeling the word in his gut. 'I thought I might, after a year. And then after two years. But I like Scotland. It feels like home now.' He glanced down at her. 'Do you think you'll go back to London?'

Ren pulled a face.

'My contract ends in October,' she said slowly. 'And I have no idea what I'll do after that. I always thought if something came up at the Natural History Museum, I'd go for it.' She glanced up at him sideways. 'I've always wanted to go to the American Museum of Natural History in New York. Maybe I could get a job there.'

Harrison's step faltered, taking Ren with him, his mind whirring. Ren put an arm around him, steadying him. The smell of her hair and whatever fragrance she was wearing filled his nostrils.

'Maybe,' he murmured. 'Or maybe I'll just take you there one day.'

Ren smiled.

'I'd like that.'

They reached her flat and Ren pulled out of his embrace to turn and face him. Mouth dry, he slowly met her eyes.

'Thank you for tonight. And I really mean that,' she told him. 'This has been the best birthday I've had in years. Since I was a kid and my parents were in charge of it all.'

Harrison laughed softly.

'I'm glad I could make it a good one.' He held her hand in his, looking down at her fingers as his thumb glided over her soft skin. His heart pounded so loud he was sure she could hear it. 'We're doing this again, right?' He looked back up into her eyes to find her smiling at him.

'I hope so,' she said.

His stomach somersaulted, the tips of his fingers tingling as Ren stepped closer to him. She lifted her chin and he leaned down. Hesitating for a moment, wondering if he was reading the signs right, he tried not to smile as Ren went up on tiptoe and pressed her lips against his in a sudden burst of warmth and pleasure.

Ren lowered and the kiss broke. Faces still close, they searched each other's eyes. Harrison leaned down and kissed her again, and this time Ren reached up and wrapped her arms around his neck, holding him in place. He snaked his arms around her waist, fingers trailing down her back over her thick coat. She ran her fingers through his hair, setting his scalp alight, chilled goosebumps running down his body. His hands stayed on the small of her back, thumbs rubbing through her coat. Ren emitted a soft moan through the kiss and, just as Harrison was considering lifting her and carrying her down the steps to her front door, she pulled away.

'I would invite you in,' Ren murmured breathlessly. 'But it's a first date.' The words came out unsure and for the umpteenth time that evening, Ren considered asking Harrison into her home.

'That's okay,' said Harrison. 'I understand that.'

Ren looked up into his eyes. Those cool blue eyes that softened when he looked at her. His hands lingered on her waist and there was a hungry look about him that sent a shockwave of pleasure through her. Slowly, carefully, Ren took his hand in both of hers.

'But...we have known each other a few months now,' she mused.

'We have,' Harrison said, his voice low.

'We know each other.'

'We do.'

'We can trust each other.'

A smile pulled at the corner of Harrison's mouth.

'We can. Absolutely.'

Ren grinned and pulled Harrison down the first

step towards her front door.

'Come in?'

Harrison's eyes lit up and he followed her down the steps and into her flat.

Ren took a steadying breath as she pulled off her coat and scarf, taking Harrison's coat and showing him to the sofa in the living room. He was looking around, murmuring in appreciation.

'I like what you've done.'

'Ha. I haven't done much. A few bits of furniture, some pictures.' Ren shrugged.

'Are you kidding? It's a rainbow in here!' Harrison declared, pointing at the bright pink and blue throw over the sofa, the vibrant blue and green rug on the floor and the floral green and purple curtains at the window.

Ren offered him a drink.

'No, thanks.' Harrison sat down and patted the sofa next to him. Ren fell into the space beside him and kissed him before she could consider being nervous about what was going to happen next. He put a hand through her hair, holding her close. Then he placed kisses on her cheek and down her neck. Her body tingled and pulsed as he gently hooked his thumbs under the straps of her dress and let them fall over her shoulders, moaning a little as he did so.

'Been wanting to do that all night,' he murmured, kissing her collarbone, his hands wrapping around her waist as she pushed her fingers through his silver hair.

Gently, slowly, giving her time to push him away, Harrison eased her back on the sofa.

'Is this okay?' he asked, his hand on her thigh, teasingly reaching under the skirt of her dress.

'More than okay,' she breathed, wishing she could tear his shirt off. He reached up and slid her dress down, kissing the tops of her breasts as they became exposed. As much as Ren wanted to stay there, to feel his lips on her, it was all she could do to stop herself from wrapping her legs around him and pulling him into her.

'Bedroom,' she murmured. 'We should go to the bedroom.'

Harrison's gaze stayed on her partially revealed breasts as he nodded.

'Okay.'

Smiling, heart pounding, Ren led Harrison through her small flat to the bedroom and left him there.

'Be right back.'

She ducked into the bathroom and before she ventured back out, she pulled off her tights, proud that she'd managed to wear them for warmth and had the foresight to take them off when she'd needed to without any awkwardness. Standing in the bedroom waiting for her, Harrison had undone his shirt. Ren bit her lip at the sight of his naked chest with its light flurry of silver and dark hairs.

She hesitated and Harrison watched her, all the

fears and worries suddenly crowding her mind. What if she wasn't any good? What if she did something wrong?

Harrison had wanted this since the day they'd met; what if she was a disappointment?

She swallowed hard and Harrison gave her a soft smile. Holding out a hand to her, he gently asked, 'Everything okay?'

Ren nodded, taking his hand and letting him pull her close. Without speaking, she pushed his shirt away and he pulled it off over broad shoulders and thick arms. Ren's breath caught and she trailed her fingers down from his shoulders to his fingers, where he took her hands and raised them to his lips.

'We can slow down if you want,' he told her.

Ren shook her head.

'No, I'm good. Unless you want to?' She looked up into his hungry eyes and her body screamed for her to press herself against him.

'I'm more than good,' he told her, moving her hair so he could kiss her neck, his cheek brushing against hers, his short beard tickling her.

She turned so he could unzip her dress and as she turned back, she let it fall to the floor. Harrison's gaze travelled down her body as he took off his trousers. They discarded what clothes remained and sat on the foot of her bed, kissing each other hard. Ren wasn't sure what to do with her hands. She knew what she *wanted* to do but still, she held back. Until Harrison's head dipped down to her chest and Ren unwittingly let out a moan.

Smiling, Harrison lifted her up and placed her lying down on the bed before climbing on top of her.

'Hang on!'

Harrison backed off, hands up.

'What? What's wrong?'

Ren sat up and rifled through the drawer in her bedside table. She brandished a condom packet. Relieved, Harrison chuckled, taking it from her. Ren positioned herself and then Harrison was over her again. She ran her fingers over the muscles in his arms that were holding him up as he leaned down and softly kissed her lips.

'You want to do this?' he murmured.

Ren nodded.

'Yes. Please.'

Harrison grinned and kissed her again, harder this time. Ren wrapped herself around him, welcoming him, breathing him in and losing herself.

She wasn't sure yet which part of Harrison's body was her favourite. It might have been the way his neck smelled as she kissed it, or the feel of his broad chest beneath her cheek. She would certainly be spending the rest of that day thinking about his hands and the way he touched her. At that moment, his fingers were idly stroking up and down her arm, taking a detour to her side and hip every now and then.

It was bliss.

Lying naked in bed with Harrison was bliss.

'We could call in sick,' she offered.

Beneath her cheek, Harrison shifted and he sighed into her hair.

'A bit suspicious if we both do it.'

Ren sighed and ran an index finger slowly from his collarbone to his hip, watching as his body reacted to her touch.

'Maybe we've both got the same bug?' she murmured, kissing his chest without moving her head.

'A bug that means we're bedridden all day?'

Ren smiled.

'Yeah.'

'That no one else has?' Harrison kissed the top of her head. 'We could tell Bonnie. She'd cover for us. She could pull a sickie in a few days, make it believable.'

Ren pulled a face.

'No. No, let's not tell Bonnie.'

There was a pause.

'Why not?'

Ren lifted her head and considered the man lying in her bed. Her leg was hooked over his, as if it was conspiring to keep him there.

'She'll make it into a big thing. Maybe it would be nice to just…be us. For a little while, you know? I'll tell her. Don't you worry. But not just yet.' She kissed his chest again. 'I want this to be just us for a little while. Is that okay?'

'Sure.' Harrison swept some hair from her face. 'That means I can't tell Mac, either. Although he does know we went out last night. I've asked him not to tell Bonnie, but we can't expect him to keep it from her for long.'

Ren smiled.

'So you don't really want Bonnie knowing either?'

Harrison grinned and propped himself up on an elbow, forcing Ren to move over a little.

'I was scared she'd go shooting her mouth off to you before I had a chance to ask you out myself. Or that she'd…yeah, make a big thing out of it.' He reached over to his phone on the bedside table and checked the time. 'I gotta go soon, need to pop home and shower, get a change of clothes before work.'

Ren groaned as Harrison laid back down, pulling her back into position.

'You can shower here,' she told him. 'And wear what you wore last night. No one will know.'

Harrison pulled a face.

'I could…' He trailed off as Ren kissed his neck, breathing him in, and ran a hand down his body so she could play with him.

'How long do we have?' she asked between kisses.

'Half hour,' he said, leaning his head back and closing his eyes.

'That's enough time.' Ren sat up and straddled him.

Harrison was half an hour late for work, but at least he'd washed the smell of sex off, changed his clothes and was on his second cup of coffee. He'd need all the caffeinated help he could get if he was going to get through the day on such little sleep. Especially if he wanted to do it all again that night, which he did.

He could still feel Ren, could still smell her despite his quick shower. He'd committed her breasts to memory, the shape and feel and taste of them, along with the way her body curved under his touch. Not that he wanted to ever have to rely on memories. If allowed to do so, he had every intention on revisiting his favourite parts of Ren as often as he could.

He strode through the office as if nothing had happened last night. Ren and Bonnie were chatting at Bonnie's desk, and Ren grinned at him as Bonnie greeted him.

'You're late,' she declared. 'Everything okay?'

'Yup,' he said, but he was smiling too much. He could feel it. Despite all attempts to wipe the smile from his face, it wouldn't leave, especially when Ren was there in front of him. His body reacted to just the sight of her and Harrison moved to hurry past.

Bonnie gasped.

'Did you have sex last night?'

Harrison's smile dropped.

'Excuse me? I did not. If you must know, my son sent through a business plan and it's faultless. Chip off the old block, that kid.' He strode past before Bonnie could respond, only slowing once he reached his office.

The grin slowly found its way back onto his face as he checked that Val wasn't around. Her desk was as empty as ever. He closed the door behind him and started humming to himself as he turned his laptop on.

Once settled, he picked up his work phone and dialled Ren's extension number.

'Hello,' came Ren's voice.

'My office. Now. Bring something so it looks like I'm asking for reports or whatever.'

'Okay. Let me find it and I'll be right there,' she said, keeping her tone even, and they hung up.

Ren let herself into the office and Harrison was on his feet just as the door clicked shut. Glancing through the glass wall behind her, he slipped an arm around her waist and kissed her lips. She kissed him back, leaving a hand on his chest as she, too, glanced behind them.

'Dangerous,' she murmured.

'Worth it,' he told her. 'Bonnie catches on quick, doesn't she.'

'Yeah. We're gonna have to tell her sooner rather than later,' said Ren, moving to sit on the small sofa against the wall. She glanced out at the view. As he returned to his chair, Harrison realised that he'd completely forgotten to look out at the castle, a habit that took place every morning since he'd been given this office. His eyes were locked on Ren.

'Did you call me here just because you can?' she asked, turning to give him an amused look.

For the first time in the office, Harrison didn't jump away when she caught him staring.

'Partly,' he confessed. 'Partly because I think we should talk. I had fun last night and I want to do it again, if you want to?'

Ren grinned.

'Of course I do.'

A heavy weight Harrison hadn't known was there lifted. Everything was going to be okay.

'Good,' he murmured. 'But we work together so it's not like we're just seeing each other in the evenings and at weekends.'

Ren turned her body to face him.

'Right. I see what you mean. We need ground rules?'

'Probably for the best,' said Harrison.

'Like...' Ren looked around the office for inspiration. 'You can call me into your office for a quick kiss whenever you want?'

Harrison laughed and Ren softened. For a moment, he thought she might leave the sofa and walk over to him, but a loud knock made them both jump and turn to the door.

Martin let himself in.

'Good morning, both. Going through some of the projections? I'm spending the day in a marketing meeting.' Martin sighed. 'Oh, and before gossip gets around, Ally's handed her notice in. We'll be advertising for her replacement shortly. I'll probably be chatting to Val about it after the big marketing meeting. So, if anyone wants me today I'll be on the fourth floor. Everything all right, Ren?'

Harrison glanced to Ren who had paled. She nodded.

'Hmm. Yeah. Any news on Billy?'

Martin shook his head, pursing his lips.

'Not yet. Good, well, I'll let you get back to work.' He shut the door and marched off towards the lift.

Slowly, Harrison turned to Ren.

'Ren...'

She was shaking her head.

'Ally's leaving? That's because of her and Liam, isn't it. Because they can't push Liam out, he's the head developer. We need him. Poor Ally.'

'She won't have been pushed out. You don't know how long she's been planning on leaving.'

'Who leaves their husband and their job in a matter of months?'

Harrison shrugged.

'Anyone. It's life. For all we know, she's moving in with Liam and has gotten a better job elsewhere.'

Ren stared at Harrison with wide eyes.

'What if Martin pushed her out?'

Harrison sighed.

'He didn't, Ren.'

'But—'

'It's not legal for him to push someone out of a job just because of who they're sleeping with. Martin wouldn't have had anything to do with it.'

'But what about us?'

Harrison's heart squeezed at the tone of her voice.

'We work closer to him than Ally,' Ren continued. 'What if us being together messes everything up?'

'Then...we'll figure it out. We have to tell Bonnie.'

'Oh, yeah, no, we do. But maybe not anyone else?'

Harrison stared at Ren for a moment. Then, calmly, he got up, made his way over and sat beside her on the sofa. Taking her hand in his, he looked into her eyes.

'I want to tell everyone,' he told her. 'I want to go up to the roof and scream it to the city. I want to be able to leave the office with you in the evening and come in with you in the morning. I want to find a room in this place that doesn't have damn glass walls so I can kiss you and do things that make you moan in my ear so I have to remind you to keep quiet. I want to tell people we're together.'

Ren had visibly melted a little as he spoke, leaning closer to him, resting her hand on his thigh.

'It's been one date,' she murmured.

'How many dates will it take?' Harrison asked. 'And on a related note, are you free tonight?'

Ren laughed softly, reaching up to run her fingers over his hair.

'Yes, okay,' she started. 'I tell you what, I'll tell Bonnie today and we'll go out tonight. Maybe with Mac and Bonnie?' Harrison's eyes lit up. 'But let's not tell anyone else. Because of Martin, yes, but also because it's no one's business. Okay? And because, yes, I'm worried. If Martin finds out and gets angry, which of us will he push out, Harrison? It won't be his finance director who helps him fix everything, will it? No, it'll be the new girl he can replace easily just as soon as Billy gives up and quits. They don't really need a palaeontology consultant, who does? He can just contact the local university and ask for some help, if need be. But don't tell him I said that. I really need this job. And absolutely yes to finding a room with actual walls for a quickie. I'm all for that. But let's not tell anyone. Okay?'

Harrison searched Ren's eyes, trying to organise his thoughts and becoming mildly distracted by her fingers in his hair. He took her hands and gently stopped her. She sat back as he sighed.

'Fine. Okay. We tell Bonnie, we go out with her and Mac. I like that. And I think there's a stationery cupboard on the third floor, or the toilets over there.' He pointed down the hallway and Ren pulled a face.

'Ew.'

A smile tugged at Harrison before he could think on it.

'When will we tell everyone?' he asked quietly.

'When we know it's serious?' Ren offered. Harrison sagged. This already was serious for him. He took her hand into his lap again. 'When my contract is nearly up?' Ren suggested. That was months away. Harrison sighed.

Ren sat forward and kissed his cheek.

'We will tell people,' she whispered. 'After this whole Liam and Ally thing has blown over. Yeah?'

Harrison brightened a little and nodded.

'Yeah. That makes sense.'

He turned his head to catch her lips in his. As the kiss broke, they bumped noses.

'I think you can call me Harry now,' he whispered.

Ren's eyes widened, lighting up.

'Really?'

'Just not at work.'

Ren grinned.

'Harry,' she whispered, kissing him.

'You go tell Bonnie,' he murmured. 'I'm gonna go

investigate that stationery cupboard.'

Ren laughed as Harrison lifted her hands to his lips and kissed her fingers. Reluctantly, she stood and left the office, looking back over her shoulder to Harrison as she went. Harrison watched her go, a ball of contentment settling inside him and spreading out. Clapping his hands, he jumped up and returned to his desk. The more he worked, the faster the day would go. The faster the day went, the sooner he'd be naked in bed with Ren.

'I knew it!'

Ren looked around in a panic but no one was paying them any attention. Bonnie was grinning ear to ear, clapping her hands with glee. 'And I was right, Harrison did have sex last night. With you!'

Again, Ren glanced around the coffee shop. She didn't see any faces she recognised but still, she shushed Bonnie.

'And we'd like to keep it on the down low, so shh!' Ren hissed.

Bonnie lowered herself to the table.

'Oh, sorry. Sorry,' she whispered, still grinning. 'You and Harrison, though.'

Ren nodded, unable to stop smiling.

'Yes, me and Harrison.'

'Had sex last night,' said Bonnie.

Ren rolled her eyes.

'He took me out to dinner for my birthday,' she told her friend. 'And then I invited him in afterwards.'

'Yeah ya did.'

Ren gave Bonnie a look, but Bonnie was too busy laughing to herself to take much notice.

'This is fantastic,' she told Ren. 'And you're so suited. Perfect for each other. Was it good? The sex?'

Ren pulled a face.

'I can't answer that!'

'Sure you can. I'll go first, if you like. Mac's incredible. The way he—'

'Ah!' Ren interrupted. 'I don't want to know.'

There was a moment of silence at the table as Bonnie stared at Ren expectantly, her grin widening.

'It was amazing,' Ren relented, and Bonnie whooped. 'And that's all I'm saying on the subject.'

'Sure thing. For now. Oh, to think, I'm the one who introduced you. I knew it. The way your face lit up this morning when he walked in. He's been staring at you for months, you know. I knew he wanted you, I just wasn't sure if you felt the same way. You seemed kinda...aloof about him.'

'Yeah.' Ren pushed her hair back from her face and sighed. 'He's not the type I was expecting to fall for, I think. Not at first, anyway. But he's actually incredibly sweet and kind.'

Bonnie was nodding.

'He is.'

'And clever.'

'Very. Pretty sure he's the person holding our

whole project together.' Bonnie sipped her coffee.

Ren smiled, the memory of Harrison's touch filling her mind.

'Yeah,' she murmured wistfully.

Bonnie smirked, giving her a knowing look.

'Have you had sex in the office yet?'

Ren startled out of her memories.

'What? No!'

'No, right. It's been half a day. Of course you haven't.'

'Why would we have sex in the office when we can spend the evenings and weekends together?'

Bonnie looked as though Ren had just asked why Edinburgh was full of tourists.

'Erm…because you can?' Bonnie rolled her eyes and then grinned happily to herself again, looking down at her coffee. 'Oh god, we should double date!' she declared in a sudden burst of noise.

Ren laughed.

'Actually, we were wondering if you and Mac fancied a drink out tonight?'

Bonnie was already nodding.

'Abso-bloody-lutely we do! I mean, I can't talk for Mac, but I can't see why he would say no. I'll message him.'

Before Ren could stop her, Bonnie had her phone out and was typing a message to Mac, and given the time it took her, she must have been telling him everything. Ren waited, sipping her coffee, wondering how much time they had before they had to get back to the office.

'Liam and Ally used to have sex in the cleaning cupboard, if that's of any use to you,' Bonnie murmured as she typed.

Ren stared at her.

'You what?'

Bonnie glanced up.

'Liam and Ally. Before they were found out and Ally quit. They used to have sex in the cleaning cupboard. It's in the corridor between our office and the developers' corner. Next to the printing room. Very quiet and no glass doors or walls or windows. Complete privacy. Val told me. Ally told her. Apparently you get used to the smell of bleach.'

Ren blinked, opened her mouth to let out a witty retort and then blinked again when no words emerged.

'I don't even know where to start with that,' she said eventually, as Bonnie put her phone on the table. 'Would you have sex in the office?' she whispered.

Bonnie snorted.

'I offered to christen Mac's new office. Told him I could hide under the table. He nearly took me up on it.'

Ren's eyes widened.

'You wouldn't actually do it, though, right?'

Bonnie laughed.

'No, probably not. Not at his desk like that. A cupboard though...' Bonnie brought her cup up to her lips and drank deep.

Ren shook her head.

'Think I'll stick to the bed for now.'

'Good idea,' said Bonnie. 'Keep the cleaning cupboard for if you need to spice things up in a few years.' She winked at Ren, who continued to stare at her in shock.

'About Ally,' Ren murmured after a moment's pause. 'Did Val say why she'd quit?'

Bonnie shrugged.

'Not really. I think it might have been a build-up of things, you know.'

'It seems strange to quit your job right after leaving your husband. You'd think she'd need the money.'

'Yeah.' Bonnie sipped her coffee thoughtfully. 'She's moving in with her sister and going freelance, apparently. I actually wonder if she's been planning it for a while and it all just coincided.'

'Oh?' Ren perked up. 'You don't think Martin had anything to do with her leaving, then?'

Bonnie looked at Ren and calmed in an instant.

'Martin wasn't happy about Liam and Ally,' she murmured. 'But I reckon that affair was the only reason he knew Ally existed. He's never had any reason to get to know the marketing team past Val. She keeps them all pretty hidden away on the fourth floor, partly to keep herself as a barrier between him and them.'

'He's not that bad,' said Ren.

Bonnie shook her head.

'No, no. It's a control thing for Val. She doesn't want him telling them what to do when she can tell them what to do.'

'Ah, yeah.' Ren drank her coffee as Bonnie gave her a sideways look.

'Are you worried?'

Ren nodded.

'Harrison and Martin work so closely together and now I'm working closely with Martin, and if he finds out...' She trailed off, looking to Bonnie for help.

'Neither of you are doing anything wrong,' Bonnie pointed out. 'You're both single and free to date and sleep with whoever you choose.'

'What if he thinks it'll interfere with our work?'

'Prove to him that it won't.'

Ren sighed.

'I can't lose this job,' she murmured, mostly to herself. 'I can't job hunt again. Not yet. But I'm definitely not giving up on Harrison.' Bonnie grinned at her. 'Don't tell anyone, okay? No one in the office, I mean. I really don't want anyone knowing. Not yet.'

Bonnie pulled a face.

'Does Harrison agree with that?'

Ren sighed.

'He wants to shout it from the rooftops, but he's in a better position than me, isn't he.'

'I'm pretty sure your wealthy Wolf of Wall Street

will help you out if for some reason Martin got rid of you, but listen, Ren, he won't. Martin has no power to fire you because you're sleeping with someone in the office.'

'Is there a company policy or something about it?'

Bonnie gave this some thought.

'I don't know. I don't remember. Why don't you find out?'

Ren drained the last of her drink.

'Yeah, I'll look into it. Probably not worth doing anything until I know we're serious.'

Bonnie pursed her lips.

'Double wedding,' she murmured under her breath.

'Heard that,' said Ren.

Bonnie laughed and checked the time.

'I promise not to tell anyone, but seriously, look it up. I'm sure it'll all be fine.'

'It's not about head office saying it's fine, though, is it. It's about Martin.' Ren gathered her coat and bag. 'Come on, we'd best get back.'

'So you can tell Harrison about the cleaning cupboard?'

Ren smacked Bonnie with the empty sleeve of her coat.

'A toast!' Mac declared, holding up his pint. 'To my new ridiculously well-paid job, all thanks to

Harrison, and to Harrison and Ren finally seeing each other naked. To new jobs and nakedness!'

'New jobs and nakedness!' said Bonnie, Harrison and Ren, holding up their drinks. Bonnie laughed before drinking. Harrison turned to Ren, his eyes soft, and Ren's stomach flipped, leaving her unable to sip from her drink. Under the table, his hand found her knee and his finger traced circles. Ren suppressed a shiver of pleasure, giving Harrison a secret smile. Or what she thought was a secret smile.

'Well, aren't you two just the cutest,' said Bonnie. Ren and Harrison turned to find their friends watching and smirking.

'Adorable,' Mac agreed.

'As opposed to you two,' said Harrison, picking up his pint.

'I'll have you know that we're dignified,' said Mac, taking Bonnie's hand, lifting it to his lips and winking at her. Bonnie giggled. 'I can't believe you two are choosing to spend your evening with us instead of in bed together.' Mac turned back to Harrison.

'Well, I wanted to tell people and we're not telling the office.' Harrison glanced at Ren. 'Yet.'

Ren nodded.

'Except Bonnie, of course.'

'Well, you had to tell me,' said Bonnie. 'I guessed. I'm very perceptive.'

'Very,' Mac agreed, and something passed between him and Bonnie that made Bonnie blush. Ren watched with curiosity.

'Did Jackson actually send you a business plan?' Ren asked Harrison. 'Or was that just a ruse to keep Bonnie off the scent?'

'He actually did.' Harrison squeezed her knee under the table and a jolt of pleasure shot up through Ren. 'It's good stuff, too.'

'Business plan? What's this now?' Mac asked, lifting his pint to his lips.

'Jackson wants to drop out of college and start up a distillery. He was looking at doing it in New York but it seems that he quite likes Scotland.' Harrison pulled a face. 'A bit too much, perhaps. He told me he has a girlfriend, but he came home late and smelling of perfume one night he was here.'

Mac laughed.

'Cut the kid some slack, Harry. If he's moving to Scotland to start a business, he probably won't be with the girlfriend long.'

'Hmm.' Harrison drank his beer. 'Anyway, he reckons we should go into business together. A whisky distillery and a craft beer brewery.'

Mac's eyes lit up.

'Smashing idea!'

'Have you ever brewed beer?' asked Bonnie.

'Nope.' Harrison filled his mouth and swallowed.

'Has your son ever made whisky?' she ventured.

'Nope.'

Bonnie raised an eyebrow.

'So what's so great about this business plan?'

'He's put real thought into it. I reckon he could get funding. And I'd be happy to invest in it, although I haven't told him that yet. He's said he'll do all the leg work and set up production, he'd want me in charge of the money.'

'Makes sense,' said Mac. 'Is he good at sales?'

'He's selling the whole idea to me.' Harrison rubbed at his beard and Ren watched him, her mind drifting back to her bed the previous night when that beard had brushed over her soft skin. 'It's a way off yet,' Harrison continued. 'But it's an interesting idea.'

'And would mean you wouldn't be working together anymore,' said Bonnie, looking to Ren.

'I reckon that wouldn't happen until my contract has ended,' said Ren, trying to focus on the conversation. 'So I wouldn't be there anymore anyway.'

'Nah, I reckon they'll probably offer you Billy's job,' said Harrison.

Ren turned to him and they studied each other for a moment.

'Well,' said Ren, looking back to the others. 'One thing at a time. Let's just enjoy this for the time being.'

Harrison smiled and, under the table, his hand slowly slid up her thigh. Ren pressed her lips together to force away a visible reaction as her body responded. She drank her drink, taking a large gulp. Harrison did the same.

Mac had levelled his gaze at Ren.

'So, do you still think Harry is capitalist scum?' he asked.

Everyone turned to Mac. Bonnie raised her eyebrows, Harrison glared and Ren slapped her hands over her mouth. Mortified, she turned to Harrison with wide eyes, her stomach dropping.

'Thanks, Mac,' Harrison growled.

'No problem, mate,' said Mac, still watching Ren.

'Oh god, I did call you that, didn't I,' she said to Harrison.

'You did.' Harrison gave her a charming smile and she relaxed a little as she searched his eyes.

'Well, you're not scum,' she told him.

'So, just a capitalist?'

She shrugged.

'Can't argue it,' she pointed out.

He laughed and nodded in agreement.

'Sure. Fine. At least I'm no longer scum.'

Her smile fell, the guilt flooding back.

'I'm so sorry.'

He softened and leaned towards her.

'Don't be,' he murmured gently.

The tension over the table lifted and Harrison leaned forward, kissing Ren lightly on the lips. The guilt evaporated, pushed away to the back of her mind for a later conversation.

'When you say you don't want anyone knowing about the two of you,' Bonnie started as they all settled back.

'Yeah?' said Harrison in a low voice.

'Do you just mean you don't want Martin to know? I mean, that you just don't want it getting back to him?'

Ren and Harrison exchanged a look.

'Pretty much,' Ren admitted. 'I don't really mind anyone knowing, but I wonder how Martin will react after this whole Liam and Ally thing. I think we should just wait a while, until all that has calmed down.'

Bonnie gave this some thought.

'Hmm. You might have a point, there.'

Ren sat back, smiling.

'Vindication,' Harrison whispered to her.

'Right,' said Ren, clapping a hand down on the table. 'Drink up, love,' she told Harrison. 'This has been lovely and we should do it again some time, but I'd quite like to have Harry to myself.'

Calling him Harry sent a wave of happiness through Ren and he grinned in response. Mac raised an eyebrow and Bonnie scoffed.

'So, can I call you Harry now, too?' she asked Harrison.

He shook his head as he downed his pint.

'Nope. Just these two.'

Bonnie sulked as Mac laughed. His grin fell at the sight of Bonnie unhappy.

'Oh, don't fret, sweetheart. C'mon, drink up and we can go have sex too.'

Bonnie cheered instantly, lifting her half-finished drink to Harrison and Ren as they pulled their coats on.

'See you tomorrow.'

Four days after they told Bonnie and Mac about their new relationship, Harrison picked up his phone and hit Ren's extension number. He stared out at the view of the castle while he waited.

'Harrison,' she answered. 'What can I do for you?'

'Well, if you really must know, I've found a hotel room we could book over lunch,' he told her, looking back to his screen and the details of the hotel.

'Isn't that a little extravagant?' she asked in a low voice.

'Fun though,' Harrison pointed out. 'Is it busy out there?'

'No. Liam's with his team and Bonnie's downstairs in a meeting with marketing.'

'So no one will notice if you come visit me? And while I would love to invite you into my office right now just so you can straddle me on the sofa, I actually have a proper work question.' He glanced sideways at the sofa, imagining the weight of Ren on his lap, her lips on his as her fingers unbuttoned his shirt and his hands explored underneath the skirt of the dress she had pulled on that morning…

'Oh? What's that?'

Harrison cleared his throat, banishing the thoughts.

'The development team's overtime sheets are in, along with their invoices for some software upgrades. I don't suppose you could share their progress with me?'

'You're still checking up on them?' Ren asked.

'Partly, but it's also technically my job.'

'They're on schedule,' Ren told him.

'Show me.'

'Hang on.' Ren hung up and Harrison did the same, leaning back in his chair and staring towards the castle. Would it be so bad to disappear for an hour at lunch to get acquainted with a hotel room? Maybe he should book them a weekend away together.

He turned at a gentle knock on the door. Ren stepped inside quickly to reveal Ari and Harrison's grin faltered. He recovered quickly, bringing up a spreadsheet to cover the window of hotel deals on his laptop screen.

'Hey,' he said to both of them.

'I'll find the project sheets,' Ren told him, taking a seat on the sofa and opening her laptop. Harrison turned to Ari.

'All right, mate? Just a quick one. I didn't realise you two were going into a meeting.'

'No worries,' said Harrison.

'Do you have the budget codes for the new battle area we're putting in?'

Harrison dug around on his laptop and tapped away at his keyboard.

'Sure thing. Just sent them to you.'

'Cheers, mate. Hey, we haven't caught up yet. Fancy a beer after work?'

Harrison hesitated and Ren glanced up. Their eyes met for a moment, and then Ren looked back down to her screen. This was turning out to be a good example of why they should be telling people. He wanted to ask Ren about this, not to get her permission, as such, but to check. That was what being in a relationship was. That was what he loved. Not just the kissing and touching and sex, but the partnership, the checking with each other, the talking and planning.

'We should be done here well before then,' Ren told Harrison, giving him a well-hidden meaningful look. 'And I'll have the final pieces to you by four at the latest.' Her eyebrow subtly twitched up.

The corner of Harrison's mouth lifted, amused. He turned back to Ari.

'Sounds like I won't be working late, so yeah, a beer would be great. Usual place?'

Ari sighed wistfully.

'It's been so long I'd forgotten we had a usual

place. Definitely. Catch you later.' He nodded to Ren and left, closing the door behind him.

Slowly, Harrison turned to Ren.

'Four at the latest, huh?'

Ren smiled.

'What? I didn't know what to say. You're allowed to see friends, aren't you, but you didn't answer him. We have our own lives. I was just trying to tell you it was okay. We probably need a little break from each other, anyway.'

'Oh,' said Harrison. 'So, I can't come to yours once I'm done drinking with Ari?'

The expression that settled in Ren's eyes sent a bolt of excitement through Harrison.

'You want to come to mine after drinking with your friend just so you can have sex?' She attempted a mock angry tone, but her grin gave her away. Harrison mirrored it, glancing back to the glass walls to find the corridor empty.

'Actually, I thought I could bring some food and then we could have sex?'

Ren covered her laugh with a hand over her mouth.

'Chips,' she told him. 'From the chippy down the road.'

'Deal.' Harrison stood and plonked himself next to her on the sofa. 'So, Bonnie said there's a cleaning cupboard we should investigate?'

Ren studied his eyes as he tried to resist kissing her.

'You can't wait until this evening?' she asked.

His gaze travelled down her body, lingering where her dress clung to her curves, and he sighed.

'I guess.'

Ren tapped away at her computer for a moment.

'I've shared the current progress the developers are making. We can talk about it more in the meeting we have with Martin this afternoon.' She closed her laptop and leaned over, catching him off guard as she pressed her lips against his. He held her in place until she made a noise. Grinning, he let her go and she quickly checked the glass walls.

'Not funny,' she murmured.

'It's fine. Martin's not in until later. You know, there's something very sexy about keeping all this hidden. It's hard not to think of all the things we could try getting up to.' Harrison took Ren's hand, stroking her long, clever fingers.

'Like booking a hotel room just for a lunch hour?'

Harrison lifted her hand to his lips.

'Exactly.'

'Let's do something this weekend,' Ren offered. 'A trip to the beach or something.'

Harrison laughed.

'I was just thinking about the weekend,' he explained. 'Great. And hey, tomorrow night, come to mine. I'll cook.'

Ren stopped and stared at him.

'You can cook?'

'I'm talented in many ways,' he told her. She

searched his eyes, smiling. 'Cooking isn't one of them but it's the thought that counts.'

Ren laughed and leaned forward, kissing him again. She glanced down at the sofa as she pulled away.

'You know, we should work late one night.' She kissed his cheek as she stood and then she sauntered out of the office. Harrison kept his eyes on her for as long as he could. When she was gone, he sat back, his mind filled with what he and Ren could get up to on that sofa after everyone had left.

'You look happy. What have I missed?'

Harrison stopped humming to himself and realised he was smiling. Attempting to pull the corners of his mouth down and straighten out his face, he turned to Ari and stepped out of the way of the coffee machine. It had been a good eight months, if not more, since Harrison had worked with Ari in the flesh, although he was more than used to seeing him on his screen during online meetings with head office. The game's head writer had been born in Greece and lived there a grand total of three months before his family moved to London. A novelist and games writer, Ari had only lived in Edinburgh for six months while he did the main storyboarding and ironed out any initial problems. Since then, he'd returned home to his wife and four children, deftly handling any issues the developers threw at him from a distance.

'Nothing,' said Harrison, trying hard not to put a question mark at the end. Ari raised an eyebrow and studied him.

'Nah, something's definitely different.' Ari grinned and sighed all at once. 'You know, I've sort of missed this place. What the hell is going on with Martin and Liam?'

Harrison laughed and, in a quiet voice, explained the affair between Liam and Ally. Ari's eyes widened as Harrison talked.

'Wow. What else have I missed?'

'Nothing much,' said Harrison. 'You know about Billy, right?'

'Right. Martin's trying to get rid, from what I can figure out. Did he get rid of Ally?'

Harrison's heart jolted painfully.

'What? No. No, Ally's left to go freelance.'

'Huh, yeah.' Ari turned to collect his full coffee cup from the machine. 'Right. And Ren is taking over from Billy? And she's a qualified, bona fide palaeontologist? I keep meaning to book a meeting with her. We need to go over the storyboards properly, I might have to pick her brain.' Ari glanced up at Harrison and added, 'She seems nice.'

Harrison controlled himself.

'Yeah, she is.'

He must have given something away because Ari narrowed his eyes at him, fighting against a smirk.

'Is she single?'

'What?' said Harrison far too quickly. He bit the inside of his lip. 'I don't know. Why? You're not looking at having an affair, too, are you?'

Ari chuckled. The man had a wonderful softness about him, in his eyes, his voice, his laugh. It almost lulled you into sharing all of your secrets.

'No,' he said. 'And I couldn't anyway because you're into her. You're sleeping with her, right?'

Harrison froze, his mind whirring. He looked around. They were alone in the kitchen area and no one was paying any attention to them, so he relented.

'Yeah,' he said, grinning. 'You got me.'

'I knew it. Don't worry, I won't tell anyone.' Ari stirred some sugar into his coffee and leaned back against the worktop, staring out into the office. 'How long has it been going on?'

'Not long,' said Harrison. 'It's very new and we're worried about Martin finding out.'

Ari nodded.

'Yeah, he's a weird one, Martin. I won't say a word. And I'll be back in London soon, anyway. So, we still on for later or would I be interrupting things?'

'No, no, it's okay. We're overdue a catch up.'

'Seeing her after, huh?'

Harrison grinned.

'I have to take food with me, though.'

Ari chuckled.

'Got it.'

'It's a shame your wife's in London,' said Harrison. 'I accidentally introduced Bonnie to my friend, Mac, and now they're a couple. We could have all gone out for dinner together.'

Ari smiled.

'I thought Bonnie seemed happier too. I'm glad things are looking up around here. Just need to sort out Martin, huh? And dinner would still be good. I can be the odd one out, I don't mind.'

Harrison patted Ari on the shoulder.

'Great, I'll ask Bonnie and Mac about it. How do you suggest we sort out Martin?'

Ari exhaled hard through pursed lips and, finally, shrugged.

'Who knows. Just do what you gotta do and then report him to HR if he causes trouble.'

With a smile, Ari left Harrison and wandered back to his desk. Harrison stared at the empty space Ari had occupied as his thoughts ran through newly forming ideas.

It was like going on an adventure. Harrison had arrived half an hour early to pick Ren up. She was only just out of the shower, washing the day of work from her, and answered the door in a towel. Ren was amazed they'd made it to her bed, although her towel had fallen off the moment the front door had closed. Body still tingling from Harrison's touch, she followed him along the dark, chilly Edinburgh streets to his place. They walked slowly, her hand in his as they talked about nothing and everything, and Ren did her best to memorise the way. Harrison squeezed her hand when she laughed at his jokes and she stroked his with her thumb, just because.

She paused on a quiet street, pulling Harrison gently to a stop. Breathing in the cold night air, Ren looked up at him and grinned.

'Thank you,' she murmured.

'For what?' he asked, stepping up to her and putting his arm around her waist.

'Everything,' she said. 'For everything over the last couple of weeks. For helping me at work, for making me feel more confident, for making me feel safe, for being gorgeous. Just...thank you. It's been hitting me recently just how happy I am. I haven't been this happy in a long time.' Ren wrapped her arms around his neck and pulled him close. 'And it might be the city and it might be Bonnie and it might be the job. But mostly, it's you.' She kissed him softly.

'It helps that the sex is good, right?' he murmured, holding her close.

Ren laughed.

'Best I've ever had,' she whispered, before leading him down the street. She walked half way down before she remembered she had no idea where she was going and turned back to him.

'Where do you live?' she asked, smiling.

Harrison was grinning, ambling up behind her.

'You're adorable,' he told her, pulling her back and kissing her. She braced for a hard kiss, but it was gentle and her insides twisted in response, her legs weakening beneath her. 'This way.'

They walked into West End, past tall beautiful buildings with black railings out front, and trees and private gardens on the opposite side of the road. Eventually, Harrison slowed and pulled out his keys. He led her up steps to the black front door of a stunning Victorian building. When he let himself in, Ren followed tentatively.

'Up the stairs,' he told her, and she followed him up a grand staircase decorated in a subtle, elegant Victorian style. She whistled softly.

'Jeez, how much money do you have?'

Harrison chuckled up in front of her. She noticed he didn't answer her question. At the top of two flights of stairs, Harrison reached a door and unlocked it, opening it and letting Ren inside first.

'Welcome to Casa Calloway.'

Ren wasn't sure what she'd been expecting but a stark white, stunningly large penthouse apartment at the top of a grand Victorian building hadn't been it. The hallway opened onto a large living room with a fireplace and beautiful big windows that drew Ren to them. The view was of the rooftops over the city, towards the castle. There was a sofa and two armchairs, all pointed at the fireplace, and a large TV over the mantle. Off to the side was a bookcase, filled with books and framed photographs of a small child progressively growing up into Jackson.

Open-mouthed, Ren followed Harrison into the kitchen, only slightly smaller than the living room, with marble worktops and white cupboard doors. There was a splash of colour on the wall but otherwise it was just as stark and elegant at the rest of the apartment.

'This is...' Ren breathed. 'My god, how much money do you have?'

Harrison shrugged.

'Wanna see the bedrooms?'

'Okay.'

The first bedroom had a plush carpet under foot and was actually smaller than Ren had anticipated, and there wasn't a bed. There was a desk and a chair, and one wall was lined with floor to ceiling shelves, each one packed with books. She looked up at Harrison.

'My office,' he explained. 'For the rare occasions I work from home. Also the room I sometimes throw junk in.'

The other bedroom had the same carpet and an actual double bed, fully made, that Ren thought she could happily sink into.

'This is smaller than I thought,' she joked, about to step in.

'And this is the master,' said Harrison, leading her away. She watched him.

'Wait, this isn't the master?'

'Nope.' Harrison opened a door onto a large bedroom with a king-size bed, which appeared just as luxurious, if not more so. There were tall windows, this time looking towards the outskirts of the city, along with the treetops in the shared private garden just below. The wardrobes were built in and there was a door which led to an exquisite en suite with two sinks.

'What do you need two sinks for,' Ren breathed, not expecting a reply.

'Yeah, they were here when I bought the place. Not had much use for two sinks when it's just me in here. But now there's you, so…'

Ren turned on Harrison.

'Bought? You *own* this? God, Harrison, how much money do you have?'

Harrison grinned.

'I told you I have money. Hell, I told you that's why my second wife married me.'

'Yeah, but…' Ren looked around the bedroom. 'But…I didn't think it would be this much. Didn't she get a load in the divorce?'

'My parents talked me into signing a pre-nup, because apparently everyone has a level head except me,' Harrison explained. 'Saved my ass. I saved a lot when I was working as a stockbroker, I invest my money and when I moved here, I invested in this place. So, I earn less here but my money's working for me.' An amused smile twitched at his lips as he watched Ren trying to process this.

Ren sat down on the foot of the bed.

'Is it a problem?' he asked.

Ren met his eyes, her mouth still open.

'Of course not!'

Harrison laughed as Ren sobered.

'But, I'm not with you for your money. I want you to know that.'

'Oh, I know,' said Harrison, gesturing for her to follow him. She left the bedroom and dawdled into the kitchen. 'I think your shock sort of proves that, don't you?'

Ren blew out her cheeks.

'So,' she said slowly, looking around the kitchen. 'What are you cooking me?'

Harrison was right – he couldn't cook. At least the chilli he'd made had been edible and followed by a shop bought chocolate cake that more than made up for it. His bed, on the other hand, was like a cloud, and for the first time since they'd started sleeping together, Ren slept for most of the night. She woke curled up into his warmth, Harrison's arm wrapped possessively around her. Ren hadn't slept that well in a long time.

It meant that she stepped into the office, fifteen minutes after Harrison, with a bounce in her step, which disappeared when she spotted Billy sitting at his desk.

'Billy!'

He looked up and watched Ren approach.

'I wasn't expecting to see you in today. How are you?' Ren smiled at him, glancing to Bonnie and Liam's desks. Both were empty.

'Been better,' Billy muttered.

Ren hovered by her desk chair and considered him.

'Wanna chat?' she offered.

Billy studied her with hard eyes and then sighed. 'Yes.'

They found a small meeting room, Ren closing the door on them while Billy took a seat. She sat opposite him as he stared down at the desk.

'Are you back properly?' she asked.

Billy rubbed a hand down his face.

'I don't know,' he admitted. Groaning, he put his head into his hands. 'My sick note ran out, HR have started calling me to talk about my contract. Martin wants me gone, doesn't he? I don't know what to do, Ren.'

Ren sighed through her nose. Billy looked up at her. 'You want my job?'

'Not really,' said Ren. 'But I need a job and I like working here, so I'll take whatever they offer me at this point. I don't want to take your job, though. I want to help. What can I do to help?'

'I don't know.'

Billy stared down at the table, a picture of abject misery. For a moment Ren considered fetching Harrison, but then she straightened her back and lifted her chin. She could do this. Thinking back through her own career and bad experiences, Ren chose her next words carefully.

'All right. Do *you* want your job?'

She waited until Billy shifted in his seat and slowly raised his gaze.

'No,' he told her. 'I used to like it but basically it's organising a load of people and it's...boring.'

'Yeah,' Ren agreed. 'I get that. So do you know what you'd rather do?'

Billy struggled, placing his hands on the table and wringing them together. Ren narrowed her eyes. 'Go on,' she encouraged. 'What do you want to do?'

Billy sighed.

'It's stupid.'

'Billy, my job is dinosaurs. C'mon.'

That got a small smile from Billy.

'Okay. I want to be a writer.'

There was a moment of silence as Ren waited for more and Billy waited for her reaction, grimacing a little in preparation.

'A games writer?' Ren asked.

Billy nodded and then jumped when Ren laughed. She put a hand over her mouth.

'Sorry. Sorry, I didn't mean to laugh. But that's great!'

'Is it? Why?'

'Ari's here! Why don't you ask him about how you can get into games writing?'

Billy pulled a face.

'He's the head writer. Why would he help me? And anyway, I didn't say I was any good.'

Ren shrugged.

'Ask me to name all the dinosaurs off the top of my head. I can't. Hell, I can't even pronounce some of them, I definitely can't spell most of them, but I'm still a qualified palaeontologist. The only way to get good is to practise, the only way to become what you want is to try and keep trying.'

Billy's brow creased.

'Sounds like something Harrison would say.'

'Does it?' Heat flushed up Ren's chest and neck, her cheeks starting to burn. She did her best to ignore it. 'Well, I'm saying it. Because that's my experience.'

'You tried and tried and lost your job and had to take a consultant job in Scotland,' Billy told her. Ren's smile fell, her heart pounding.

'That may be so. I didn't have much in London,' Ren told him. 'And now I have not only an interesting job but great friends and…' She took a quick breath. 'An amazing boyfriend.' It was the first time she'd referred to Harrison as her boyfriend and damn, it felt good. She hid the smile well. 'And that's because I didn't stop trying—'

'Because you needed a job,' Billy pointed out.

'And so do you,' Ren told him. 'What's the difference? Stop finding excuses. Ari seems like a lovely bloke. Go talk to him.'

Billy shook his head and Ren sighed.

'So what are you going to do when Martin gets his way and you're out of this job, hmm? Are you looking at other project management jobs?'

Billy squirmed some more.

'I've been writing a novel,' he murmured, barely audible.

Ren considered him.

'If I talk to Ari and he agrees to chat it through with you, will you talk to him?'

Billy slowly met her eyes and nodded.

'Do you want me to keep helping you with the

project management?' Ren asked.

Billy sighed.

'You can do all of it for all I care. I tried so hard to do a good job but it's impossible with Martin throwing his weight around and Liam shagging his way around the office. You can't get hold of anyone except for Bonnie and Harrison, and Harrison picks holes in everything. *Everything!*'

Ren had almost stopped listening.

'What do you mean, "Liam shagging his way around the office"?'

Billy avoided her gaze.

'Nothing. I didn't mean anything. I meant him and Ally, that's all.'

Ren's eyes widened.

'He's sleeping with other people?' she whispered, leaning forward. 'Who?'

'I don't know.'

'Billy, come on. I'm trying to help. I've been covering for you all this time and I'm going to talk to Ari so you can try to get into professional writing. The dream! So, tell me.'

Searching her eyes, Billy relented.

'Fine. Kate in HR. They've been doing it on and off for about two years, and what's-her-name, Fiona, in accounts. That didn't last long. I think he traded her in for Ally.'

Ren had stopped breathing.

'That's why Ally moved in with her sister instead of Liam,' she said when she finally took a breath.

'Probably.'

They left the meeting room a few minutes later to find both Bonnie and Liam at their desks. Ari was heading down the corridor towards Harrison's office, or maybe Martin's. Bonnie stood with her coffee cup as Billy reached his desk. Ren gave her a look and they met in the kitchen.

'What's going on with Billy?' asked Bonnie.

'He's miserable as sin,' Ren told her quietly. 'Really unhappy. But I'm going to try and help. Turns out Liam's not just been sleeping with Ally.'

Bonnie's eyes widened.

'What do you know? Tell me everything.'

Ren smiled.

'Not here. Later. Pub, tonight?'

Bonnie nodded.

'You got it.'

'Great. God, I haven't even had a morning coffee yet but I need to go find Ari. See you later.'

Bonnie gave Ren a strange look, but Ren was already striding towards Harrison's office. Ari was sitting in Val's chair, laughing with Harrison. They both turned as she knocked on the door.

'Hello, there,' said Harrison, looking her up and down.

She flashed him a smile and turned to Ari.

'Hey. Sorry to interrupt, I don't suppose I could have a moment when you're free?'

Ari glanced at Harrison, surprised.

'Sure, what's up?'

Ren turned on Harrison.

'You're not to say a word of this to anyone.'

Harrison raised an eyebrow but mimed zipping his mouth closed.

'Billy wants to be a games writer, or at least a published writer, although I think he's a little embarrassed by it. I wondered if you would have a chat with him? Maybe boost his confidence a little, talk options with him?' she asked Ari.

A grin spread across Ari's face.

'I had no idea Billy was the creative type. Definitely, I'll go chat with him.' He stood. 'Is he at his desk now?'

Ren nodded and Ari left the office, heading towards Billy.

'You're perky today,' came Harrison's voice from behind her.

'Yeah,' she murmured, closing his office door so that they were alone. 'I think I should sleep in your bed more often,' she told him, wandering over as he grinned at her.

Harrison stepped into the lift, shocked to find Ren inside next to a couple of women from marketing. He gave her a look and she subtly lifted a cup of coffee – she'd taken a detour on her way into the office despite the plan for her to arrive earlier than Harrison that morning. Smiling to himself, Harrison turned to face the front.

'Hold the doors!'

Harrison shot out an arm as the lift doors began to close and Dougal ran inside. Breathing hard, he thanked Harrison. The doors closed and the lift began moving up. The only sound was the quiet chatter of the two women in the corner, who weren't as quiet as they should have been. It soon became evident they were talking about Liam.

'Is he still news?' Dougal asked them. 'C'mon, that was months ago now. Surely you girls have got something new to gossip about other than my boss?'

The women glared at him.

'He was sleeping with Kate in HR as well as our Ally,' said one of the women. Harrison flinched, wishing he could glance back to Ren. How had that news gotten out? 'Your boss is the office bike,' the woman continued.

'I would say HR need to get involved but it turns out they already are,' said the second woman, snorting at her own joke.

Dougal frowned.

'None of our business who's sleeping with who,' he muttered.

A silence descended. Out of the corner of his eye, Harrison watched Dougal turn back to look at Ren.

'How's it going?' he asked. Ren must have smiled because Harrison didn't hear her speak and Dougal continued. 'I think we're nearly done with coding all the dinosaurs, which is kinda sad. Are you still taking over from Billy? So you'll still come visit us to boss us around?'

'Probably,' came Ren's voice. 'We're working out the finer details.'

Harrison rolled his eyes. The finer details being what Billy would be doing while Ren did his job.

'Great. Hey, have you been to Loch Ness yet? My camping group are going up in April. Want to join us?'

There was a pause as Harrison held his breath, his heart thumping wildly.

'Oh, you go camping there? Thanks for the offer, it's very kind, but I'm not really a camping person,' said Ren.

Dougal nodded.

'Fair enough. But if you ever fancy giving it a go, I have a spare tent. It's fun. We sit around the fire, tell stories, have a little barbecue, get drunk. It's a great way of meeting people.'

'Sounds it,' said Ren. 'Okay. I'll think about it.'

Harrison wondered if that was true.

The doors pinged open and the women from marketing stepped out onto the fourth floor, around Bonnie who had been waiting for the lift's arrival.

'Oh, Doug.' She stopped the doors closing. 'I was coming up to look for you. Can you come look at something for me? I need your opinion on some graphics I've used in a mock up that was just delivered. Marketing say it's great, but it doesn't look right to me. I want it to look like the game.'

'Sure.' Dougal flashed a grin to Ren as he stepped off the lift. Ren stepped forward as the doors closed and exchanged a look with Harrison as they both let out a breath. Reaching out, Harrison slipped an arm around her waist, pulling her close and stepping behind her. He gently put his arms around her, sliding his hands underneath her top. She melted into him under his warmth, leaning her head back against his chest as pleasure reverberated around him.

He kissed her neck as his hands explored.

'If this was a book, we would stop the elevator,'

he murmured in a low, husky voice. 'Do it against the wall.'

Ren moaned.

'What sort of books are you reading?' she asked breathlessly.

Harrison gave a short laugh against her neck. Ren turned in his arms, forcing him to move his hands, and kissed his lips.

'And it's a lift,' she corrected, grinning as Harrison's eyes narrowed.

'It's a good thing you're incredible,' he told her.

Ren laughed and kissed him again.

They stepped apart as the lift doors opened with a ping. Walking out, they headed towards Ren's desk and, coincidentally, the corridor towards Harrison's office.

'So, you don't want to go camping at Loch Ness with a developer?' Harrison checked. Ren gave him a look.

'Maybe. If Bonnie hadn't befriended me. And if I hadn't met this amazing man who swept me off my feet.' She grinned at him, throwing her bag onto her desk. Billy lifted his head at the sudden noise, scowled at Harrison and went back to staring at his phone.

'There are some nice hotels near Loch Ness,' Harrison told her. 'Much better than camping. Might want to tell your boyfriend.'

That was the first time Harrison had referred to himself as Ren's boyfriend and it just slipped out, catching him off guard. He hesitated as Ren's eyes softened before she turned back to her desk.

'Hey, Billy. How did the chat with Ari go?' she asked, taking off her coat. Harrison used the diversion as an excuse to collect himself and head towards his office.

'Good,' came Billy's voice from behind. 'Actually, really good.'

Harrison smiled. Good old Ari. Which reminded him, he needed to make a dinner reservation for them all. He'd do it when he'd had his coffee. He shoved his coat on his chair and turned on his laptop, before returning to the open-plan office and making his way to the kitchen with his coffee cup. Billy had his head down over his phone again and Ren was already at the coffee machine.

'Is that his plan for the rest of the day?' Harrison asked quietly as he joined her.

'He's waiting for Martin to come in so he can talk to him about some things Ari suggested.'

'Oh?'

'Yeah, some courses and stuff. And the possibility of a secondment. He's really nervous. Cut the guy some slack.' Ren took a deep breath. 'And wish me luck. I've got to pin down Liam today for an update, and if what Billy says is true, it might be tricky.'

Harrison made a noise of agreement.

'Depends on who he's sleeping with now.'

'Hmm. I guess if I can't get hold of him, I could

ask the other developers. Dougal's helpful. I'm sure he'll point me in the right direction.'

Harrison grimaced at the mention of Dougal's name.

'Oh yeah, he's real helpful, that one.'

Ren turned to him.

'What does that mean?'

Harrison sighed, looking into her bright, green eyes, wishing he'd kept his mouth shut.

'Oh come on, Ren, he asked you to go camping! Don't worry, though, he has a spare tent. Sorry, a "spare" tent.' Harrison made air quotes and Ren frowned.

'You don't think he does have a spare tent?'

'I'm surprised he didn't offer to share his with you, that's all.'

Harrison jumped when Ren laughed. She stepped close to him so she could lower her voice.

'I know this might be hard for you of all people to believe,' she told him. 'But men don't usually want to sleep with me. I don't think you have anything to worry about.' She chuckled to herself.

Harrison leaned close to lower his voice.

'I know this might be hard for you to believe,' he told her. 'But you're beautiful and I'm not the only man here who thinks so. Trust me. I've seen the way Doug looks at you. It's the same way I look at you.'

Ren searched his eyes, their heads still too close together considering they were in the office.

'No,' she whispered. 'He doesn't. And I prefer the

way you look at me.'

If they'd been anywhere else, she would have kissed him. Harrison bit his lip.

'If we told people, we wouldn't be having this conversation,' he suggested.

Ren's smile fell.

'News is getting out about Liam. You really think now is a good time to tell everyone about us? Maybe we should wait to see how Martin reacts first.'

Harrison sighed hard.

'You know, maybe we could just tell people and to hell with Martin.'

Ren looked up at him, shocked. She kept her voice low but matched Harrison's accidental harsh tone.

'And to hell with my job?'

'We don't know that'll happen, and you're not in this alone. I'm right here with you.'

'With not as much to lose!' Ren's voice rose a little.

'I mean I'll fight for you.'

'I know, but that's easy for you to say when you have a secure job and a ton of money,' Ren hissed.

'That's got nothing to do with it!' Harrison growled. 'Martin can't fire you over this. If he tries anything, we report him to HR.'

Ren opened her mouth to respond when Martin stormed into the office.

'Liam! Where's Liam?' The executive producer looked around, glancing from Ren to Harrison as they jumped apart. 'Is he in yet?'

'No idea,' said Harrison. 'I'm only just in.' He waved his coffee cup and then moved to the machine.

Martin turned to Ren who shook her head.

'I haven't seen him yet,' she told him.

Martin huffed, looking to Billy who turned away meekly.

'If you see him, tell him to check his emails. I've booked a meeting with him.' Martin marched towards his office.

'Everything all right, Martin?' Harrison called after him.

'No! It isn't!' Martin shouted over his shoulder. As he left, Harrison turned back to Ren who was staring up at him.

'We're definitely not telling anyone yet,' she said, and Harrison sighed.

'Fine,' he muttered, taking his coffee and heading back to his desk.

The week passed quickly and each day, the tension in the office built. Most people kept their heads down, working towards the new deadline with vigour, making the most of the promises of paid overtime. Ren stayed over at Harrison's most nights and by Friday, she knew the way to his by heart, although he still insisted on collecting her even as the evenings became lighter. Her palaeontology work was becoming less about the dinosaurs and more about the environment they lived in, their behaviours and reactions, which were being coded into the game, and small details that Ren didn't have a clue about. She found herself swinging from plucking pieces of knowledge and research from the back of her head, to smiling and nodding at something a developer was saying, before perhaps asking Dougal to explain it in hushed tones later that day.

That Friday morning, after another blissful night in Harrison's bed when she'd tried to decide if she preferred his cotton sheets or his naked body against her skin, Ren prepared for a senior meeting. Picking up her laptop and coffee to take into the meeting room, she marvelled at how far she'd come since that nerve-wracking first day.

'Ready?' asked Bonnie.

Ren nodded, glancing back.

'No Liam?'

Bonnie shook her head.

'No Billy?'

'That doesn't bode well,' Ren murmured, following her friend through the corridor to the glass meeting room. As usual, Harrison was already there, tapping his fingers against the table, staring through his laptop at his thoughts. Ren couldn't help but smile at the sight of him, still, after all these weeks of spending practically every day, evening and night with the man. He smiled at both of them as they sat at the table, Ren taking the seat opposite him despite the urge to be next to him. He gave her a wink as she sat and her insides curled up with pleasure and warmth, a grin fighting its way onto her face.

'You two,' said Bonnie with a smile, sitting near Harrison.

Before they could talk, Val entered the room followed by Ari and then Martin. The executive producer bustled to the end of the table and arranged himself with a sigh.

'Everyone here? Good.'

The others looked around.

'Erm, Liam's not here,' said Bonnie.

'Or Billy,' said Ren.

Martin pursed his lips.

'They won't be coming.'

They all exchanged looks across the table. Martin turned his laptop on, evidently avoiding eye contact with any of them for the time being.

'What's going on, Martin?' Harrison asked. 'Anything we should know?'

'All will become clear,' said Martin, finally content with his arrangements. He sat back and surveyed his small team. 'Well, I thought we could start with an overview of where we're at with the game right now, but I suppose we can start with staffing updates.'

Ren's bowels dropped.

Martin took a deep breath as everyone watched him expectantly.

'Liam has handed his notice in,' he said with more calm than Ren felt. She glanced at Harrison who gave her a sideways glance back.

'Why?' he asked before Martin could say more. Martin looked up at him.

'You would have to ask him.'

A silence fell over the table.

'No, Martin, really,' said Val, leaning forward. 'Is this because of...what he's been doing?'

Martin pursed his lips.

'It is by mutual agreement that Liam has handed his notice in. He's been placed on garden leave and will not be returning to the office. Obviously, this is bad timing for the game. We're now without a head developer.' Martin sighed. 'I've asked Dougal to prepare an update for us. And we're discussing what to do about the vacancy that Liam is leaving. It might be that we promote within.'

Ren's stomach twisted. She risked another look at Harrison. He was staring at Martin, the muscles in his neck taut as he gritted his teeth. To her horror, when she turned back, Martin was looking directly at her.

'Ren? Could we start with an update from you?'

Ren cleared her throat, her voice coming out weaker than she'd have liked.

'What about Billy? Where's he?'

'Billy is held up elsewhere,' Martin said. Ren waited for more, but apparently that was it. Martin raised a questioning eyebrow and Ren cleared her throat again.

'Okay,' she said, opening her laptop. 'Update. A project management update?' she checked.

'Please,' said Martin, his tone growing sterner.

Across the table, Harrison sighed hard, and when Ren glanced up he had levelled his gaze at Martin. It was a warning, not that Martin seemed to have noticed. Butterflies bounced around inside Ren as she tried to take some comfort from Harrison's obvious annoyance at the situation.

'Well,' she started. 'We're pretty much on schedule.' She flicked through her data. 'Everything's coming along nicely, from what I can see, but everyone is working overtime.' She glanced up at Harrison. 'And I mean everyone. And everyone's getting exhausted.' She looked at Martin who, again, pursed his lips. 'Basically, the marketing team are doing great things, the game is now getting to a stage where we can start doing proper tests and Billy's given me the information for the testing team, so I'll be in touch with them soon. I'll leave the full updates for the others to give, but it's all looking good so far. I just wonder how things might change without Liam leading the development team.'

'Don't worry about that,' said Martin. He turned on the marketing director. 'Val, what's your update?'

They went through each of them. Ari gave an update on the new storyboards and some ideas he was running past development. Bonnie explained how she had moved on to the final, finer details of the game and was now working on mock ups with the marketing team. There came a knock on the door as Bonnie was finishing and Dougal entered carrying his laptop. He connected it up to the big screen on the wall while Bonnie explained her last update, then everyone turned to Dougal.

'Err, hi, everyone,' he started. 'Take it easy on me, I've scraped all this together just now from Liam. So, erm, we're basically done with all the original designs. We're now working on the new storyboards from Ari.' Dougal nodded to the writer who smiled back. 'Working with Bonnie and Ren to design anything new and make sure it's all as authentic as possible. For example...' Dougal tapped away at his keyboard and brought up a design of an Edmontosaurus wearing something sparkling green. Ren's brow creased as she tried to work it out. 'Our lovely Ed here is wearing the new harness design. She'll be one of the mounts available to our players and they can choose from a variety of harnesses, from the basic plain leather, to more extravagant ones with bonuses, such as speed and aggression or how docile they are, depending on the dinosaur type. And they come in different colours, so players can style their dino mounts.'

Harrison leaned forward on the table.

'Tell me we're charging for those harnesses.'

Dougal did a quick double take at him, frowning. He opened his mouth, but Val got there first.

'Sort of. There are different coloured ones that can be bought, but the bonuses can often be won in battles and through quests.'

Harrison pulled something of a face, shrugged and sat back.

'Any idea on the price of the ones we're selling?'

'Not yet,' said Val shortly.

'We'll discuss,' said Harrison. 'Sorry, carry on.' He turned back to Dougal.

Dougal steadied himself and continued, taking them through some of the other new designs and details. Once he was done Bonnie asked a few questions, which led to some discussion on time-scales, to which there were no clear answers until something was done about replacing Liam.

They thanked Dougal and he made his escape.

Next, Harrison gave a detailed update on the amount of pre-orders they had, along with their expenses, and told Martin that they'd need to discuss the amount of overtime that was being done. Ren lifted her hand up and Harrison hid a smirk behind his coffee cup.

'Yes, Ren?' asked Martin.

'I'd like to be in on that meeting, please.'

'Well,' said Martin. 'There is more, but I was waiting for the any other business part of the agenda.' He looked around the table. 'Are we all done? Can we move on to any other business?' No one complained, so he continued, turning to Ren and smiling, which was now possibly more dis-concerting than his pent up anger. 'Ren, as I'm sure you'll all agree, has been doing a fantastic job over the last few weeks, taking over from Billy.'

Everyone smiled and nodded, and Ren flushed, fighting the urge to lower her gaze.

'Your aptitude and hard work has not gone unnoticed,' Martin continued. 'And, as I under-stand it, your skills as our resident palaeontologist are being used less and less as the game progresses, as is natural. Which is why I've been talking to head office—'

Ren's heart skipped and she held her breath, meeting Martin's smiling eyes.

'—And there happens to be a vacancy for a senior project manager in London. We'd like to put you forward for it.'

'No!'

Everyone snapped round to look at Harrison who sat forward, breathing hard, eyes wide, realising what he'd just done. Ren watched him, her chest tight.

'No?' Martin frowned.

'I mean, it would be a great loss for us if Ren were to leave our project,' said Harrison carefully.

Martin nodded.

'Of course. I wouldn't let you go, Ren, until we'd at least found a replacement for Billy or until this project was over. We'd need to discuss it, if you were successful, but this could mean a contract extension. It's all hypothetical, of course. But I thought you might be happy about it – the chance to move back to your family in London, hmm?'

Ren gathered herself, forcing herself to breathe. She gave Martin a small smile.

'Thank you, Martin. That's so lovely, to be appreciated and offered such an exciting new opportunity. I'll certainly think about it, although I've actually grown very fond of Edinburgh and our project team.'

'Yeah, you can't leave,' said Bonnie. 'I'd miss you.'

Ren smiled at her friend.

'Plus, she has a new boyfriend here,' Bonnie told Martin.

Martin turned back to Ren who was staring wide-eyed at Bonnie, her smile fading.

'Oh? I didn't realise. Maybe a London move wouldn't be so appealing, in that case. Not if you've settled here so quickly. And, of course, I'm aware it's not a palaeontology role. But it wouldn't be the first time a gaming newbie has joined the company and stayed on in a career change, would it Harrison?'

Harrison looked up from the table, bewildered.

'Hmm? What?'

'You did that, didn't you. Weren't you an investment banker in New York? And you came here to work in the finance department and, okay, so it wasn't a big career change, but still. Investment banker to finance director of an arm of a gaming company. Not bad, huh? So, career changes like that can be good.'

Harrison blinked and quietly said, 'Stockbroker. I was a stockbroker.'

Martin shrugged.

'My point still stands.' He turned to Ren. 'Have a think about it, anyway. I'll see what head office says.'

Ren nodded.

'Thank you. Maybe we can talk about it later?'

Martin agreed, turning his attention back to his

laptop. As the spotlight of his gaze shifted from her, Ren turned on Harrison but he had returned to staring at the table.

'Does anyone have anything else?' Martin asked.

'When will we know about Liam's replacement?' Val piped up.

Martin exhaled in a puff.

'Soon. In the meantime, any requests should probably go through Ren and Dougal.'

Ren kept her eyes on Harrison, which was why she saw his eyes go hard. He gritted his teeth again, the muscles working in his jaw. Ren swallowed, her fingers tingling, eager to be out of this damn meeting.

Harrison couldn't collect his thoughts.

'The hell was that about?' Ren hissed. She turned to check that the door to Harrison's office was definitely shut and that Martin hadn't suddenly appeared in the two seconds since she'd last checked.

'I know. I'm sorry.'

'For a man who is so great at so many things, you suck at keeping secrets.' She approached Harrison who was leaning over his desk.

'I'm sorry.'

'And it's not really that, though, is it,' Ren continued. 'I'm allowed to make my own choices! Whatever job I take is up to me.'

Harrison nodded.

'I know.'

'Then what the hell?' Ren stopped herself, straightening, waiting for an explanation.

Harrison clenched his eyes shut, wishing to go back to when he'd held Ren in his arms, and everything had been happy and right with the world. He took a deep breath but the muscles in his jaw wouldn't relax.

'I don't want to lose you.'

'You're not going to lose me.'

Harrison looked up at her.

'Look, I'm happy for you. I'm so happy that things are going well. The fact that they want to keep you on, that they're considering you for a promotion. These are all great things! But I just can't...' He blew out his cheeks. 'I shouldn't have done that and I'm sorry. It just slipped out. I'll be more careful. Although, you know, if we told Martin, we wouldn't need to be careful anymore.'

'No, I'd just find myself unemployed like Liam.'

They stared at one another, Ren breathing hard, Harrison far too still for comfort. He forced himself to relax and closed the gap between them. He studied her beautiful big eyes; they still made his stomach flip.

'We're not doing anything wrong,' he told her gently. 'If he did anything like that, we'd report him to HR. To head office. Which, arguably, is what Liam should be doing.'

Ren hugged herself, looking away. Just her turning her head from him tore at Harrison's insides.

'Please,' he begged. 'I'm sorry. Forgive me. It won't happen again. If you want to take that job and move to London, then...I'll learn to live with it.

Even if it means I lose you. Because I want you to be happy, and you're right, this is your choice.'

Slowly, Ren turned back to him, searching his eyes.

'I don't want to move back to London,' she told him softly, the fight gone from her. 'I don't want the job. I want to stay here with you. I like it here.'

Harrison gave a small smile.

'Good. Because I like you being here.'

Ren tentatively reached forward and brushed her fingers over the shirt on his chest.

'Be more careful in future, yeah?'

Something inside Harrison gave way – relief, perhaps. He nodded and resisted the urge to wrap his arms around her.

'Yeah. I will.'

Ren stepped closer, lifting her chin as though she wanted him to kiss her. He glanced up into the corridor beyond the glass wall and door.

'Is anyone there?' Ren whispered.

Harrison shook his head, then leaned down and kissed her lips quickly. Ren took his hand and squeezed it before turning and leaving him alone in his office.

He fell onto the small sofa with a *thunk* and a heavy exhale, dragging his hand through his hair and down his face. After a few minutes of deep thought, he pulled his phone from his pocket and brought up his message chain with Mac.

He hit send and considered going to his desk to return to work, but his legs refused to move. After what felt like far too long, Mac replied.

Harrison smiled, quickly typed out a reply, and discovered his legs were more than happy to move if it meant carrying him out of that building. He walked past Ren who turned a little to watch him go, and while he offered her a smile, he didn't stop. Bonnie was in the kitchen and opened her mouth as if to call out to him, but he rushed past, stepping into the lift just as someone else stepped out, before the doors could close on him.

In the middle of Princes Street Gardens, he bought two coffees inside the gallery café while he waited for Mac.

Mac strode through the door dressed in what looked like a new suit, and seemed relieved to spot Harrison immediately. They found a table among the few tourists and groups of elderly locals having a morning coffee, scraping back chairs in the echoing gallery entrance area and keeping their voices low.

'Thanks,' said Mac, adding sugar to his coffee. 'I'm kinda glad you messaged me. I needed to get out. I'm not sure about this new job, you know.'

'Oh? How come?'

Mac waved him away as he sipped his coffee, grimacing at the heat.

'No, no. You first. What did you do? How mad is Ren?'

Harrison explained what had happened during the meeting and the discussion with Ren that had followed.

'Sounds like you're okay,' said Mac. 'She's forgiven you. What's the problem?'

Harrison shifted on his chair.

'Do you think I'm controlling?'

Mac's laugh echoed, bouncing off the walls, making everyone seated around them glance over. He waved an apology, lowering his head and his voice.

'I mean, you won't let Bonnie call you Harry despite how long you've been friends—'

'Work friends.'

'So? And now she's my girlfriend. Come on!'

Harrison frowned down at his coffee.

'Do I do anything else?'

Mac gave this some thought.

'You're not controlling, Harry. You're in love. It's okay that you don't want Ren to leave, of course you don't. And it's understandable that you shouted out when you didn't mean to. I don't know what you're worried about.'

Harrison stirred his coffee absent-mindedly.

'I've been so concerned with spotting red flags in women, I forgot that I have some of my own,' he murmured.

Mac shrugged.

'We all have red flags. But I mean, they're not major red flags, are they? So you're a little protective and loud. So what? Bonnie's accused me of not taking some conversations seriously enough.'

Harrison looked up.

'Really?'

Mac nodded.

'She called me immature. We fought, words were said, we apologised, we had sex. It happens in relationships. And we're better for getting it all out. I try my hardest to be serious when she wants me to be. And she's been trying to give me a little more breathing room. And we're good again.'

Harrison sighed.

'I didn't know you two were fighting.'

'We're not, Harry. It was one little argument. My point is, it happens and you come out the other side. It's fine. Stop overthinking it.'

A smile touched Harrison's lips.

'Yeah,' he murmured.

Mac studied his friend.

'You really want to tell everyone about you two?'

Harrison nodded without looking up.

'I just don't see the problem. The more I think about it, the more I think we should tell people. I got it at the beginning. There's no point telling anyone if it then all falls apart really quick. But enough time has passed now and...'

'And?'

Harrison sipped his coffee, not meeting Mac's eyes.

'I still feel like I could marry her.'

When Mac didn't respond, Harrison risked looking up. Mac was smiling.

'Have you told her that?'

Harrison scoffed.

'Of course not! That's bound to scare her off. We haven't even said we love each other yet. I'm pretty sure that has to come first.'

Mac nodded.

'Yeah.'

'Have you told Bonnie you love her yet?'

To Harrison's amazement, Mac flushed, looking down to his coffee and clearing his throat.

'Might have done.'

'Did she say it back?'

Mac nodded.

'Yup.' He looked up and laughed at Harrison's expression. 'I said it by accident, but she said it back immediately.'

'By accident?'

'Yeah. She made me laugh and the words just slipped out. Sort of like what happened to you today, but less embarrassing and more kissing afterwards.'

Harrison shot his friend a look. Mac leaned across the table towards him.

'What would you tell you to do if you were me?'

Harrison groaned, sitting back.

'To talk to her.'

Mac shrugged.

'And there's your answer.'

Harrison pulled a face.

'Now,' Mac continued. 'What would you tell me if I told you this job was getting to me?'

Harrison took a quiet, deep breath, pushing thoughts of Ren to one side so he could focus on Mac's problem.

'Okay, let's start at the beginning. What about the job is getting to you?'

Mac sighed.

'I don't know. The people, I think. I'm working all the hours, which used to be fine but now I find myself at work missing Bonnie.'

Harrison smiled.

'Well, that's to be expected. You know, this job is really new to you. There'll be a settling in period.'

'Yeah.'

'And I would normally say that in our industry, you have to work the hours.'

'Hmm,' Mac grumbled.

'But.' Harrison waited until Mac looked up at him. 'There's Bonnie to think of. I reckon you've got a choice. One, you plan something of a future with Bonnie, put a time limit on this job and save as much money as you can. Two, you reduce your hours a little, which may not be possible.'

'It isn't,' Mac confirmed.

'Or three, you find another job.' Harrison studied his friend. 'Which of those seems right for you?'

Mac drank his coffee, thinking it over.

'I kinda like the first one.'

Harrison grinned.

'There you go.'

'But how long would I have to stay?' Mac asked, glancing up at a group of tourists heading towards the gift shop.

'Probably depends on how much you want to save. You'd need to discuss it with Bonnie. But I'm more than happy to help you figure out a plan once you two have decided what you want to aim for.'

A grin slowly spread across Mac's face.

'I've never been in a relationship like this,' he murmured softly.

Harrison looked past his friend, out the window towards the gardens.

'No,' he said. 'Me neither.'

As the days passed, Ren had all but forgotten Harrison's accidental outburst. Every day was the same blur of rushing around the office organising people, catching Bonnie in the kitchen and sneaking into Harrison's office for a hug and a chance to stop for a moment. She'd managed to speak to her parents at the weekend, but hadn't told them about the possibility of moving back to London – she wasn't sure how they'd react. She had, however, kept them up to date on her relationship with Harrison. At least, she'd divulged as much as they needed to know, and then sent some photos of Harrison's apartment to her mother.

That Friday morning, with the senior meeting cancelled until the following Monday, Ren had managed to slow her pace. She was just drinking the last of her coffee when Martin appeared over her shoulder.

'Can I have a word, Ren?'

It was a good thing her cup was empty or the contents would have ended up all down her dress. Nodding, calming her panicked heart, Ren locked her screen and followed Martin to his office. Glancing to the right, Harrison's office was empty and Ren wondered where he was. Had he disappeared off for a secret coffee with Mac again? He had told Mac he'd help him with a financial plan. Ren had to wipe the smile from her face as she took the chair opposite Martin's desk. Her first inclination, during that conversation, had been to ask Harrison to look at her finances and help her make a plan. Until it had dawned on her that if this relationship continued as it was, maybe her finances would become his, that his finances would become hers, and she wouldn't ever need to ask.

'I have some news,' said Martin, placing his clasped hands on his desk. Ren waited, trying to ignore the coffee bubbling in her stomach. 'Billy has handed his notice in.'

Ren's eyes widened.

'What?' She gawped, about to ask why he hadn't asked for a secondment before realising that it wasn't any of her business and that Martin might not react well to such a question.

'Hmm. He's been offered another job. A writing job at a marketing agency, or something.'

'Oh.' Ren sat back and tried not to smile. Good for Billy.

'Which means I can now officially offer you the

permanent position of project manager.' Martin grinned. 'What do you think?'

'Oh, that's... A permanent role?'

'Yes, to start as soon as possible, of course. We'll have to take you off this contract and give you a new permanent one.'

Ren could hear her heart beating in her ears. Her first reaction was to jump up and punch the air, so she squeezed her hands between her legs and stayed put.

'That's wonderful! Thank you so much.'

Martin exhaled sharply.

'Oh, good. I was a little worried you'd say no.'

'Oh, no. I would really love to stay here. I'm enjoying the job.'

'Good, good. I'll send you the salary details and have a chat with HR to get your new contract sent over. Congratulations!'

'Thank you so much, Martin. I really appreciate this.' Ren, unable to hold back her wide grin, stood and shook Martin's hand.

'Well, you've been a god send, Ren,' he told her. 'It makes me so happy you'll be staying on with us.'

Ren left the office on bouncing steps, as if she could float away with each stride. Annoyingly, Bonnie was missing from the office and Harrison was still nowhere to be seen. She grabbed her empty coffee cup and skipped into the kitchen.

'Hey, I had a thought. Let's have a weekend in New York.'

Ren wheeled round to Harrison and he hesitated at her happy face. 'What's going on?' he asked, smiling.

Ren went to tell him when her brain caught up.

'I—what? New York? For a weekend? First of all, no, I'm not flying all that way for two days. That's insane. Are you going to visit Jackson?'

'Actually,' Harrison said, leaning back against the kitchen worktop and lowering his voice. 'My parents would like to meet you and I'd love you to meet them. Mom's not been well lately and it's a wonder my stepdad can still pick up a golf club. I thought we could have dinner with them and make a romantic weekend out of the rest of it.'

Ren had only heard part of that. She stared at him, open-mouthed.

'You want me to meet your parents?' she hissed, her voice far too high.

Harrison chuckled and nodded.

'Is it too much too soon?' he asked.

'In New York?'

'Well, that's where they live.'

'But you... You didn't want to go back to...'

'Yeah, well, I don't mind so much about going back to the scene of my disaster of a second marriage when I have a beautiful woman on my arm.' Harrison winked at her. 'It'll be fun. We'll get an expensive hotel suite, dine out, we can see a show if you want. I can take you shopping. You can Sex and the City it.'

Ren sobered and raised an eyebrow.

'Yuck,' she told him.

Harrison laughed.

'I don't need any of that,' Ren continued. 'A normal hotel room would do, and we can see a show if you want but I'd rather do the museums. No shopping, although maybe some proper tourist New York clothing. Honestly, I'd rather be in the New York sewers than shopping Sex and the City style.'

Harrison's brow creased.

'In the sewers? With the rats?'

'With one rat,' Ren said, smiling, wondering if he'd catch on. 'And four turtles.'

Harrison, still confused, opened his mouth to respond when Dougal appeared by their sides.

'You're a ninja turtle girl? Let me guess, Leonardo.'

'Donatello,' Ren told him. 'I like my ninja turtles at genius level.'

Dougal laughed, reaching past her to the coffee machine.

'I prefer Mikey.'

'Makes sense,' said Ren.

'What does that mean?'

'Oh come on, you're a party dude!' Ren gave him a surf's up hand gesture and Dougal laughed.

'In my defence, yes, I am. And I can skateboard too.'

'Naturally,' said Ren.

There was a pause as they smiled at one another and something heavy dropped into Ren's gut. Dougal looked her up and down, still smiling, before he reached for his coffee.

'Hey, I know you're not a camping girl, so how about I stop trying quite so hard and just take you out to dinner instead?'

Ren's smile froze. Beside her, Harrison shifted but he kept quiet. The voice at the back of Ren's head was impressed; if a woman had asked Harrison out in front of her, she would have done something. Especially if she'd spent all that time warning him about it, as Harrison had done with her.

'Oh, that's really sweet,' she told Dougal carefully. 'But I have a boyfriend.'

The light in Dougal's eyes dimmed a little. He looked away and nodded.

'Of course you do. Look at you! My fault that I waited so long to ask you properly, huh?'

'Sorry,' said Ren.

'He's a lucky guy,' said Dougal. 'I hope he appreciates that you know Jurassic Park by heart.'

Ren laughed but didn't respond. She was pretty sure Harrison didn't fully appreciate that about her. She wasn't even certain he knew who the ninja turtles were.

'He does,' said Harrison, with a tension in his tone that Ren hadn't heard before. She snapped up to look at him.

'Harrison,' she warned quietly.

'He appreciates her,' Harrison continued, not hearing her or not caring. Dougal looked from Harrison to Ren and back to the finance director.

'Good,' he said, unsure.

'*I* appreciate her,' said Harrison, full of emphasis.

'You?' Dougal looked to Ren who opened her mouth to explain, but Harrison got there first.

'Yeah, me. The boyfriend you just asked her out in front of.'

'He didn't know,' Ren murmured, placing a hand on Harrison's arm. 'Remember? People don't know.'

'No, but I want them to know,' Harrison said, glancing down to her. 'And partly because I don't like guys asking you out because they don't know about us, but also because I'm in love with you and I want to tell the whole world.' Harrison's voice grew louder and Ren's heart thumped harder with each word. Her breath caught at his declaration and she softened, forgetting for a moment where they were and that Dougal was still in front of them, looking bewildered.

Harrison turned to her and lowered his voice.

'I love you, Ren.'

A wave of pleasure swept over Ren as her insides melted.

'I love you too,' she told him softly.

Harrison beamed.

'Then nothing can stop us,' he told her. Ren watched, horror dawning on her, as Harrison moved around Dougal, climbed up on a chair to step onto the nearest desk where he stood to his full height and got the attention of every single person on the fifth floor. 'Hey!'

'Harry!' Ren hissed, stepping up beside Dougal. 'Get down!'

'I'm in love with Ren Bradley!' Harrison shouted. 'We're in love and we're in a relationship. I want everyone to know that I'm in love with Ren!'

From the other side of the office, Bonnie applauded loudly.

Dougal glanced at Ren.

'It's okay,' she told him. 'You didn't know.'

Dougal rubbed the back of his neck.

'Actually, I think everyone knew,' he told her quietly. 'I just didn't know if it was true.'

Ren stared at Dougal as he gave her a sheepish smile and then quickly walked away before Harrison could climb down. She watched the developer go for a moment and then turned back to Harrison as he stepped down off the chair, holding onto her for balance.

'You gonna shout at me now?' he asked.

Ren didn't know whether to laugh or cry. So instead she touched her fingers to his cheek, brushing away nothing with her thumb, and then nodded behind him. Harrison turned to see what had just become apparent to Ren; Martin was standing on the other side of the office, his arms crossed, his glare fixed on the two of them.

'I'm going to get fired.'

'You're not going to get fired, don't be ridiculous,' Bonnie told Ren, handing her a biscuit from the pack she kept hidden in her desk drawer for emergencies.

'As good as,' said Ren. 'He's going to push me out, isn't he.'

'Then we report him to HR and head office,' Harrison soothed. He sat on the edge of her desk, holding her hand in his, stroking her skin with his thumb. The thrill of being open about their relationship, to the extent of holding her hand in the office, ran through him and he had to keep forcing away a smile. Ren saw it, though.

'I'm glad you're happy,' she told him. 'But I finally thought I'd found a job I was good at and I could stick with. Martin's offered me a permanent contract. I haven't had a permanent contract in... I've never had a permanent contract.' Ren took her hand from Harrison's to bury her face. Over the top of her bent head, Harrison and Bonnie's eyes met.

'He offered you a permanent contract?' Harrison repeated.

'Does that mean...?' Bonnie attempted.

'Billy's quit. Another poor soul Martin has pushed out,' Ren whined.

'I thought he was going to try for a secondment,' Bonnie murmured.

'But that's great!' said Harrison at the same time. 'He's offered you a permanent contract. He thinks you're doing a good job, which you are. It's all going to be all right, Ren. You'll see.'

Ren shook her head.

'I haven't signed anything yet. He could just take it away.'

'I know how it seems but Martin really isn't that vindictive,' said Bonnie, pulling out her phone.

'What are you doing?' Harrison asked, his hand now a reassuring presence on Ren's back.

'I just want to ask Billy if he bothered asking for a secondment.'

'He probably didn't,' Ren admitted. 'I think he was a bit scared of Martin.'

Bonnie gave her a look.

'There's no reason for you to be scared of Martin,' she told her. 'You'll be fine. You both will. He likes both of you, you're both great at your jobs and, quite honestly, I can't see Martin crossing Harrison.'

'Harry,' Harrison murmured awkwardly, his

mind whirring.

Bonnie's eyes widened.

'Really? I can call you Harry?'

Harrison smiled and Bonnie threw herself at him for a hug. For a moment, everything was forgotten as Bonnie knocked the thoughts out of him. Ren laughed as Harrison tentatively hugged Bonnie back.

'We're going to be the best of friends-in-law,' Bonnie told him, still holding him tight.

Over her shoulder, Harrison gave Ren a look and mouthed, 'Help.'

'Harrison! Ren! My office!'

They all froze as Martin shouted over to them before he vanished towards his office without even a glance back to check they were following.

Ren stood, placing a hand over her stomach. Harrison knew the feeling as his own bowels loosened.

'Oh god. Oh god, oh god,' Ren murmured under her breath.

'It'll be fine,' said Harrison, standing and taking Ren's hand. 'Come on. Let's get this over with.' He lifted her hand and pressed it against his lips to give himself a shot of confidence as much as to reassure her.

'Good luck.' Bonnie watched them go, concern etched into her brow, and then shoved a biscuit into her mouth.

'If need be, I'll quit,' Harrison murmured. 'That

job is yours. Whatever it takes, I promise you.'

Ren looked up at him and he did his best to give her a smile, holding her hand tightly, walking tall and with purpose, despite his shaky breaths. His mind flashed back to all of the boardrooms he'd sat in, the deals he'd made, the negotiations he'd won. Compared to those, this was nothing, and yet there was so much more at stake.

Martin wasn't alone in his office. Neil, the Edinburgh branch's head of HR, was sitting beside Martin's desk, and he gave them something of a comforting smile as Ren walked in behind Harrison. Martin gestured to the two chairs set up on the opposite side of his desk and they all took their seats.

'So,' started Martin. 'About that little outburst earlier.'

Harrison was going to wait, to see what Martin had to say, but then Ren was talking, words falling out of her. He turned to look at her and she glanced sideways at him, but he didn't stop her.

'Martin, can I speak first? We've – me and Harrison – have been in a relationship since January and you have to agree, it hasn't affected our work. As far as I'm aware, no one's known unless we've told them. We're both free and single to see who we please and no one's getting hurt, not even the game.' She lifted her chin. 'So I do hope this isn't going to affect our jobs in any way.' She glanced at Neil who gave her another smile in return.

Martin sighed.

'Are you finished? Good. No, Ren, this isn't going to affect your jobs. You're right. I had no idea about the two of you and it hasn't affected your work.'

'You can't lose your jobs because you're in a relationship,' Neil explained. 'Unless there's a conflict of interest, in which case we would simply move you to another project. You don't have to worry. I'm Neil, by the way, we haven't met yet.' He extended a hand and Ren shook it, eyes wide, looking to Martin and then glancing to Harrison.

'Harrison.'

Neil and Harrison nodded at one another before turning back to Martin who was busy pursing his lips.

'We do, however, have a policy on relationships in the workplace which is why I invited Neil to this meeting.'

Ren turned back to Neil as Harrison smiled. He had meant to look up the HR booklets he'd been given when he first started, but with work being so busy and spending most of his free time in bed with Ren, it had slipped his mind.

'I should have known,' he murmured.

'Well, why would you? Unless you were planning on getting into a relationship when you first started here,' said Neil, riffling through some paperwork he'd brought. 'Most people tend to forget there's a policy or they just didn't read that part of their contract when they signed it. Here we are. You both need to sign these forms declaring the relationship, that it is consensual and that there are no conflicts of interest with your jobs.' He handed the forms over and Martin clicked a pen, offering it to Ren.

She looked at Harrison who was already reading through the form, searching for the fine print and any traps they could fall into.

'It's that easy?' Ren murmured.

'We would have preferred you to have declared the relationship a little earlier,' Neil explained. 'But it's really not a problem.'

Harrison met Ren's eyes and then signed his form. Ren looked down at her own.

'And it's fine that Harrison and I work so closely together?' she wondered out loud. Harrison's heart leapt into his mouth.

'Well, as you're moving to the London office, I don't think it'll be a problem,' said Neil, taking Harrison's form from him.

Both Harrison and Ren stopped, staring at the head of HR.

'What?' Ren breathed.

'But you said our jobs wouldn't be affected?' said Harrison.

Neil looked to Martin.

'I was told that Ren has been offered the permanent role?'

'She has,' said Martin. 'Although she hasn't accepted yet.'

Harrison was looking at Ren, his heart pounding in his ears, his mind running through all the scenarios far too fast to make any sense of them.

'But that's for this team. In this office,' she said breathlessly.

There was a hint of a smile on Martin's face.

'Yes, but come the end of the year, when the project is finished, the job moves to London,' Neil explained. 'You weren't told about that?'

Ren stared at Martin.

'No,' she said. 'I wasn't.'

Harrison swallowed on bile threatening to rise up his throat.

'Oh. I thought Billy would have mentioned it,' said Martin. 'He told me you were doing such a great job at helping him that you wouldn't have any problems taking over, and that you'd encouraged him to ask for a secondment and seek a different career path.'

Ren hesitated for a beat.

'Did he ask you for a secondment?' Harrison asked before she could.

'He did.'

'And you said no,' said Ren quietly.

'There aren't currently any secondment opportunities in the writing department,' Neil explained. 'All we have right now are unpaid internships, which obviously aren't ideal for Billy.'

'So Billy would have been going to London after the project finishes, and if you take the job and stay on here, so will you,' said Martin, his eyes on Ren.

Ren blinked and then looked to Harrison. He watched her but, for once, didn't have the answers. This was up to her. There wasn't much else he could do.

'Will Harrison be staying here when the project ends?' she asked meekly.

'Yes,' said Martin. 'Harrison will move to the next project here.'

'Then why can't Ren do that?' Harrison asked, putting far too much effort into keeping his voice steady. Martin met his gaze.

'Because that's not the job, Harrison.'

Harrison shook his head.

'Billy was here before this project started.'

'Hmm. He was project managing the game we made before, but he came up here from London a few years ago.'

When Harrison, clenching his jaw, turned back to Ren, she had brought her hand up to her chest.

'So if I stay with the company, I can't stay in Edinburgh? There are always two projects going on here, though, right? Why can't I project manage the other game in production?'

Martin looked to Neil who gave this some thought.

'We could do a reshuffle, but it would depend on that project's existing manager. They're not due to complete for another two years. If their project manager fancies a change of scenery, you could potentially come back to Edinburgh after a year or so.'

Both Ren and Harrison shook their heads without realising.

'No,' said Ren. 'Why can't I swap with them? We could swap now.'

'I...I don't think they'd want to,' said Neil carefully.

'We won't know unless we ask.'

Neil sighed.

'It's unorthodox.'

'It's a no, Ren,' said Martin. 'These are the terms. If you want to stay on permanently, you'll have to go back to London. Even if only short term.'

'A year isn't short term!'

Harrison's heart jolted as Ren raised her voice.

'Hey,' he murmured, taking her hand and squeezing it gently. 'It's okay. We'll figure this out. Can she have time to think about it?' he asked Neil.

The head of HR nodded.

'Of course. You're already on the project management contract temporarily, we can change it to a secondment until October, when your existing contract runs out, and you can make a decision then, if you prefer.'

'Really?' Ren sniffed, and Harrison realised she was holding back tears. 'I can really think about it for that long?'

'Well.' Neil shifted in his seat. 'It's not ideal. Really, we'd like an answer sooner rather than later.'

Ren nodded and squeezed Harrison's hand. His heart leapt at the sensation.

'Okay,' she said. 'Okay. And we can carry on as normal until then.' The men all stared at her. 'What?' she asked, looking between them.

'You need to sign the form,' Harrison whispered, nudging the declaration of their relationship on her lap.

'Oh. Right.' Ren signed the paperwork without reading it. Harrison was glad he'd taken the time to study the fine print. She handed the form to Neil who went to stand.

'Any questions, get in touch. But please let me know as soon as you've decided.'

Ren nodded.

'Thank you.'

'Thanks, Neil,' said Harrison.

Neil gave them both a warm smile and left the office. Martin leaned forward on his desk.

'Why didn't you tell me?' he asked quietly.

Harrison almost laughed.

'After all that Liam business? Why do you think?'

Martin sat back as if stung, and Harrison and Ren left him alone in his office, deep in his thoughts.

Ren needed to sit down but suddenly her desk was too close to Martin's office, which meant that Harrison's office was definitely out of the question.

'Can we go to the coffee shop?' she asked quietly, turning so that Harrison could hear her as he followed her out. His eyes were glazed, just as bewildered as her.

Bonnie pounced on them as they appeared.

'What happened? Are you okay? Do you still work here?'

They both nodded and Bonnie frowned.

'Tell me everything,' she urged.

Ren glanced up at Harrison.

'Our relationship is fine. We had to declare it and sign some forms,' she explained.

'Oh,' Bonnie breathed. 'Well, that's a relief. So, everything's good? Celebration drinks tonight?' She grinned.

'Not quite,' said Harrison in a tone so low that it brought the butterflies back into Ren's stomach.

Her fingers fidgeted over her gut in an attempt to calm them.

'That permanent contract I was offered?' she said.

'Yeah?' Bonnie's eyes were wild, waiting for the punch.

Ren sighed.

'Apparently it means me working from the London office.'

'No!'

'Yeah.'

Bonnie opened and closed her mouth, processing the information. Eventually she gave a small shrug.

'Billy did come up here from London.' She frowned. 'Is that Martin's doing?'

'Probably,' Harrison muttered. 'And me quitting my job probably won't have any affect on it.' He gave Ren an apologetic look.

'You're not quitting!' Bonnie declared.

Ren smiled and stepped closer to Harrison, entwining her fingers in his.

'I would never have allowed you to quit anyway. You love your job. This isn't worth that. No,' she said, looking back to Bonnie. 'I don't know what I'm going to do, but I have time to think about it.'

'And talk about it,' said Harrison. 'Come on. Coffee shop. Just us,' he added to Bonnie. 'Then pub tonight with you and Mac. Yeah?'

Bonnie nodded.

'I'll update Mac.'

'Thanks.' Harrison led Ren to the lift and they stood inside in silence, Ren wishing the two developers in there with them would hurry up and get off on another floor. Unfortunately, they were also going down to the ground level and they all stepped off the lift together.

As soon as they were out of the main entrance, Harrison took Ren's hand and pulled her to a stop. He looked down into her eyes and gave a sad smile.

'I don't know what to say,' he said quietly. 'I'm sorry. I'm not sorry. I love you.'

Ren reached up and stroked his whiskered cheek with her fingers. He leaned into her, closing his eyes.

'I'm glad you did what you did,' she told him, reaching up on tiptoe and wrapping her arms around his neck.

There, right in front of their office building, she pulled him down for a deep, long kiss. Harrison's hands found the small of her back and held her close.

He smiled as the kiss broke.

'That was good,' he told her wistfully. 'We should do that more often.'

Ren grinned.

'It does feel freeing.'

Harrison raised an eyebrow.

'So, I was right all along?'

'Don't push it.'

Harrison laughed, taking her hand as they walked towards the coffee shop. Ren ordered the drinks and a sneaky couple of muffins while Harrison found a table in the corner, away from the other corporate workers, a handful of freelancers and a wave of tourists who had wandered in. He smiled at the sight of the muffins.

'Blueberry for you,' said Ren. 'Because you're strange and like that sort of thing. Chocolate chip for me.'

Harrison grinned, pulling a piece off his and popping it into his mouth.

'You're the strange one for not liking blueberry muffins. But I wouldn't want you any other way.'

Ren smiled, staring at this wonderful man she could somehow call hers.

'I do love you,' she murmured, grinning as he looked up at her. 'It feels so freeing to finally be able to say that too.'

Harrison nodded, reaching for his coffee.

'I've been trying to not say it for a while. I didn't want to go too soon. Is it too soon?'

Ren shook her head.

'I'm pretty sure I've been in love with you for a while,' she admitted. 'Right after I realised you weren't capitalist scum after all.' She gave him a playful grin.

Harrison laughed. That belly laugh that still did it for Ren, every time.

'Yeah, well, I've been in love with you since the

day I met you. I just didn't know if I could trust it. I'm glad I can.'

Ren leaned forward and kissed his coffee lips.

'I really don't want to move to London,' she murmured, making a start on her muffin.

'I really don't want you to, either,' said Harrison. 'But I'll understand if you change your mind.'

Ren shook her head.

'Are you kidding? I'm not leaving you. No way.'

'I could come to London with you,' he offered, but he grimaced as he said it. Ren smiled.

'No. If I'm going back to London, it's to work in a museum. Not for a gaming company,' she told him. 'And I'm not going back. Sure my family are there, but if I'm not up in Scotland, they won't have an excuse to visit, will they? And I haven't actually spoken to any of my friends since I moved up here, so I think that's all over. And if not, they'll probably enjoy a visit up here too. And we can go visit London, nothing to stop us doing that. Just like how we'll visit New York to see your parents.'

Harrison grinned and reached over to take her hand. Ren squeezed his fingers and then took her hand back so she could drink her coffee.

'What about your contract, though?' Harrison asked.

Ren took a deep breath and felt a weight that had been on her shoulders since she'd lost her job at the Natural History Museum lift. Somehow, everything was suddenly easier. She was pretty sure Harrison was at the root of that.

'I'll find something else when my contract ends. Somewhere else. Something will come up, so I can stay in Edinburgh and we won't be working together. I love this job, honestly, but I'm beginning to think that this job came into my life so I could meet Bonnie and you, not because I'm meant to be a project manager. Let someone else do that. As long as you don't fall in love with them.'

'Nah,' said Harrison. 'I think I'm done.'

They stared at one another, smiles growing into grins, Ren's body fizzing with a warm, quiet comfort she hadn't felt in such a long time.

'Come on,' she said. 'We should get back to the office before people notice we're gone. They'll think we're in the cleaning cupboard.'

Harrison hesitated as he stood.

'Damn. We never did do that.'

That evening, Harrison and Ren arrived in the pub before Mac and Bonnie. Harrison ordered the drinks, explaining to Ren the delicacy of that specific ale while she tried hard to pay attention. She smiled and nodded and sipped the pint he offered her, making yummy noises at the appropriate moment.

'You really don't care, do you?' he asked as they found a table.

'No. Sorry. It is nice, though. Do you hate me

now?'

Harrison laughed.

'Don't think I could if I tried.' He leaned over and kissed her.

'Are these for us?' asked Mac as he swept over, pointing at the two untouched pints among the four on the table.

'They are,' said Harrison.

Bonnie wrapped her arms around Ren from behind in a quick hug before taking her seat.

'So, it's been a big day, I hear?' said Mac, sipping his pint and giving Harrison an appreciative nod. Harrison lifted his drink and they clinked glasses.

'It has,' said Ren. 'A big, emotional day.'

'Bonnie said you got up on a table and declared your love for Ren to everyone in the office.' Mac grinned.

'I did,' said Harrison.

'Good thing you waited instead of doing it the week Ren started, like you wanted to, huh?'

Ren laughed as Bonnie, eyes widening, looked between them all.

'You what?'

'Don't worry, sweetheart, I told him to wait.'

'And wise words they were,' Harrison told them, looking adoringly at Ren. She grinned and reached over to take his hand. 'So, what about you? Any news on the job?'

It was Mac's turn to grin at Bonnie.

'Yeah, we talked about it. I'm going to stay at this

job for a year, maybe two, and then I'm going to find something else. Maybe something bigger, definitely something grand with a salary to match.'

'Aim for the stars,' said Harrison.

'Yup. Save my money, invest it wisely, and then quit. So I can buy the house my wife and children deserve and then spend time with them.'

'And he better mean me and our future children by that because if he has a secret family there will be hell to pay,' said Bonnie.

Ren and Harrison laughed as Mac kissed Bonnie's lips.

'Great. Because I don't think we need our gentleman's agreement anymore,' Harrison told Mac.

'I'll drink to that,' said Mac, holding up his pint glass. All four toasted, clinking their glasses, and just as Mac went to sip his drink, he added, 'But you'll still help me with job stuff.'

Epilogue

Ren glanced down from her screen to the engagement ring on her left hand, smiling to herself as the office light made the diamond sparkle. Harrison claimed to have bought it the day after he stood on a table in the office and declared his love for her. Although he waited another month before taking her away to a luxurious hotel in Inverness for the weekend, getting down on one knee on the bank of Loch Ness.

The answer had come easy.

There wasn't a doubt in Ren's mind that she wanted to spend her life with Harrison.

Things had settled after that. They'd found a routine in the office, now that everyone knew about them. The game was on schedule for release and Martin had promoted Dougal into the vacancy Liam had left. It meant that he now sat behind Ren and they could shout film quotes at each other throughout the day. Harrison hadn't so much as flinched when he'd heard the news.

'Hey.'

Ren jumped as Harrison pulled her from her thoughts. He moved from her left to her right and sat on her desk. Wrenching her gaze from the ring on her finger, she looked up at him, putting on her best professional work expression. Harrison passed her his phone and, brow creased, she looked at the screen.

'What am I looking at?' she asked before she had time to process what was on the phone. It was a house for sale with the photos and details listed. Ren sat back to study it as Harrison watched and waited for any sort of reaction.

The house itself was beautiful. A four bed detached with a double garage, but it was the garden that made Ren's eyes widen. The house came with land and minimal neighbours, in the countryside. She checked the location and looked up at Harrison.

'You want to move to the Highlands?'

Harrison leaned forward to see which photos she'd gotten to.

'It comes with two barns,' he said, as if that was an explanation. 'And four acres.'

Ren's eyes kept widening.

'That's...a lot.'

'We could convert the barns, one into a distillery for Jackson, one into a brewery for me.'

Ren looked up and met Harrison's eager, nervous eyes. She smiled and he visibly relaxed a little.

'You're going into business together?'

Harrison nodded.

'I'd like to. I haven't run this past him yet, I wanted to get your thoughts first. Look at the gardens, and views. We could see if we could get planning permission for some wooden lodges or something, rent those out. And it's still fairly close to Inverness, if you wanted to keep the corporate job.'

'What about Mac? And Bonnie? And your job here?' Ren murmured. Although this plan would certainly give her something to do when her contract ended.

'I'll quit. C'mon! To go into business with my son? If he's up for it, and if you're up for it, that's absolutely something I need to try. And look at this house.'

'Look at the price!' said Ren, spotting it for the first time. 'We can't afford that.'

'We can.'

Ren looked up at her fiancé.

'With one hell of a mortgage?' she wondered out loud.

Harrison shook his head.

'With a reasonable mortgage. And that's only because I'm going to invest in the Calloway whisky and beer business, and converting those barns won't be cheap..'

Ren blinked up at him.

'You can afford this?' She showed him his own phone, just to make sure.

Harrison grinned.

'Yeah.'

'You never did tell me how much money you have,' she murmured, studying him for a moment. These were possibly questions she should have asked before saying yes to marrying him. They were definitely questions she'd need answering before the wedding.

'No, but if we do this, I'd still have enough to keep us going for a while. There's a lot of work that needs doing. We'd be running on savings to begin with. But I've got enough investments that it shouldn't be a problem.'

Ren stared up at Harrison. She wasn't even sure what most of that meant.

'Okay,' she said slowly. 'What about Mac and Bonnie?' She glanced back to Bonnie's empty desk; she was downstairs in a meeting with marketing.

'They can come visit. We'll come back to Edinburgh regularly. I've already got a list of places I want to try and sell our whisky and beer to.'

'Okay. Where will Jackson live? With us?'

'That's up to him. He might want to live in the city,' said Harrison. 'Or we could build an annex for him or something.'

'Or something,' Ren murmured, flicking through the photos again.

'Look, we don't have to decide yet. But it's an

idea, right? A good idea? You like it?'

'Well, yeah. I love it,' Ren admitted. 'We'd be our own bosses.'

'Freedom,' said Harrison. 'And you'd have an equal share in it all. I think the law protects you if you're my wife, but we'll get it all written up, just in case.'

'I could run the holiday rentals,' Ren mused out loud.

Harrison grinned.

'Absolutely. So, you want to view it?'

Ren had to stop herself doing a little dance.

'Yes! I mean, yeah, okay. We should go look at it. Because you can afford this.'

'We, Ren,' said Harrison. 'Once we're married, it'll be we who can afford this.'

'We'd wait until we're married?'

'No. I just want you to stop referring to our money as mine.' Harrison slipped off the desk, took back his phone, kissed the top of her head and wandered towards his own office, humming softly to himself.

Ren watched him go, her legs twitching to follow him and maybe finally go find that cleaning cupboard. Looking around, finding everyone busy in their own worlds, she slowly stood and made her way down the corridor, following Harrison, her insides fizzy with the anticipation of what she wanted to do and what was to come.

If you enjoyed this book, please leave a rating or review on your favourite distributor to help other readers find Jacob and Sophie's story.

Find your next romantic read at
www.jennynicebooks.co.uk